1976

Dutch Uncle

Marilyn Durham

DUTCH UNCLE

Harcourt Brace Jovanovich, Inc.

New York

For my grandmother, who always liked a good clean story
But mostly for my mother, who doesn't

Dutch Uncle

1

The dust was usually ankle deep in the streets of Tucson when the wind wasn't blowing it around. The merchants tried putting planks down at the corners for the ladies to cross on, but every wagon that came along knocked them apart and stirred the dirt over them until they were nearly invisible. It had been a good thought, though.

The Mexican woman stood looking down at the drifted filth between the boardwalk and the first plank, as if of a mind to settle where she was rather than risk her skirts and boots in an attempt to cross. She was dressed in such unrelieved black, from bonnet to shoes, that she might have been on her way to Juárez's funeral, and she clutched two equally somber children by the wrists, holding them back from the plunge.

Jake Hollander had already given her a full minute of his attention when she boarded the train at Yuma. She had sat across the aisle and one seat forward, eyes closed, riding backward while her kids ogled him tirelessly over the near seat. Her face was sallow, almost waxy, and her eyes when she opened them were large and fierce, as if with pain or grief.

She hadn't acknowledged his examination of her or even appeared to notice it, nor did she speak more than a few terse words to her offspring. But Jake had formed one of his quick professional conclusions about her before turning his mind to other things.

In spite of her rigid propriety and puritanical black dress —perhaps in some way even because of them—Jake Hollander had pegged her as a reformed whore. There was no shade of malice in the judgment, no reproach, and no interest; just the practiced eyes of a man who made his living on quick estimates.

Now, when he drew even with her on the walk, she still seemed to be hesitating on the verge of a leap, so he circled her and made a long step out to the first board ahead of her. He was halfway across the street when he heard a high-pitched wail from one of the kids.

"Ma*ma!*" Still walking, he glanced back.

She had fallen. She was crumpled face down in the street, with the two spindle-stick boys hopping and crouching around her like a pair of worried crows.

Nobody was running to her rescue. A few of the other train passengers had stopped some yards back, consulting their nerve. There had been random outbreaks of smallpox all over the Southwest that summer, and people who fell over in their tracks weren't necessarily just drunk.

Jake stopped. He was pretty sure she wasn't drunk, and smallpox was no threat to him. Still he hesitated, looking at the little heap she made in the dirt. Some of the others began to move forward slowly on the authority of their varied consciences, but by then Jake had already started back for her.

She had been saved from asphyxiation by falling across the cheap, fat carpetbag she carried, but she was heavily floured with the dun-colored dust when he picked her up. Her eyes fluttered and closed as she sagged in his arms. The bystanders hustled up to see, now that she was safely in somebody else's charge.

"What's the matter with her, mister? Too much sun?"

"I don't know," said Jake. "Is there a doctor around here?"

2

"Just got off the train myself, same as you. There ought to be one in a town this size. She your little woman?"

"No," Jake said irritably, scanning the clapboard-faced street for a doctor's shingle. He saw none, but directly across from them were the hotel and saloon that had been his own destination. "Somebody pick up my bag for me." He carried her there, trailed by five or six interested transients and the two Mex kids. One of them was hauling both pieces of luggage while the other one trotted beside him, squalling with dismay.

Inside the cramped hotel lobby he put her down on a settee that wasn't long enough to include her feet, then brushed the results of their contact off his good black coat. She was drenched in a breath-stopping perfume that seemed to confirm his first estimate of her, but overriding that was the unmistakable stench of a fever. He stepped back as the clerk and manager bent over her. "If you've got a doctor around here I guess you'd better get him," he told the manager. "And if you've got a room left, I want it." He set his own black leather valise up on the desk and wrote "Jcb. Hollander, Sn. Frsco." in the register.

"Yes, sir. Elmer, you run down to the billiard parlor and see if Doctor Cheathem's having office hours now." He looked at the slight bulge under Jake's breast pocket. "You can either check your weapon in with me, or down at the sheriff's office. Or you can keep it in your valise. Just don't wear it out on the streets. That'll be three dollars." Jake looked at him coldly. "That's the rules here, mister. I don't make them, but I won't say they aren't good ones."

"Three dollars for a single room?" Jake echoed with cool scorn. He slipped the gun from its shoulder holster and dropped it into his open valise, then locked it up again.

"No, sir, that's three dollars for a double. And of course we put in a day bed for the little ones, too." He demonstrated the smile of a tolerably forgiving man.

"What little—" Jake caught the drift of the manager's eye.

3

"They're not mine, they're hers. No connection. How much is the single room?"

"Dollar and a half. Fifty cents more if you take a bath."

Jake nodded, satisfied, and stacked three half dollars on the desk beside his valise. Then he made the shortest path across the lobby to the adjoining bar.

He had a beer first to clear his throat, and a judicious sample of the free lunch on the bar while he looked around. There was nothing of any interest to him in the hotel bar. He left it and tried the saloon next door.

The saloon held more promise. Though it was still early in the day for a serious game, in the back of the long, wainscoted room there was a table encircled by a body of earnest-looking poker players. They displayed two characteristics Jake was always pleased to find. Each player telegraphed his current luck with little twitches and grimaces of unconscious candor, and they were playing for cash. He watched them from the anonymity of the bar, his thin, cold face gradually softening into an expression that was almost affectionate.

In time he moved their way, drink in hand, to stand behind the most successful player and observe how he bet his hand. He wore a look of respectful attention. The one who was winning asked him to join them—smelling fresh meat—and Jake did so with mannerly caution.

Travel was expensive, and he was determined not to dip into his money belt until he reached El Paso. Still, he let them take a bit out of his pocket cash before settling down to work.

When he returned to the hotel it was after midnight. There was no one in the lobby. He went straight up to his as yet unseen room, tired now, but satisfied with the evening's profit.

The cards had come his way all afternoon, so that he stayed far enough ahead to allow a pot to go from time to time to keep somebody happy. It hadn't been his intention to clean out the rubes. With them he was friendly, even talka-

4

tive, not too lucky, and a good sport when somebody else claimed a pot.

He had discovered years ago that the good opinion of a rube was a free ticket to the bigger games in a strange town. The more accomplished and well-heeled players then took him for a lucky yokel himself and welcomed the opportunity to relieve him of his undeserved wealth.

Luck had about as much influence on Jake's game as rumors of the Second Coming. Not because he tried to force the cards, although when it came to that he had the hands of a conjurer, but because he put his confidence in the odds.

By nine o'clock the hobbyists had begun to leave the table, and the serious players took their places. After a short period of testing on both sides, the blood flowed freely. The losers were silent, according to their code. They might also have begun to grow doubtful toward the end, but they could find no fault with his dealing or his punctilious observation of the rules. By the time the game closed out he had won, if not their friendship, at least enough money to take him another hundred miles in comfort along his chosen way.

When he put his key in the hotel-room door and found it already unlocked, he frowned. But the moonlight coming through a long window inside showed the room to be undisturbed. The bed was turned down and his valise sat at the foot of it, unopened. He felt a moment of regret that his gun was in the valise rather than snug against his chest, but after another second spent listening to the silence behind the door and in the direction of the closet he went in with a sigh.

No one had any reason to wait for him up here. Assault in a hotel room would be too noisy. The best place for a poor loser to recoup his losses was outside in the dark street.

Without bothering to light the lamp, he undressed, hanging his clothes over the foot of the bed. Under his shirt and vest was the chamois money belt, which he unfastened and put beneath the pillow. Just to feel more secure about it he opened the valise and felt for the gun. He put that under the

5

extra pillow so he could slide his hand up to touch it without effort.

Naked, he fell into the bed and stretched out long legs that ached from inactivity. Just before sleep drowned him, he thought there was a subdued outbreak of voices somewhere down the hall and the jar of feet hurrying past. But they didn't stop at his door. They were the last thing he heard that night.

A floor board creaked. He heard that, and the strange wordless whisper that followed it. He didn't move or allow his breathing to alter while he listened. Sometime in the night he must have grown cool, because he could feel the slight weight of a cotton quilt thrown over his shoulders.

Someone brushed against the bed, and the odd vocal noise was repeated, almost like a hum. Whoever it was must think he was drunk or dead to be so careless. The quilt pulled up to his chin helped to cover his right hand's careful movement up under the pillow next to his head.

His gun was gone.

At the same instant he realized that, he heard the unmistakable cluck of a hammer being cocked. He opened his eyes while he still had time to see who it was that was about to use his own gun on him.

The muzzle was at eye level with him but aimed higher. It wavered in and out of focus between him and the face of the person holding it—a damned kid! One of those Mex kids he had seen yesterday. He'd erased them from his mind so effortlessly that now he had to spend another second trying to recall how or where he had seen them.

Anger flooded in with the memory, and he drew his breath for a shout that would send the little bastard flying. Then he let it out again, carefully.

The gun, on half cock, was swinging back his way again. The kid was trying to pick out its cartridges with his fingers. He was breathing heavily with concentration, and again there was that sound; he was humming or mumbling to himself, but not in English.

Jake tensed for a snatch at the weapon just as the boy raised his eyes and saw him awake. Jake's hand snaked out from under the pillow and grabbed the gun, getting his little finger between the hammer and the cylinder and jerking up, just as the boy's two thumbs brought the hammer back to full cock and slipped off.

"What the hell are you up to, you little bastard?" Jake yelled, making a futile swing at the brat's head with his other hand as he sat up in bed.

The boy started back with a rabbity shriek and fled around the bed, where he collided with the second boy on his path to the door. Jake had locked the door, and it was still locked.

They fell against it, sobbing, as he released his pinched finger from the pressure of the hammer and flung back the quilt. He intended to rush them, knock their heads together, and throw them out. They seemed to see their death in his face, because they screamed in unison and fought the door handle, pulling at it instead of turning it.

On his feet and towering over them Jake had a sudden sense of himself, a naked man threatening two mindless little animals with a pistol. He paused, still outraged, and glanced around to see how they had got in, then saw the cot against the far wall. Baffled, he stabbed the gun in its direction.

"What the hell? You slept in here! Who put you in here?" But they saw the gesture as a command and obeyed it, darting around him like terror-stricken cockroaches to throw themselves back on the cot and cling to it wailing.

Amazement disarmed Jake. He threw the gun down on the bed and snatched up his clothes. His questions needed no answers. Who else could have put them in his room but the goddamn manager? In his room and on his bill, no doubt. He hauled his pants up to his lean waist and crammed in the tails of his crumpled shirt while he stoked his rage with more questions.

Where was their mother? Why, nicely recovered from her little faint and working out her own expenses down the hall somewhere. He'd bank on it. Was this her standard routine in every new town? Flop out flat in front of some passing idiot and trust him to carry her in to a good bed, then kennel her pups for her while she went to work on her back!

When he reached for his vest he saw that his pockets had been rifled. His winnings from the previous night were stacked and laid out on the floor decoratively, with his watch as a centerpiece. He grabbed up the money and counted it, glaring at the two brown faces on the cot between times, but it was all there and the watch still ticked. He stuffed the money and the watch back into his pockets, then got out the door key. They didn't move when he unlocked and swung open the door.

"Come on, get out of there. Out! *Fuera! Pronto!*"

They slid out together and bolted for the freedom of the hall. At the head of the stairs they passed the manager, just arriving with a pale, greasy smile.

"I want to see *you* in about one minute!" Jake snarled at him before he slammed the door again.

He hadn't touched the hidden money while they were in the room. He got it out now and pulled up his shirt to fasten it around his waist. With his savings snug against his body again he felt better. He tucked in the shirt, strapped on the shoulder holster, then put on his coat. He hadn't shaved yet, but that could wait.

When he jerked the door open again the boys were gone and the hotel man was still waiting, hands folded like some undertaker waiting to be paid.

"Why did you put those two little greaser pickpockets in with me? Do they work for you? What do you do with them, run some kind of switch on the badger game?"

"Mr. Hollander, we—I had no wish to inconvenience you. Naturally, there's no charge for them to you—"

"There damn well better not be!"

"—and of course we—I should have obtained your permission first—"

"You'd have played hell doing that!"

"—but you were so late coming in, and there wasn't another room, and their mother, as you know, was so ill—"

"I'll bet she was!"

"—that we didn't think you'd object. When you didn't complain last night, I assumed that you had spoken to the boys and understood how it was with them. I must say, I thought it was very kind of you, indeed."

Jake looked at him with slowly ebbing suspicion. "All right. Fine. I've been kind. We'll call it even, then, if you just take them back to their mother and tell *her* to kindly keep them out of my way from now on."

"But, Mr. Hollander, that's just what I was on my way to tell you. Their mother is—" his voice dropped to a whisper—"dead." Jake looked at him stonily, once more suspicious of a catch. "We were very much concerned last night that her fever might prove to be something contagious and the whole hotel would have to be quarantined. It's happened before."

"So you thought you'd just test it out by putting those two fever blisters in here with me?"

"No, oh no! But it was necessary for the doctor to examine her thoroughly, and children of that age can't stay in the room at such a time. Of course, you know you would already have been exposed, anyway, carrying her in here."

"Thanks a lot."

"But there was no need for alarm, as it turned out. Doctor Cheathem was able to determine the cause of the fever, and her unfortunate death. She had recently lost a child—an unborn one, that is. She had a childbed fever." He sighed. "One can only wonder what it was that forced her to travel in such a grave state of health. It's very sad, of course, but we *were* relieved to know it wasn't something like smallpox or typhoid." He smiled wanly.

"Lucky for you."

9

"The poor little ones don't know the truth yet. We felt it would be needlessly cruel to wake them in the middle of the night with such terrible news."

"Yeah. Well, I guess you better tell them now."

"Indeed. Yes. Poor boys. Ah—Mr. Hollander, as I was coming up the stairs a moment ago, I said to myself that, since you had already made some slight acquaintance with them, *you* might be better qualified than I to—" He was talking to no one. Jake had closed and locked the door again.

Inside the room Jake was still trying to smother an anger that should have died promptly at the sight of the hotel man's fraudulent grief. He stripped off his coat and opened his collar so he could shave. He would have to do it with the cold water from the wash pitcher, but he would rather chip ice for the job now than have his room invaded by more of the hotel half-wits.

He wasn't able to decide whether he believed the story about the whore being dead. In truth he could see no good point in the man's feeding him a plate of fish, but he knew that any good confidence trick depended for its success on the confusion of the victim. He thought he knew all the flim-flamming angles there were, but he also knew that anybody who thought that was ripe for a picking and deserved it.

He lathered his face with the pine-tar soap he carried in his kit and began to reap a two-day growth of graying stubble from his long jaw.

The act of shaving usually soothed him with its meticulous ceremony of movement and posture. But now he found he was unable to give it the concentration it demanded. His hand wavered for an instant, and he cut himself just under the left ear. He swore and dabbed at the cut with a towel. As he did so he glanced at the cot that had harbored his uninvited guests.

There was a large wet stain on one side of it, spreading toward the middle, fresh and tinged with amber against the rough white sheet. Tumbled in confusion beneath the cot was a collection of worn socks and shoes, their laces mended in several places with knots.

He felt the revulsion of an unwilling pity. Poor little bastards, he thought in spite of himself. He'd scared them out of both piss and boots. But he hoped he would never have to set eyes on their sad, dirty faces again.

2

The Southern Pacific railroad was driving steel eastward across the wastelands of the Arizona and New Mexico territories at top speed in spite of common sense, the terrain, and the concerted opposition of the Apaches, but as of that day in early March, 1880, the trains went no farther than Tucson.

Jake Hollander took his valise down to the office of the rapidly shrinking Texas and California Stage Company and bought a ticket for the next leg of his journey. The price of the ticket hardened his heart against the stage company's plight. After the comfort of the train it was like paying to be arrested by the Spanish Inquisition.

He had an hour to wait before the stage came, so he spent it consuming a breakfast of steak, eggs, and the worst coffee he had ever tasted. He rinsed the flavor of it out of his mouth with a double whiskey, because he was feeling unaccountably depressed.

There was no good reason for the mood that he could discover. He had enough money hoarded around his ribs to buy his way into the saloon business of El Paso if he still felt like it when he got there, or to move on to someplace else if he didn't.

That was the system by which he made all his business

decisions, the way in which he managed life itself: to do what he felt like doing at the moment he wanted to do it. That was freedom. Anything more was a shackle. He did consider his word to be binding. But since he had no wish to be bound he never gave his word on anything if he could get around it.

He had no ties of friendship or family in El Paso or any other place in the world, nor had he ever wanted any. But he did have one or two acquaintances in that border town whom he was willing to see again for business purposes.

He had no friends. But it was equally true that he was no one's enemy. For the most part of humanity he felt the contempt of the sane man for the fanatic. The human race irritated him, but it was the irritation of a man tormented by mosquitoes because he must dredge treasure out of a swamp. He expected nothing else.

Even so, his temper felt circumstances warm it with a kiss when he approached the stage depot for the second time and saw the hotel manager sitting there on a bench with the two Mexican pups and an arm of the law.

The men stood up as he arrived. The orphans gaped at him dull eyed, as if they thought Jake had come to finish them off and were resigned to it.

Their twin expressions of idiocy were partly due to tear-inflamed eyelids and to swollen noses that forced them to breathe with open mouths. The noses were running. He looked away from them with disgust.

"Mr. Hollander," the manager began, "if you would be so kind—" but his companion cut him off.

"Hollander, what do you know about that woman who died last night at the *ho*tel?"

"Not a damn thing."

"You brought her in here, didn't you?"

"The train brought her in, the same as it did me. She passed out in the street and I picked her up. I've been sorry ever since."

"Now, don't get huffy, mister. I'm just doing my job. When

13

people come into town and die of a sudden, I've got to try to find out who they are. Here's the thing. She didn't come here to stay. She had a piece of paper in her pocketbook with a name and address on it. It appears like she was going to see somebody over in Arredondo."

"Never heard of it."

"It's a new silver-strike town just over the border in New Mexico Territory. One of them jumped-up-out-of-a-hole tent-and-shanty towns."

"I'll try to avoid it."

"No, no! You'll be going through it, the way you're heading. And that's why we're down here now. These two poor little fellers—they can't stay here. Their mama's dead and they got no kin here. This county has already got all it can do to take care of its own dead and their orphans. We can't go fostering everybody's child that stops off here to die."

There was a miaowing wail from one of the two children. The deputy glanced down at them guiltily.

Jake waited with cool patience for the end of the speech. It had to come soon because he saw the stage just turning onto the broad street two blocks away, churning up a tan storm around its wheels to choke the pedestrians.

"Now, I could take the two of them up to the county orphanage next week until somebody comes asking for them," the lawman said. "I get a dollar for it, going each way. But meantime they're at the town's charge to feed and bed. What we propose instead is that for the same amount—a dollar a day—you take them on into Arredondo with you and turn them over to whoever is waiting there for their mama to come."

The stage rattled up from the livery stable with its fresh team and driver. As soon as it stopped, Jake opened the door and got in.

"That's a mighty uncharitable attitude to take, mister," the lawman said accusingly through the little window. "Might be that I ought to send a wire on ahead of this stage to some

14

friends of mine along the way that there's a jackleg gambler on this stage who rakes in the chips a little too easy and could bear watchin'.''

Jake paused fractionally in the act of putting a thin cigar in his mouth. The deputy's eyes caught the small hesitation and twinkled. "Anyhow, they got a paid-up ticket to Arredondo now, whether you like it or not, and I'm putting them on this stage. If you let 'em wander off at the wrong stop or get hurt along the way, it'll be your business—and maybe somebody else's.''

Jake snapped a match head on his thumbnail and said nothing.

The children were boarded after a huddle between the lawman and the stage driver. Other passengers came and took their seats, until the stage was filled. The express box was stowed on top along with a mail sack, the whip cracked, and they lurched forward in a dun haze.

For the next two hours they were the common prey of the transit line. A way station, solitary as a turtle in the desert, provided water and a brief rest from the jarring and rocking before they resumed the journey.

The midday stop was made in a town so small it could support only two saloons. Jake waited to see which would be favored by the majority of the travelers, then entered the other one. It was a Mexican cantina, with peeling, faded red paint blotching its adobe face, and black as a monte dealer's heart on the inside. The atmosphere was morose; exactly to his taste.

He ordered a beer and whatever they had to eat, which turned out to be tortillas and red beans. In ordinary circumstances Jake was as indifferent to food as he was to people. He would eat anything that was reasonably priced and served on a clean plate. But he discovered in himself a sudden aversion to Mexican cooking and left the beans scarcely tasted.

He was watching the minuscule explosions of gas in his second beer when a small hoarse voice behind him said,

"Tío." He raised his head and exchanged stares with the bartender.

"Tío."

"What are you doing in here?" he growled, still staring at the bartender, who was beginning to frown.

"Tenemos hambre, Tío."

Jake flushed under the bartender's measured look. The conversation at the other end of the bar came to a stop.

"Look, whatever he said, I am not that damn kid's uncle."

The bartender looked away from Jake to smile down on the two brats. "Get up on the stool, *chicos,*" he said with sudden heartiness. *"Tío* is playin' a little trick on you, no? Slipped off and left you on the stage? I'll get you some dinner. *Frijoles y tortillas, no? Muy buenos,* eh?" His overlarge smile now included Jake in the joke. Jake remained tight lipped.

"I am not—" he began again, then stopped. To hell with explanations. He started to slide off the stool and found two of the three other customers had suddenly moved up behind him. He looked at their sun-reddened faces and faded blue eyes. They seemed to be cattle hustlers of a medium-low grade. He considered the .36 Colt strapped against his heart. Having his coat on was going to slow him down. How much?

It hardly seemed sensible to send two men to the undertaker over a couple of plates of beans—or to go there himself. He sat down again.

The bartender slid two steaming dishes under the pups' noses, and they attacked them as if they hadn't seen food for a week. He wondered when in fact they had. One of them—the one he thought had tried to shoot him that morning—stuffed his mouth until he choked. He wheezed and wept as he coughed, while Jake watched with repugnance, wondering if he was going to vomit it all up again.

"Bring him something to wash it down," he said to the bartender.

"We don't keep no milk."

"Then bring him a beer!"

16

The man grinned at him and pulled two beers. Jake laid a fifty-cent piece on the pitted bar without returning the smile.

When their plates were mopped dry with the last bit of tortilla and twin belches testified to the satisfaction of both stomachs, he stood up again. They followed him outside, wiping their crusted noses, until he turned on them.

"How's your English, kid?"

The larger of the two grinned sheepishly.

"I talk it good," he said in his croupy voice. "I know all American plenty much, *tío*. We ain't Mex, goddamn no, Mama says. We gringo kids, hell yes; born in America. I talk good American or she beat my ass!"

Jake waited a second to let the dust of that settle. It wasn't any more than he expected, he thought.

"Well, since you know so plenty much, you'll understand this. If you call me 'uncle' again you're going to be catching your teeth in your hat. *Comprende?*"

"Yes, *tío*."

"What!"

"Yes, I-don't-know-what-to-call-you-then, *tío*."

"Don't call me anything. Nothing! Just get back in that stage and shut your mouth. Both of you!"

It occurred to him on the way to the next town that the way to be rid of them was simple. He wouldn't board the stage again after supper. He would stay the night wherever they stopped and get another stage tomorrow. The resolution lightened his mood to the extent that he even consented to answer one or two questions put to him by the older boy.

By now everybody else on the coach must believe they were his, he decided. So he diverted himself for the next few miles by examining the complacent lot of travelers one by one; calculating the effect on each of them if he should find himself chosen to be the next *tío* of the little leeches tomorrow.

At supper the leeches dined at his expense more like ravening wolves, devouring two plates of stew apiece and an equal

17

number of small beers. The beers were to make them sleep, he hoped, until they were well on their way without their conscripted *patrón*. While they gobbled, he returned to the stage, got his valise, and checked it into the only hotel.

He escorted the children back to the empty coach, well ahead of the other passengers. "Get up in there and stay there, understand? I've got to look up a friend I know here, and I don't want you two along."

"Yes, *tío*."

"Go to sleep. You look tired. Get some rest while you can. Stretch out on the seat and don't get out of here. *Comprende?*"

"*Comprendo, tío*. I know all you say in American, I told you." He smiled confidently at Jake. Two of his front teeth were missing.

"Good."

He left them staring out the window after him. He had no compunction about ridding himself of them in this way. They were expected in Arredondo, and the stage was headed in that direction. They would arrive just as surely without him as otherwise. And otherwise was beginning to get too expensive.

He re-entered the familiar haven of the saloon to attend to the real business of his life.

But he found little profit in the business that evening. The locals were dull, cautious, and incurably penny ante. Raising the pot scared them out. Bluffing made them call. When he did have a hand to play, the pot he raked in was hardly worth the effort.

He folded early and went up to bed in the barracks simplicity of his room. The bed was passable, the noise from the street wasn't too loud compared with San Francisco, but he couldn't sleep. His morning depression had returned, to join with a midnight sense of foreboding. The futility of his journey to El Paso suddenly assailed him.

What was the sense in putting himself through the misery

18

of traveling a thousand miles to a new town when he already knew that all towns were alike for him? And if he had to move, why El Paso? Why not someplace nearer and bigger, like San Diego or Sacramento?

The quick answer to that was that he had already been there. He had stayed there as long as he ever stayed anywhere. They had been good-enough places, for a while. San Francisco had been even better. But he had left an easy spot there, a pleasant climate, and a companionable woman, a month ago, to come this far on a tail-busting stage and lie in a bed alone because it was *time* to move.

For him, time would seem to sleep like an aged dog, or it would be a trumpet in his ear. He was forty-five years old and there was a clock inside him ticking away the days and years, faster all the while. He couldn't put a name to the apprehension he felt, but it was more acute lately.

He thought about the woman he had been living with for the past two years in San Francisco. Her name was Maureen, but it was possible for him to think about her now without giving her a name.

He could have brought her with him; she would have come. It had never occurred to him to do so. Yet she had been good for him while they were together. She had been reliable. Warm. Good looking. Sensible, for a woman. He could admit that he was going to miss her for a while longer. But he didn't ask himself what his feeling for her had been otherwise.

He had thought it was likely she would cry or make some kind of fuss if he told her he was leaving town. She seemed to think he would be around forever. She had begun to act that way. So to avoid the angry embarrassment he always felt when other people paraded their emotions to no purpose, he had simply left without telling her. It was the best thing to do, when he knew he would never write to her, never see her again unless by accident in some unlooked-for and undesired way.

19

He twisted restlessly on the bed, determined to shut off that line of thought. There was nothing wrong with what he had done; nothing wrong with him, except that he was having a sleepless night again. They said age did that. And he was stuck in a rotten town that played rotten poker. He was a man who had to change his surroundings from time to time, yet hated to travel. Who the hell didn't? But tomorrow he would be halfway to El Paso. A week from now things would be taking shape again, and he would forget he had ever been in this hole.

There was a knock on the door.

"Sir? Mr. Hollander, sir? Are you still awake?"

He sat up quicker than there was any need to, the feeling of doom suddenly icing down his brain.

"What is it? What do you want?" It was the desk clerk from downstairs; he remembered the voice.

"Why, ah—there's somebody out here I guess you've been waiting for."

He was up and across the room with his hand on the door in an instant, but he didn't open it.

"Who is it?"

"*Tío?*"

The sensation that prickled through his flesh at the sound of that voice was almost as nasty as fear. "Oh, Jesus," he breathed, eyes closed. Then he opened the door. They stood close together in the dim hall in their rusty black clothes with an anxious shepherd behind them.

"The ticket agent said they were left on the stage by mistake, but he must have meant they just came in earlier than you expected. They were down at the stage office for a couple of hours before they told the clerk they had an uncle here in the hotel. I guess you've been worried about them."

Jake let them in. The clerk handed him their mother's frayed old carpetbag, examining him with fresh curiosity at the same time. Jake didn't see how anybody could mistake him for a spick's uncle, but it seemed to be happening again.

20

"The ticket agent didn't know your name, and the funny thing is they couldn't tell me what it was, either. But they're pretty small to be traveling by themselves. I guess they were just scared and tired. I knew they had to be yours, though. You're the only new gentleman in here tonight."

Jake closed the door with the briefest thanks and turned to look down at the children. He wasn't even angry, he realized. Of course they'd turn up on him again, like a couple of bent pesos. He should have known the damned driver would be watching to see if he came back. Even if he had forgotten about Jake, the Gringo Kid here would have told everybody that his *tío* had just gone off to see a friend in town.

He had felt it all the time. It must have been the reason for his unease.

"Get off that bed!" he snarled at the little one, who was just starting to make a nest in it. "If you piss in the bed you're not going to sleep with me!"

They watched, heavy eyed, while he snatched off the covers and folded them up to make a pallet on the floor. He threw in both pillows for good measure, because this time he had put his money belt under the mattress.

While he sat hunched on the edge of the bed, they pulled off their shoes and socks and obediently lay down together on the pallet. Jake was trying to remember something he had heard once, about a poor bastard who unwittingly committed some kind of crime and had to go around for the rest of his life with a dead bird tied to his neck. It didn't make any sense.

"Are you mad at us, *tío*?"

"No, I'm not mad at you. But why in the hell do you keep calling me *tío*? You don't even know me."

"Mama said. We got a lot of *tíos*. Mama says they like it better than when we called them all papa."

"Yeah. I guess. Well, my name is Jake. You call me that."

"Chake?"

"That's close enough."

"My name is Paco Robles." He was the bigger one, with

21

the missing teeth. He looked about the right age for them to have come out naturally instead of having been kicked out, which Jake felt would have otherwise been a reasonable assumption.

"How about your brother over there?" He had never heard the little one speak; only hum or cry.

The older one laughed.

"He ain't my brother. She's my sister, *tío!* She is María Concepción, that Mama calls Urraca because she like to hide every damn thing she can find. Mama says—" He stopped under the intensity of Jake's stare. "You mad at me now?"

Jake groaned and leaned over to blow out the lamp, then stretched himself out on the bare bed fully clothed.

"Chake?"

"Shut up and go to sleep."

There was no more talk from anyone. Surprisingly enough, Jake himself was asleep in five minutes.

3

Paco Robles was curled up like a cub at the foot of the bed when Jake woke. The smell emanating from his sleeping sister explained his daring. She had sopped their pallet again. Jake stepped over her and shoved open the window to let in some fresh air. The sound woke Paco with a start, but after a careful examination of Jake's deadly morning face he confined his ever-ready tongue to a "Good morning, *tío*," which Jake did not answer.

The girl woke while he was shaving, and the two of them watched him perform the ritual in a rapt silence. They were not used to the presence of men in the morning. Their chins lifted in unison as Jake lifted his and carefully scraped himself from Adam's apple to chin. When he was finished he looked critically at María Concepción.

"Has she got any extra clothes in that bag?"

"Yes, Chake."

"Well, get them out. She smells like a coyote's pantry."

While they were busy rifling the carpetbag he slipped his money belt out from under the mattress and put it on, tucking his shirt in hastily as he caught the little girl's mouse-bright eyes watching him over her brother's shoulder. He buckled on the shoulder holster and put on his coat while Paco buttoned up his sister.

23

"What should I do with the old wet stuff, *tío?*"

"Leave it here." It would be his gift to the management for surprising him last night. He picked up his own leather valise and reached for their old carpetbag. It seemed unusually heavy for being half empty. "What the hell have you got in here, a cannon ball?" He looked inside, but there was nothing except the usual things: underwear, the woman's purse, and a cheap jewel box full of worthless trinkets. He closed it again.

"Let's go find some breakfast," he said.

When they were replete enough to begin licking the dark molasses from between their fingers Jake asked a few necessary questions.

"Who are you going to visit in Arredondo?"

"Tía Deel," said Paco.

"Who?"

"Tía Deel. Mama's fren'. We gonna live in her house."

Jake remembered something the Tucson deputy had said about a name and address in the woman's purse. He opened the bag again and took out the beaded, fringed pouch. Inside it there was a bottle of something that smelled like licorice, a packet of thin Mexican cigars, and an envelope. No money at all, not even a stray penny.

The envelope was addressed to Mrs. Rosana Robles in care of the postmaster in Yuma. There was no return address, no postmark, and no letter inside. On the back someone else had scrawled, in an illiterate hand, "The Golden Moon."

He put the empty envelope in his vest pocket and threw the purse back into the bag. Once again he weighed it on two fingers hooked through its handles, then put it down with a slight frown.

"Who is this Tía Deel, your mother's *comadre?*" Paco looked blank. "I didn't think so. Is she a relative? Have you got any relatives?"

"What's a relative?"

"Your mama's family—her brothers or sisters. Her mama

24

and papa." Paco blinked twice at the novel thought. "How about your papa? Do you know who he is?"

Paco brightened. "We got two papas. Urraca's runned off a long time ago with a skinny bitch and Mama hopes he got the clap, and—"

"Hey, that's no way to talk in front of your sister!"

"—and my papa is with the devils in hell," Paco finished. "I didn't say nothing bad to Urraca. Anyway, she don't listen. She watches," he explained as an afterthought.

"What's Urraca mean?" Paco was again at a loss. "I mean why do you call her Urraca if her name is María whatever?"

"Oh. Mama says she's like some kind of a little bird that steals stuff and hides it and cusses out all the other birds. Only Urraca don't cuss."

"Does she talk?"

"She don't any more. Not since Mama got so mad at her for crying so much when she got her fingers mashed in the door. Man, she sure yelled and hollered then! Mama closed the door because a *tío* was there, and Urraca was right behind it. Mama pick her up and tried to hush her up, but she wouldn't stop crying. Then Mama got mad and yelled, and Urraca yelled louder, and the *tío* got up and went away. So then Mama got really mad and boom-bam!" He clapped himself over the ears in demonstration. "Mama can hit you pretty damn hard when she gets mad, man."

Jake looked at Urraca guzzling sugared coffee, his distaste for "Mama" and the whole family growing rapidly.

He had never had the slightest contact with children before. He scarcely remembered even his own childhood, except that it ended when his father died and his mother took him to live on a Pennsylvania farm with her brother. His uncle had worked him there as hard as he worked his mules or himself, and had beaten him regularly by way of instruction, until the day Jake slammed the back of a manure fork into the old man's lean belly and ran off before his tormentor could start breathing again. He had never returned.

25

In the thirty or more years since that day he had acquired a number of aversions other than those he had to manual labor and relatives. These two voracious whore's whelps embodied most of them.

He had little use for Mexicans or Indians and, whatever Paco's mother had told him, these two were about as gringo as Montezuma. He disliked helpless things and maimed things. The sight of beggars or cripples was enough to make him cross the street to avoid them. He had nearly starved after he ran away from his uncle's farm, wandering from place to place like a stray dog, looking for work he was able to do. He had slept in barns and haystacks in the country, and in alleys and doorways in the towns all one winter until he was as lame as an old man from the cold. It was a memory he had buried under years of deliberate forgetfulness, but one that still affected him with a black shame when he thought of himself in such a condition. He had taken care of himself afterward—so well that in later years he never admitted to having had a day's illness in his life.

Now here he was saddled with two creatures he didn't care to call human. One of them was either deaf or witless, and the other—it was as if a dog could talk! Some callous whim of fate had decided he had to be stuck with them for a little while, but the end was almost in sight. Arredondo, whatever else it might be, was going to look like one of the seats of mercy to him. They should reach the place sometime tomorrow, and there he would leave them to whatever kind of blowsy madam it was that lived at an address like "The Golden Moon."

Arredondo was like a hundred other mining towns in the territories in every respect but one. All of them were founded on the labor and shifting whim of the earth's most fickle yet most persistent economic agents: the *minero*, the *cantinero*, the *ramera*, and the *jugador*.

Ordinarily, the *minero* was the founder of such places,

wandering there with his pick, his mule, and his quenchless optimism. At his hoarse call to wealth the others came, and a new spot was marked down on the maps for a time.

The *cantinero* followed wherever there were thirsty men; dispensing whiskey from the back of a wagon or from under a tent until he could get his saloon roofed. Without his comfortable retreat, even an El Dorado looked like barren ground.

When the saloon doors were on their hinges the *jugador* swung through them, his pockets full of dice and cards, his baggage a dealer's box, a keno layout, a bird cage, or a Hieronymus bowl. He made the wealth seem real by taking it away from the miners.

Hard on his run-down heels, or even there already to meet him, was the whole herd of whores, the *rameras;* crowding into the miners' dreams with bright eyes and hard laughter; pandered by the legend that there was a soft heart hidden in their easy flesh.

And when the ore ran out they left in reverse order. The gamblers and whores went first, sensing a lessening of the tide of fortune sometimes even before the miners themselves knew it. The saloonkeepers followed later, and with regret, being property developers. But they had to be on the alert for the next coming thing, the next big strike; the next promise of permanence, somewhere.

The only difference between Arredondo and the rest of such places was that there the cantina had come first. Built at the crossing of two ancient trails, it had been there longer than the few original inhabitants could remember.

It seemed to be a remnant of some larger building, but what kind no one could say. Some thought it must have been a church, others a fort, others even a monastery. Whatever it had been, it was now pared away by ruinous time to a peculiarly graceful though shapeless tower of adobe, two stories high, with walls a yard thick; a large, cool, gloomy

27

court of a room on the first floor, and a rabbit warren of small, ugly hiding places overhead.

It had no particular name. It was *la sola cantina a la redonda*—the only place around.

When the Texas and California Stage Company opened its line of stations, gringo ears misunderstood that claim and entered the place on the map as Arredondo. The company built stables next to the adobe building and put its proprietor on the payroll as a station keeper. For the benefit of travelers, even he answered to the name Arredondo.

One day a passenger with a long memory passed a few minutes there, waiting for the change of team, and asked the man if he was related to the famous Mexican inspector general Don Joaquín Arredondo, who had created his own version of the Black Hole of Calcutta in San Antonio thirty years before, for the insurgents of the Texas Rebellion. The *cantinero,* whose real name was Hernando Sánchez, amiably confessed that he was that don's great-nephew.

It was a moment of peculiar satisfaction to both the antiquarian and Sánchez, who afterward made such frequent mention of his noble ancestor—whose name he had never heard until that day—that he almost came to believe in the relationship himself.

The addition of the stage line didn't increase Sánchez's business greatly, because of the vast expanse of uninhabited land between the terminal points of the route. But when the miners found silver in the hills surrounding his old ruin Sánchez's life was changed.

He imported a dozen or more ignorant country women from the outlying starving villages and opened a laundry for his new customers. The women lived in a row of kennels behind the *lavandería* and attended to their clients more directly in the rabbit warrens of the second floor at night.

They were not a very attractive pack of whores, but they were the only available women for fifty miles around. In recognition of this distinction, and because he was a lenient man

28

at heart, Sánchez allowed them to keep one-eighth of all they could earn from both their jobs.

Meanwhile the railroad was opening up the territory from the north for those fortune hunters who were weary of harsh Colorado winters.

Strike towns began to bloom and fade like cactus flowers from Santa Fe to the Mexican border, and suddenly merchants were jerry-building their false-fronted stores along the old north-south trail that had become Hassayampa Street because it led the way to the Hassayampa Mine, the first and still the biggest in the area.

Sánchez was in no way the mythical lazy *indio*. The competition of the Anglos whetted his appetite for trade. Expanding on the stage business, he opened a livery stable, employing a cousin who was a farrier. It was said that his horses were the safest in the territory because they were so poor and dispirited not even the Apaches would steal them. The horses were certainly elderly and calm, but Sánchez had an understanding with the Apaches that he didn't care to advertise.

When the Wells Fargo express company first proposed, in addition to its usual services, to freight in perishable foods daily from the approaching railhead, Sánchez's fertile brain labored and brought forth the notion of a wagon train loaded with ice and fresh produce hauled in from the Sonoran mountains by his tribe of cousins.

The ice sold for five cents a pound, a stiff price; but the fresh fruits and vegetables went for a pittance—to the ice customers only. The express company protested, outraged, and even went so far as to drop its own produce prices as much as good sense allowed. Sánchez smiled and continued to make three-quarters-of-a-pittance profit on the sale of his groceries.

The Anglos of the community were both ungracious and ungrateful. They bought his low-priced goods, to the ruin of the express business, but they loathed him for beating out the freighters at the old American game.

In spite of the Apaches, in spite of the extremes of heat and cold there, and in defiance of the probability that the strike would peter out before they got their rooftrees nailed up, the people of the great silver hunger rolled into Arredondo. The trail crossing filled with raw pine shotgun stores, ramshackle lean-tos, cabins, shanties, tents, and even massed wagons. The noise of hammers day after day made the thin air quiver at the madness of industry in the Anglos. They labored from first light to dark as if there were no burning sun searing their pale skins scarlet. Siesta was a word of contempt to them.

What they were building was not yet a town. It was a concentrated busyness in the eternal torpor of the desert. It had no government, no school, no church, no set of laws, and no recognition from the territory in which it thrived.

There were more than five hundred people on the spot by the end of the first year after the strike was made. Fewer than two dozen of them were children. Fewer than fifty of them were wives, strictly or casually.

When Jake Hollander forced himself out through the narrow stage door and looked on the place for the first time, he saw it having one of its good days.

The street was full, as if for a holiday. The hammers were awake and singing. The sun was up in an unblemished sky. For all of a day the wind had not blown. The temperature was a benign eighty degrees, and the people were taking advantage of it, and each other. He looked out on a complex of human aspiration and human greed that would have sent philosophers to their dictionaries and theologians to their knees for a definitive word. But Jake was neither of these.

"Naked Ass Alley," he said under his breath to the haphazard collection of saloons and grab shops before him.

4

He ran a businessman's eye along the saloon fronts of Arredondo. They were the most-represented markets on the main street, all well advertised with brightly painted signs. But the Golden Moon wasn't among them.

Across the street a crowd had assembled. Jake glanced past them without interest, then looked a second time when he realized they were watching him. They were miners, logically; but miners combed, pomaded, dressed in their Sunday best. Their absorption in him was beginning to stir the hair at the nape of his neck when Paco and Urraca scrambled out of the stage behind him and the driver dropped their filthy, fat carpetbag into the dust at his feet. Jake turned quickly to catch his own valise before it got the same treatment.

"Thirty-minute stop here, mister, if you want to get a bite to eat. But don't take any longer than you have to, will you?"

Jake nodded. "What's that across the street?" he asked. "A lynch mob or a shotgun wedding?"

The driver glanced at them and grinned. "A little bit of both by this time, I expect. If you eat in the station here, it's on the ticket. Anywhere else and it's on you. Thirty minutes." He reached for the mailbag as two stable hands came out for the animals.

Hernando Sánchez stood in the doorway of the cantina

31

picking his teeth and greeting the incoming passengers with a casually raised hand. He was a small, slender man with the assurance of a bullfighter and a face that wore the benign melancholy of a plaster saint. The face and hand gave casual absolution to each arriving guest until he saw the two children.

"Hey, *mocosos*. Be off!" he snapped with a quick turn of the hand into a fist.

"They're with me," said Jake as he entered. Sánchez was instantly contrite.

"A thousand apologies, *patrón*. I thought they were my own. Come in, little soldiers. Forgive my mistake, eh? Such fine strong boys! Almost big enough to be *caballeros*. What is your pleasure, *patrón?*"

"A whiskey and two beers. Small ones."

Sánchez turned in the direction of a bundle of rags at the end of the bar. *"Un aguardiente y dos cervezas, por favor."* The bundle stirred and raised itself into the specter of a skeletal old woman in a colorless *rebozo,* who had been dozing on a stool. She drew the two beers and brought them to the *cantinero*'s hands, then returned to get the whiskey.

"What will you have to eat, *señor?* We have an excellent stew today. Very nourishing and wholesome. There is nothing in it that I would not eat myself." Sánchez had been taking lessons from patent-medicine advertisements that a store clerk read to him.

"A little information, first," said Jake.

"Whatever you wish." Sánchez turned his head to check on the old crone fumbling a bottle off the shelf. As he looked, she uncorked it and started to put it to her fallen mouth. Sánchez picked up a small revolver from the shelf beneath the bar and put a shot into the wall over her head. There were startled cries from some of the customers, the old woman squawked like a parrot, and Sánchez repeated distinctly, *"UN aguardiente, por favor."* She poured out the drink hurriedly and tottered forward with it. Jake noticed that the wall was heavily pocked with holes in that corner.

"*Gracias,* little queen," murmured Sánchez, taking it and setting it before Jake. He seemed to notice the heavy silence in the room for the first time.

"It is nothing, *señores,* nothing at all. Relax yourselves and have good appetites." To Jake, he said, "My little mother is so deaf, sometimes she doesn't hear my voice. Ah, the frailties our loved ones have to bear when they grow old. Also, she drinks a bit too much. It is very bad for her liver. If I did not care for her so tenderly, she would be dead by now. What did you wish to know, *patrón?*"

"Is there a place in town called the Golden Moon?"

"A den of iniquity. Yes. A house of shame and great expensiveness. You should have nothing to do with such a place. I have heard that they"—he leaned forward to whisper—"put drugs in the drinks there. A man goes in—they drug him, they rob him. He gets nothing of what he went for, because they are all witches, you know. They only do it with the devil.

"When he wakes his pockets are empty, and they throw him out in the street." His voice rose suddenly. "Get out, you pig! You have no money. We don't want you." Jake froze, the focus of every eye in the room. "Like that," said Sánchez, concluding in a normal tone. "Also, the *bruja* who runs it, she has the evil eye."

"Where is it?"

Sánchez put his hand to his heart. "*Patrón,* why do you wish to go there and become diseased and cursed? Here, we have everything you could wish for, at little expense. Food, drink, soft beds, someone to wash and mend your shirts—Prudencia!" He snapped his fingers to a stoop-shouldered slattern carrying a tray of stew bowls. "Attend to this gentleman."

Jake stood up hastily and put sixty cents on the bar. "Never mind. Thanks anyway."

Sánchez followed him to the door. "Let it be as you wish,

33

then, *patrón*. But when you have ruined your health come back to see my sainted mother for a remedy. She is the only *curandera* in Arredondo."

The crowd across the street was beginning to drift away as Jake came out of the cantina. There were several shots fired in parting, and the sound of breaking glass. Paco and Urraca fell together behind Jake's knees, but there was no further demonstration. The men scattered in groups of twos and threes to the various saloons.

They left behind them a window, already much cracked and taped, now freshly punished with bullet holes. It bore the words THE ARREDONDO ARROW in semiprofessional letters across its width. He started for it, as a better information source than the barkeeper. When he was still several yards from the walk he could read the smaller inscription, *Clement C. Hand, Publisher*.

Behind the ruined glass a compact body stood on guard at bulldog readiness, his arms in gartered shirt sleeves, his eyes invisible behind the reflective shield of spectacles.

Jake came to an abrupt halt at the sight of the name and the figure, then turned and angled off down the street instead. "Come on, hurry it up," he growled at Paco and his sister. Behind them the *Arrow* door swung open and there was the clatter of light boots on the walk.

"Hey, there! Wait! Dutch, is it you?"

"Is he after us?" Paco panted hoarsely at his side.

"Dutch Hollander! Hold on!"

Jake slowed down reluctantly, then came to a halt. People on the street had begun to stare at him and his pursuer. He turned and looked back as the smaller man closed the gap between them. "Hello, Hand," he said in a voice that mustered all the heartiness of a bored consumptive.

Clement Hand was more demonstrative. "Dutch Hollander, it is you. I thought you looked familiar when I saw you get off the stage, but how long has it been now, fifteen—twenty years? A hundred? No matter, you look the same. I'd know

34

you anywhere. Where have you been all these years, and what are you doing in Arredondo? Planning to stay? Say, come on back to the office. Carrie's there. You'll really give her a surprise!"

Paco listened to the stream of questions with a frown. He tugged on Jake's coat so sharply that Jake barely restrained himself from kicking him. "He don't even know your name right, *tío*. Maybe he's some kind of damn *loco*."

Clement Hand beamed down on the boy, not understanding his throaty mutter. "Say, are these your little ones, Dutch? I never thought you'd settle down to raising young. They're a fine pair of boys, though."

Jake looked frostbitten. "They're not mine."

"They're not?"

"I'm trying to deliver them to somebody who lives here. Maybe you know her."

"I know everybody there is to know around here. But come on back to the office, first. Look, there's Carrie now, standing out there wondering at me. She didn't know what made me rip out of the place like I did. She'll be fretting. I suppose you saw the little rumpus that took place a few minutes ago. It wasn't anything serious. It's just that the boys are getting a bit keyed up. But Carrie worries. Come on back."

He took Jake's arm and pulled him back to the office door, where the slender figure in a severely tailored shirt and skirt stood waiting for them.

"Carrie, dear, look who's here! Speak of the devil, hey? What do you think of this? Providence. Couldn't be anything but providence."

Providence was not a term Jake had ever heard applied to himself, but his mind was less occupied with the word than it was with the fair-haired woman waiting for them. Seeing someone like her again was an accident so rare in his life he had nothing with which to compare it. He didn't think he was going to enjoy the novelty.

Carrie Hand's face betrayed no more emotion than Jake's.

35

She put out a long-fingered, cool hand smudged with ink and said, "Hello, Mr. Hollander. Are you planning to stay here in Arredondo?"

He shifted some of his luggage so he could take the hand, relieved that she had come to the point so quickly. "No, I'm just passing through, Miss Hand. Or is it something else now?"

Her fingers slipped out of his. "No. It's still Miss Hand."

"I'm only here until the stage leaves. I'm looking for a place here called the Golden Moon. Could you direct me?"

Her eyebrows lifted. "The stage only makes a half-hour stop, Mr. Hollander. Will you have the time?"

Jake's mouth twitched into a fleeting smile, but her brother was taken aback. "Carrie, what's got into you? And what's all this Mr. Hollander–Miss Hand business?"

Jake ignored him. "I'm not asking for myself, ma'am. I'm trying to direct the boy, here."

Her whole posture tightened at that, and even Clement Hand's face grew sober.

"You're not really taking these children down to the Moon, are you, Dutch? Do you know what kind of place it is?"

"I've got a fair idea. But don't worry about it. They're expected. Where is it?"

Clem pointed down the street to a two-story house, still unpainted. It was already the most imposing structure in town except for the oddly shaped cantina. Carrie Hand turned on a pivotal foot and went back into the newspaper office. Jake made a movement to leave, too.

"Stay a minute more, Dutch. Please," Clement Hand begged, and urged him through the door and into a chair near his own desk. In the corner farthest from the door a yokel the size of a grizzly bear was cleaning type. He stared at them uncomprehendingly. Paco and Urraca joined him and began a minute inspection of the printing equipment.

"How long have you been here, Clem?" Jake asked with faint interest. He was still enduring a silent summing up from Carrie across the room.

36

"A year this coming May."

"Have you always been this popular?" Jake indicated the seamed window.

Clem laughed too quickly. "Oh, that's nothing. If I'd packed up and left town every time somebody felt like putting a hole in my window— Why, when we first came here and went to press, half the men in the area took off from work just to come see how the machine operated.

"I ran off a special edition for them, with all their names and their claim names and a headline that said, 'We Struck It Rich in Arredondo.' Some of them got so happy they shot out all our lamps and peppered the roof with so many holes we nearly drowned when the rains came." He laughed again and looked at Carrie. She said nothing.

"Look, Dutch, when I said to Carrie it was providence that sent you here, I meant it. I don't know where you're headed or why, but if it's a job you need I believe we've got just the thing for you right here. And I know you're just what the League has been praying for." He seemed to look for Carrie's support before continuing, but she remained silent, watching Jake. Jake made a steeple out of his fingers and waited.

"Where are you from now, Jake, if you don't mine me asking? Tombstone? Tucson? Phoenix or Flagstaff?"

"San Francisco."

Clem whistled. "Had you been there long?"

"Two years," Jake said, with no intention of expanding any further on his history. Carrie turned back to her desk, but he saw she was still listening.

"Well, I guess in that case Arredondo doesn't look like much to you. I don't know if you've had any experience with mining towns. They're a lot different from cattle towns like Willow Bend. Steadier, for one thing, since they don't have to depend on a seasonal influx of roughnecks for their money.

"The money is here, and more of it stays here, even if we don't have a regular bank yet. But that's only because we're

37

so new. You see, Dutch, Arredondo is still so fresh out of the ground that we don't even have any kind of proper local government! We're not incorporated into a town; we don't have a mayor. We've yelled our heads off to the county and the territorial government for some attention so we can begin to have a little law here, collect taxes, and make something of the place that would attract more people. But they're all so busy up in Santa Fe, playing railroad and seeing Indians behind every rock, they haven't taken the time for us.

"It's the damnedest thing—oh, sorry, Carrie—but we can't even get a sheriff's deputy out of the county. They say they don't have the money. We offered to pay the man's salary out of our own pockets—and they haven't even had the courtesy to answer our last letter! Here we are, a growing, booming town with a major industry that would turn most other towns green with envy; new people coming in every week, new buildings going up every month—and it's just as if we didn't exist."

Jake sighed faintly. Clem didn't notice, but Carrie did.

"So, to make do for the time, some of us have formed the Citizens' Government League to represent the town's interests the best way we can. No authority, of course. There are five or six merchants, several saloon owners, the foreman of the Hassayampa Mine when he bothers to come, me, Carrie, and a few others.

"We do what we can when a problem comes up, but a handful of sober citizens meeting once or twice a week over a saloon don't have much influence on the bunch of drunks down in the bar." He took off his glasses and began to polish them vigorously.

"Now, I don't want you to think that this is one of those wild places like Tombstone and some others. It isn't. The men work hard here. There aren't any vagrants or loafers. The town is too isolated for them. I guess that's something we can thank the Apaches for: making it too rough a trip for a saddle tramp looking for trouble. The men are honest and

38

good workers, but on weekends they do want to blow off steam, and then the ladies and children have to keep out of the streets. No real trouble yet, but the danger does exist, and some of us have been concerned about it." He looked myopically at Jake.

"What we need here is somebody to represent the law until the politicians in the capital are ready to give us a little help. We scraped up the money to build a jail six months ago, but we can't keep anybody on the job to run it. Oh, we had a fellow who lasted a couple of months, then got a fresh attack of the silver fever as soon as he had a grubstake and took off to the hills again. We hired another one, just a kid. He took the job seriously, but he wasn't old enough to make the men take *him* seriously. He tried to stop a fight between the Gebhardt brothers and got his arm broken. He quit. It was just as well he did, but—"

Jake was shaking his head, already standing up again. "I'm not in that business any more, Clem. Haven't been for a long time. Sorry. Thanks for your offer, though. It's been good to see you again." That was as far as he could decently go with a social lie.

Clem was looking at him in astonishment. "What do you mean, you're not in that business any more? You're Dutch Hollander, aren't you? What other business could you be in, as long as anybody remembers Kansas?"

Jake smiled faintly. "That's just it, friend. Nobody remembers, least of all me. And I don't use that name, either. It never was my choice to begin with. The name is Jake. Jacob Hollander. And I stay well by keeping out of other people's fights."

"What do you do now?" It was Carrie asking.

Jake turned in surprise. Several sharp answers sprang to his mind, but he put them away. "I play poker," he said simply.

She gave a ladylike sniff of disapproval. "That isn't an occupation; it's a vice."

39

He smiled. "Miss Hand, you're right, as far as most people are concerned. Many are called and few are chosen, as the preachers say. I'm one of the few. I get by, and I don't take anything from people except what they want to give me—like those preachers." He touched his hat brim to her and finished the motion with an imperious gesture to Paco, who reluctantly let go of a handful of inky type.

"But, Dutch—" Clem began again doggedly.

"You've been refused politely, Clem," his sister said. "Mr. Hollander is eager to get down to the Golden Moon, and you're detaining him."

Jake gave her the ghost of a bow from the door before closing it behind him.

The Golden Moon bore no sign to show it was a place of business, but, looking at the size of it compared with the rest of the town, Jake could see that it would need none. Especially when it was painted. He did wonder about the owner's plans in that direction; a bright pumpkin yellow, or maybe just an old-fashioned, honest cow-yard red. He handed the carpetbag to Paco and knocked on the door.

There was some vocal disturbance at the back of the house, then the shuffle of feet approaching. The door was opened by a fat, brown old woman in *zapatos* and a calico skirt. He examined her doubtfully.

"Who's in charge around here?" he asked, deciding she wasn't.

"She's asleep. Come back later."

"Wake her up. I've got something for her."

The old hag grinned at him nastily, and Jake snorted.

"Not that! Tell her there are a couple of her relatives out here to see her." He put his foot in the door before she could close it, and repeated quietly, "Wake her up, *mama grande,* or I will."

She scowled like a totem pole, but she let him and the

children come into the hall while she retreated to the back of the house again.

The walls inside were covered with an ornate wallpaper the color of raw liver, veined with nameless vines. The carpets were of the same shade, crawling with arabesques, and the walls were heavy with gilt-framed mirrors and pictures of absent-minded-looking nudes. Beyond the hall was a large game room that mocked the gentility of a parlor, with Austrian lamps and plush-bottomed chairs. But Jake could also see an excellent faro layout and several other green-felt-topped tables big enough to seat six or more. The room, which he thought must take up most of the downstairs, was overcrowded in spite of its size, and stale with cigar smoke, sweat, and perfume.

To his left was a stair leading up. Paco and Urraca dawdled on it, running their inky fingers up and down the white banister spindles. Jake remained standing in the middle of the hall with the patience of his trade, listening to the silence and watching the door at the back of the parlor.

After five minutes a woman opened it and sauntered across the game room toward him. She was tall and plump, with a milky skin and still-uncombed carroty hair. She was dressed in a purple-and-gold silk Chinese robe of appalling gorgeousness, and she sucked vigorously on an orange that was only a shade or two lighter than her hair. She drained it of the last of its sweetness, her cheeks hollow with the effort, skinned out a strip of pulp with her teeth, and tossed the rest into an ash tray, wiping her fingers delicately on her hips.

"Good morning, or afternoon—whatever it is. What's the joke?" she asked pleasantly enough, while her eyes gave him a thoroughly professional examination.

"No joke, Mrs.—?"

"Moon. Delia Moon. What's yours?"

"Hollander."

"Pleased to meet you. I don't get many calls from such de-

41

voted family men." She was looking at the two children now. Paco smiled at her toothlessly when she winked at him.

"That's the whole point of my visit, Mrs. Moon. They're not mine."

"No? Well, they're real cute, anyway. Whose are they?"

"Yours."

She spat three orange seeds into her palm with deliberation and cast them away.

"Take that bone to another dog, honey, like the greasers say around here. I never saw them before in my life."

"No? Well, according to them, they're your niece and nephew. And according to the sheriff in Tucson their mother was headed for your place when she died suddenly. I was delegated to bring them along to you."

She ran one hand through last night's coiffure, yawning. "I know this is some kind of flimflam, mister, but I'm still too sleepy to figure it out. Why don't you just tell me the catch and save us both some time?"

"The mother's name was Robles. A new employee, maybe?"

She sucked orange pulp out of a tooth, her eyes narrowed thoughtfully. "Robles? I nev— Wait, now. Gringo Rosie? Is that who you mean? Rosie, uh—Rosita—Rosana Robles?" She gave a peculiar little coughing laugh. "Sure, I knew her. I just never thought about her having a last name."

"She had a letter from you, addressed to her as Robles."

She bridled at that. "Not from me, she didn't. I haven't seen her or thought about her for years. I never even knew she had a couple of kids, if that gives you any idea. You say she's dead? That's a shame. What'd she die from?" Jake shrugged. Medical details bored him. The woman ruminated for another moment. "Look, mister, you want some coffee? I haven't had mine yet, and I'm a dummy without it. *Angelina!*" she bawled over her shoulder. "Bring some coffee in here." She waved him to a chair.

Jake shook his head. "Thanks, but I don't have the time. I'm just passing through town on the way south. I brought

42

them to you, like the sheriff asked me. Whatever money their mother might have had I guess he took, to bury her. I've got her bag and purse, but there's nothing in them. The kids ran up a little bill on the way, if you'd like to settle it now." He reached into his vest pocket for the scrap of paper on which he had made a list of their share of his travel expenses.

She was staring at him as he unfolded the paper. Suddenly she laughed, a genuine lilting sound, though a bit loud. She put her hands on her hips and threw back her head, pealing out like a rather pretty fishwife.

"You really think you can waltz in here and palm those little scuts off on me, don't you, Highpockets? You must think I just got off the boat. Who are you, anyway, Rosie's new easy man? Well, if you want to get rid of her kids, take them down the street to that big mud hut and sell them to Sánchez. He'll buy anything! Then tell your brass-assed girl friend I said she's as dumb as she ever was. Trying to play dead, and thinking I could be sucked into taking her brats after what she and her—" She brayed again, angrily now.

Jake didn't laugh.

"The Robles woman is dead and buried in Tucson. Her kids had a ticket to come here, and I brought them. Now, if you'll excuse me, I've got a stage to catch." He dropped the paper on the floor and turned to go. Behind him the Irish laughter died.

"Wait just a minute, mister. Don't think you can walk out of here and leave those brown brats on my step—you can't! They're nothing to me."

He grinned back at her. "Or to me either, sweetheart. Looks like you're stuck with them. Unless you can get me arrested." He glanced at the stairs as he approached, but the children were gone.

A scream of outrage from upstairs told him where they were. There was a second scream, followed by a chorus of curses in two languages and a crash of crockery. Feet trampled the floor above. Delia Moon pushed past him and took

43

three jumps up the stairs before an enraged female face was thrust over the upper railing at her.

"What's the matter up there, Chica?"

"What's the matter is that I got two goddamn *chicos* runnin' into my room while I got a customer, and he don like it so much to have company come and watch him while he's trying to—" She made a wry face. "It's old man Patterson," she confided in an earsplitting whisper. "You know he likes to come in while there ain' nobody else around."

"What got broke?"

"Oh, I threw that ugly vase that Jimmy gave me at them, and it hit the door. Chipped the paint a little, *siento*."

"Where'd they go?"

"I don't know. Down the back stairs, I guess. If they run into Angelina, tell her I like her to bust their heads together, just for me." She retreated to soothe her flustered client.

"*Angelina!*" Delia roared again. "Hold on there, Highpockets, now I got a bit of a bill for you. Let's see. One imported vase—from Nogales, that is—at maybe two bits. One busted paint job on my new door—two dollars. That's one for the paint and one for the painter. One embarrassed customer who's probably lost the calling card he came in with, and at his age won't be able to find another one like it for a month. I don't know what to charge for him, because that sort of thing is priceless." She started to laugh again, leaning on the newel post. Jake smiled back at her reluctantly, his hand on the doorknob.

"What are you, really? Some kind of dealer?" she asked. He gave a bare nod. "That's what I thought. Did I insult you when I called you Rosie's easy man? Well, maybe I'm going to insult you again. You couldn't be. You're not her taste. Is she really dead?" He gave assent to that. "Well, that's too bad. And you say she died broke?" Her chocolate eyes studied him. "She was a real good-looking girl the last time I saw her, but she had a weakness for big blond Americanos. That's how she got her name, Gringo Rosie. She was all *india*, that girl.

You really didn't know her?" He shook his head and turned the knob a little. "Tch. There really is one born every minute, like the man used to say.

"Listen, what's-your-name—Hollander. If you're a dealer, and a good one, I've got a spot for you right here. The man I've got now has been tipping up his glass more than I like to see. I don't have anything against drinking in the proper place, which is the customer's side of the table, but a drunk dealer is like a whore with the hiccups—it spoils the action. You drink?"

"Only when I'm sober."

"I could get along with you, Highpockets. You want the job? It beats peddling kids."

He shook his head again gently. "This is my day to turn down good jobs. I worked in a parlor house once. I think I'd rather pass out temperance tracts at an Irish wake."

She was laughing at that as he went out the door. His own laugh was silent but more satisfying, since it was the last one, he thought. He had rid himself of the brats. She had them somewhere in that house, hiding in a closet, maybe. And she had forgotten them for a moment while she tried out her fine brown Irish eyes on him.

He wondered if she still worked at her trade, or just played the lady madam. Dressed in something less garish than that sleazy wrapper, she would be a good-looking woman. He also wondered where she'd got the money to build such a place. She looked a little young to have earned it all herself.

A heavy rumble in the street ahead of him made him glance up, then start forward with a yell. But he was too late. The damned stage had left on time, without him.

5

He sat in Hernando Sánchez's place, with his back to the wall out of old habit, smoking one of the late Señora Robles's little black cigars. He had fastidiously moved the chair away from the wall because of the random parade of cockroaches that galloped up and down the mellow clay.

Paco and Urraca slept with their heads on the table, behind an array of ravaged bowls and beer mugs. Paco's lip was swollen and wine colored where it had met the back of Jake's hand. For this Jake's conscience smote him and added to the bleakness of his mood.

He had never considered himself to be a potential child beater or dog kicker, but the timely arrival of the two little whelps at his heels just as he was absorbing his defeat by the departed stage had been too much for him. He had stopped Paco's cheerful mouth with a hand that moved faster than his brain at that moment. That worried him, too.

The whorehouse cook had caught them, put tacos in their hands, and turned them out the back door in time to run after him. To make amends for the blow he had fed them, and fed them again. They had raced through the streets all afternoon with a cannibalistic-looking brood of brats from behind the cantina, and now they slept. Their presence beside him had helped to fend off Sánchez's laundresses, and the scowl on his face had discouraged even Sánchez. He had been sitting there for hours sipping tequila and smoking up Gringo Rosie's last cigars.

When Clement Hand swung through the door Jake gave him no sign of recognition until he had pulled up a chair beside him.

"Sit down," Jake said belatedly.

Clem was looking pleased. "I've been searching for you, Dutch. I heard you missed your stage."

Suspicion began to form in Jake's mind. "Yeah. The driver took off like somebody turpentined him."

"They have very strict schedules to keep to, or they lose their contract for the mails. It's too bad. For you, I mean. But otherwise, I was wondering if you've had time to think over what we talked about earlier?" He wore thick-lensed spectacles that magnified his pale blue eyes.

"About me becoming the town bearkeeper? What is there to think over?"

"Does Deel's offer suit you better? It might not be impossible to combine the two, I suppose."

Jake looked at him with interest for the first time. "How did you hear about that? Don't tell me that Carrie lets you be buddies with the head whore?"

Clem looked evasive. "Delia Moon is a member of the Citizens' League." He let Jake laugh at that, his own eyes shifting away to the bar. Sánchez caught the look and sent one of his drabs to the table with a bottle and a glass. For some reason Jake was surprised.

"You're a regular customer down here, too, aren't you?"

"I come in sometimes. Sánchez hears everything that happens for miles around. He's as good as a straight wire for a newspaperman." He poured and swallowed quickly. "I came in tonight because I was looking for you. I wanted you to know that I called a meeting of the Citizens' League this afternoon and told them about you. I know—you're not interested in a permanent job—but I told them, anyway. I thought

47

that since you missed the stage, you might like to know they would all be dead pleased to get you for town marshal, even temporarily. I even got them to raise the salary quite a bit, on the strength of your experience and reputation."

"Reputation!"

"That's fifty dollars a month and a dollar a day for any prisoners: twice what the last man got. And there's a little room in the jail where you could sleep rent free. You could be on to a good thing here, Dutch. Especially if Delia—"

"The only good thing I want to be on to here is the next stage out," muttered Jake, thinking of that woman's laughter.

Clem sighed, his fingers beginning to tap out some meditative code on the tabletop. He looked at the sleeping children. "What are you going to do about them?"

"Nothing." This wasn't enough for Clem. "I go. They stay," Jake told him. "Simple. Maybe your Citizens' League would like to take over for me. It'd give them something else to have meetings about."

"You could do that? Just go off and leave them here?"

"They're not my kids. They're up for grabs and that's too bad, but it isn't my fault. Do you want them? Madam Moon doesn't. Take them home to Carrie. I remember how she used to get worked up over worn-out horses and stray dogs. If she still does, this is her meat."

"Oh, Dutch." Clem sighed as if in shame for him. Then, "We don't have the room."

"Ah!"

Clem chose to ignore the irony in that one syllable. "Well, I'm sorry if I've intruded on your privacy, Dutch, but I just couldn't let the right man for our job go without trying one more time." He seemed to be on the point of leaving the table, then changed his mind and leaned back again. "You sure do stir up my curiosity, though. You know how it is with newspapermen." There was a look of amusement on his face that faded as he studied Jake.

"What bothers you?"

"Oh—why you left Willow Bend without a word to anyone. Why you left a profession you were born for, to gamble for a living, when you had the respect and admiration of a whole county—"

"And a salary of twenty dollars a month."

"That wasn't bad money for a young man in sixty-two."

"It depends on what you had to do for it."

"What do you mean? You did what you had to do, well enough. The way you could use a gun was the reason you had the job."

"Oh, it wasn't that I minded shooting people, Hand," Jake said sarcastically. "There just wasn't enough sport in killing crippled kids that were sicked on me by you and your damned paper."

Clem turned red and began to blink his weak eyes in a nervous way that Jake remembered and detested. "Sicked on you? The Yaeger kid was a mean-tempered little punk who used that leg of his as an excuse for everything. He tried to kill you just to make himself a reputation."

"And who gave him the idea it would? You did!"

"Dutch, I didn't—"

"Don't call me Dutch, damn it! That was another one of your inventions. 'How Dutch Hollander Tamed the McNaughton Gang'! There *was* no McNaughton gang. There were a bunch of red-necked farmers in a personal fight with a ragged-assed jayhawker named Benson who ran off their stock and put buckshot into their prize bull. You made *him* look like the victim; you made a little back-forty fight look like the Mexican War; and you tried to make me look like Tom Smith cleaning up Abilene singlehanded. 'Killed Six of Them Without Reloading'! For Christ's sake, no wonder that little bastard couldn't resist me. He'd been picking off prairie dogs with a Walker Colt since he was twelve years old."

"He wouldn't have thought any more of picking you off the same way! And you did kill six of the McNaughtons. I didn't exaggerate that."

49

"And Jesus walked on the water!"

Clem blinked and tapped for a few seconds, then poured himself another drink. Jake was beginning to feel embarrassed for allowing himself to feel so much resentment against an ancient abuse. In fact, his own outburst had surprised him. Clem was watching him closely. After a moment the amused look returned to his eyes. His mouth quirked.

"Dutch—"

"Jake!"

"Jake, then. I must say, I imagined a lot of reasons why you left Willow Bend so suddenly, but I never thought of out-raged modesty. Is it too late for me to print a retraction?"

Jake's snort of amusement blew all the tension out of the atmosphere. They drank together, and Jake, at least, did not notice the rapt attention being paid to their conversation by several people in the cantina, including Sánchez.

"So you'll be off on the next stage," Clem mused. "Where are you going, if you don't mind saying?"

"Down to El Paso to buy half interest in a saloon, if I like it. Someplace else, if I don't," Jake answered without rancor. "Put it in your paper if you like. 'Famous Former Second Deputy Sheriff Passes Through Arredondo. Stops Long Enough to Abandon Orphans and Disappoint Do-Gooders. Hopes Dashed He Would Stay and Die Here.' How's that?"

"A three-line banner? Not bad, for an amateur. Maybe I'll run it. So you're going to become a saloonkeeper? That takes quite a bit of money, doesn't it? Do you have that kind of money on you, Jake? I guess you must have. You don't look like a man who'd write checks. You must be walking pretty heavy. Better be careful while you're here. You know we don't have any law around here." He smiled blandly. "Sorry. None of my business, is it? Let's change the subject again. Where are you going to stay while you wait for that stage? There's no hotel here, either, though Ezra French keeps talking about building one."

Jake looked around with distaste. "Anyplace would be better than here, I guess. But I can manage for tonight."

"Tonight? What will you do the rest of the time?"

"What rest of the time?"

"Why, you don't think that stages run through here like carriages on the streets of San Francisco?"

"When's the next one come in?"

"Didn't Sánchez tell you? We get four a month. Two going west and north, two going east and south. The next two are due in a couple of weeks, but they're going back the way you came. You won't see another one for El Paso for a month."

There was a profound silence.

"I'll be a sonofabitch," Jake said at last.

Clement Hand cleared his throat. "As I was about to say, Carrie and I don't have the room, just two little cubbyholes and a kitchen behind the office. But our brand-new, unattended jail is empty, if it wouldn't bother you to stay there. There's the room I mentioned, and there are bunks in the cells that the little ones could use, for now. I have the key. Unless you'd rather stay here or try for a berth at the Moon."

Jake felt properly humbled. "Thanks for giving me the choice. Jail sounds good to me, right now. I'll pay you for the bunk."

"Oh, it's better than a bunk. And there's no charge. I'll put it in the paper that the famous Dutch Hollander once hung up his gun in our jail. Or don't you wear one now?" Jake tapped his chest. "Of course. Less conspicuous. A man in your present profession must try to look like a gentleman."

He pushed back his chair and stood up while Jake was weighing the stress put on the verbs in that sentence.

"I'll get the key and some extra blankets and open the place up. You can bring the boys over whenever you're ready. Do you know where it is? Across the street and past my office four doors. Adobe, with bars. If you give us twenty minutes or so to get things aired out, you can put the boys straight to bed."

51

Jake watched Clem leave the cantina. One or two of the customers looked up as he passed, but he hurried by them without acknowledgment. He was certainly a regular member in the place, unlikely as his appearance made that seem.

He was younger than Jake, but looked older now, with his gold-rimmed spectacles and his blond hair fading rapidly into gray. He was a shopworn edition of that young fireball who had so transformed his father's bland journal with his abolitionist fervor and attacks on the unrighteous that some Willow Bend wit had dubbed him "the Daniel of the Cowpens." Time should have rendered some of the fat out of his head, but Jake thought not.

He poured a last drink and shifted his weary tail on the chair, preparing to give Clem the time he asked for before going over to the jail. The free accommodations were a minor piece of luck, but he didn't plan to use them long. It was ridiculous to think he'd wait a month in this hole. Tomorrow he'd find somebody he could hire to take him out of Clem's anxious grasp, and out of Carrie Hand's sight, too. He didn't relish being watched for a month by a woman he had known too long ago to remember clearly but who looked at him as if her memory had survived the years intact.

After a while he glanced down at Paco, whose eyes were too tightly closed. "You're not asleep," he said. The lids quivered. "Listen, kid. I didn't mean to hurt you. You just took me by surprise," he added. He was feeling a bit drunk on the tequila. Paco's eyes opened, mirroring Jake.

"It didn't hurt."

"Yes, it did. And I'm sorry. *Lo siento*. Okay?"

"Okay."

They were silent together.

"Are you a famous man?"

"No, I'm not a famous man! Where the hell did you get that?"

"You said."

"Oh. Well, I was mocking the *señor* for his *loco* ideas. If

52

you heard that, then maybe you heard that we're spending the night in jail here. How do you like that?"

"I ain't never been in jail," said Paco soberly.

"Neither have I. By God, that's a fact." He laughed then because he knew he must be drunk. "Come on, wake up Urraca and let's go see what it's like."

Urraca was slow to stir, being drugged with beer and sleep, but Paco was wide awake and suddenly in a tearing good mood. When they got outside he took her hand and began to gallop around in the street, hooting and singing tunelessly, while Jake walked behind with deliberation—and a suitcase in each hand to keep him balanced. The air felt twenty degrees cooler than it had that afternoon. He hoped it would clear his head a bit before they reached the jail.

There were no lights on the street and no lanterns hung by the doors or in the hands of pedestrians. The saloons were all going strong, but their small, dingy, oilpapered windows gave no light to the night.

The street looked empty at the moment. He wondered how late it was. A mining town this quiet in the shank of the evening hardly seemed to merit so much concern on the part of Clement Hand's tea-drinking Citizens' League. Their law-and-order money would be better spent on street lamps. He couldn't see Paco or his sister any longer, but he could hear them sneaking up on him from behind.

At the last moment he realized the footsteps were too heavy and too stealthy for a pair of prank-playing brats. He dropped the valise in his right hand, but before he could reach the gun under his coat his whole head seemed to explode in pain and a kind of reversal of light. He fell heavily, fighting to hold on to consciousness. He felt himself being grabbed and rolled over, then nothing more.

He could hear again, but he still couldn't move. Someone was crying and clutching at him, while others were running on the wooden walk. The jarring of their feet woke the pain in his head like a wild thing. He was cold and sick. When they hauled him to his feet his legs were like a baby's, and he had to put most of his weight on whoever it was that had Jake's arm pulled over his shoulders.

Paco was jabbering somewhere in front of him, and a woman's voice answered briefly. The nausea overwhelmed him. He got his legs under control long enough to pull away from his supporter, then fell to his knees and vomited in the street.

"He's sick!" wailed Paco. "That damn *cantinero* try to kill him."

"He's drunk," said the woman coldly. Carrie. It would be Carrie.

"He had been drinking quite a bit," temporized her brother. "But I don't think he was drunk."

When he was empty and shivering with cold sweat from the reaction they got him on his feet again and piloted him to the jail. The door was open, and a dazzling kerosene lamp on the table made him close his eyes in pain. Somebody put a chair under his knees and he fell into it, with his head and arms on the table.

Clem touched the back of Jake's head carefully. "Look, he's bleeding here. And he's got a lump the size of a plum. Somebody hit him."

"Oh, nonsense," said Carrie. "He must have hit his head when he fell down drunk. You can smell it. Judd, run and get me a jug of water and a clean cloth. And a piece of ice from Mr. Sánchez. Wait! Here's a penny. I know he'll want something for it."

Jake groaned and tried to sit up to see who Judd was, but felt himself restrained by a cool hand on the nape of his neck.

"Sit still, you idiot," she said in a voice that shook slightly, "or you'll just be sick again, and on this clean floor." She pulled off his coat with Clem's help, removed his collar, and began to massage the back of his neck gently.

"Little boy, when that water comes I want to see you use

54

some of it, too. And your brother. You're both absolutely grimy." There was no reply from Paco.

By the time the water and ice did arrive Jake was determined to escape from her controlling hands. He took off his shirt and washed his face, then doused his head while Clem made an ice pack for his skull.

His brain wasn't working at peak efficiency, but he had corralled enough of his scattered wits to realize one thing: his money belt was gone. His luggage, his watch, and the small roll of bills and coins in his pockets were still there.

Whoever had rolled him had done so with a minimum of time lost and a maximum danger of discovery, with witnesses so near. Somebody had known what he had and got it without wasting any time searching him.

Who knew? Urraca? She couldn't talk and Paco couldn't roll him. He had to be addled to waste time thinking of them.

Clem. He'd asked about Jake's money. "You must be walking pretty heavy. Better be careful." Was that a thing to say to a man you were planning to rob twenty minutes later? Maybe; if you were a self-possessed sonofabitch like Clement Hand.

"How do you feel now, Dutch?" Clem asked, hovering over him with the ice pack. Jake twisted around painfully and examined him. He thought Clem's eyes seemed overlarge, even considering the glasses. His face was slick with sweat and had a greenish pallor. He looked almost as sick as Jake felt.

"I'll live," Jake growled. "But I won't be so heavy on my feet now."

Clem blinked at him, then nodded slowly with understanding.

"Yes, that's what I feared when I saw you weren't wearing a money belt. The marks of it are still there on your skin. Did you lose much?"

A shadow moved behind him, and Jake noticed Judd. He was the big ox who had been sorting type in the office.

55

Haven't the two of you had time to count it yet? he thought. Aloud, he said, "Ten thousand."

The ox looked stupid. Clem looked incredulous.

"My God, that much? And you won it all?"

"I earned it. And it took a while." How long would it take to earn it again, if he had to play for it against two such poker faces as these?

Carrie hadn't put in a word, but he didn't realize she was gone until she came back through the door with another bucket of water, a pillow, and some clothes.

"Here you are, young man," she said to an unnaturally quiet Paco. "Water to wash with and something to use for night-clothes. Take off those filthy things you have on and I'll wash them tonight. Then climb into those beds in the first cell." She plumped the pillow energetically.

"Jacob, you had better go to bed, too. Here's a pillow for your head. You'll feel better when you lie down."

Whatever it had been that had made her voice quiver ear-lier, she seemed to have it well under control. No female had spoken to him with such cool command since he escaped from the schoolroom. But he obeyed without an argument, relieved to get away from the naked glare of the lamp.

He heard her shoo Judd and Clem out. There was some clanking and splashing from the cell area, then a sudden ex-clamation of surprise from her and a laugh from Paco.

More water was poured. Small rustlings. Near silence. He was beginning to drift into a limbo of concussive sleep when he felt her presence in the room with him. She bent over him, so close he could feel her breath on his face.

"Jacob Hollander, what in the world are you up to with those two children? Do you know one of them is a female?" she whispered.

The snort that escaped him jarred his battered head. "Run back and check on the other one, Carrie. I think he's dif-ferent."

She left without another word.

6

When he woke, his head felt like a belfry where the bells had just stopped ringing. He sat on the edge of the narrow cot and felt his damaged scalp with careful fingers, waiting for the vibrations to stop. There was a local soreness on the back of his skull, but it was nothing to the rage inside it. He found his boots and his shirt, then went out to look for medical aid.

The nearest saloon was called the Red Front. It was open and dispensing the only pain reliever he could tolerate. He took the first dose quickly, and the second with greater care while reasoning with his panicked stomach. The staring eyes of a plateful of sardellos on the bar made him cringe. When he had won out over the fire in his belly, he paid and went to find and shake the stolen money out of Clement C. Hand.

Their seamed office window showed him Clem and Carrie at work on the press. Paco's and Urraca's bobbing heads were just visible beyond the railing that separated the office from the print shop. He hadn't missed their presence when he woke. They weren't a habit yet, and they weren't going to become one.

He threw open the office door and thought about slamming it, but he already had their attention. Clem had just unhooked the swinging frisket and brought it down to cover his

57

margins. Carrie stood ready to pull the freshly printed sheet.

"Good morning, Dutch. How's your head? Be with you in just a second." Clem rolled the press bed under the platen and heaved on the devil-tail lever that pressed them together, then rolled back the bed: *clunk, clink, BANG*. When he released the sheet Carrie reached forward and took it, holding it up for a brief inspection. She didn't look at Jake.

"The kids woke up early and came over. Carrie fed them. Have you had your breakfast yet? How about some coffee?" Clem wiped his fingers on a rag and came through the swinging gate into the office, smiling. Jake stood in the middle of the small room waiting for him.

"I'll bring some coffee in here," said Carrie and vanished through a door to her right.

When she was gone Jake grabbed Clem by the necktie and jerked him close. "All right, where is it?" he snarled. "And don't say, 'Where's what?' or play innocent behind those glasses, or I'll stick your damned head under that press!"

Clem's arms and shoulders were well developed from years of rolling his press. He tore himself free at the expense of his necktie, but Jake caught him again, both hands around his throat this time, and pushed him back against the rail.

"I—don't—have it!" Clem wheezed through the pressure of Jake's thumbs.

"Don't bullshit *me!* You had that big ox club me and take it. Now where is it?" He shoved him through the gate to the press. Clem's glasses were lopsided and steamed from the heat of his scarlet face when Carrie returned from the kitchen with the coffee. She dropped the cups, and in another second Jake had a tiger on his back. Her arms clamped off his own windpipe as she swung her weight from his shoulders. Her nails made vicious sweeps at his head and ears. She had more hands than a heathen idol.

Overbalanced and strangling, the three of them fell against the press to the accompanying cries of Paco and Urraca. Jake was forced to release Clem to defend his own head from

58

Carrie's fists. When rescue came its source surprised him.

"Stop it! Stop it, Carrie! You don't understand," Clem gasped as he tried to catch her wrists.

She drew back, glaring at Jake. "I understand that you might well have saved his life last night, and this ungrateful whiskey sponge came in here this morning and tried to kill you."

"Well, he's—understandably upset, Carrie. You didn't hear, last night. Whoever hit him took his money, too. Quite a lot of money. And he thinks it must have been me or Judd."

For an instant she stood perfectly still, looking at Jake. Then she rallied. "What? Of all the stupid—! Your filthy money was right there in your pocket with your ticket and your other trash. I saw it when I came over this morning to pick up your filthy shirt and wash it."

"I had ten thousand in a money belt that your big brother inquired about no more than twenty minutes before it was taken off me. Ask him!"

Carrie's face went a deeper pink as she looked at Clem. "He's telling the truth about the belt, Carrie. I mean, I could see the marks it had left on him last night. And I'm afraid I did ask him if he was carrying a lot of money. I told him it could be dangerous here."

"Dangerous!" Jake snorted. "Damned near fatal, with that two-legged sledgehammer you hired to get it. Where is he?"

"Oh, stop shouting, you—you sot! You *have* been drinking already this morning, haven't you?" Carrie's voice was full of angry tears.

"Please, Carrie, dear. Try to see it from Jake's point of view. He has been robbed of a great deal of money, apparently. I'm afraid I *would* look bad to him, in such circumstances. But, Dutch, I give you my word I didn't take your belt. And I'm sure Judd doesn't have it either. He's not very bright, it's true, but he's always been honest."

Jake was not convinced. "Is that the kind of fine-haired truth that's kept you out of jail all your life? You didn't take

59

it and Judd doesn't have it. Try it the other way around. Judd took it and you have it!"

Carrie stepped between them and drew herself up to within six inches of Jake's accusing eyes.

"My brother was in the jail with me the whole time. When the children came and you didn't follow, we sent them out to see why, and they ran back and told us you were lying on the walk.

"Judd sweeps out the Red Front and the feed store at night, besides working for us. He's a little simple. He came out of the Red Front on the corner and saw us bending over you. I think there might have been several other people on the street by then. None of us was alone with you after we found you and brought you to the jail. That is how it all happened, exactly. Unless you think I'm in on the theft, too. Do you? Do you want to ask me whether I have your money belt?"

Jake had nothing to say. He slumped against the press, his head a merry dancing hell.

"Carrie, dear, since the coffee seems to have got spilled, would you get us some more, please? We could all use it." Her brother's voice was soothing, almost apologetic, as if Jake had already made the charge against her. She moved to obey him, her eyes still fierce on Jake. Paco and Urraca followed her.

"Where is Judd this morning?" Jake asked into the succeeding silence.

"He only comes in a couple of times a week, to help set up for a print and to clean up after."

"You're printing today."

"It's a special edition. I decided on it after Judd went home last night. It's nothing." But Jake reached for the proof anyway.

It was a one-page edition devoted entirely to the issue of progress and order in Arredondo. There was an editorial recounting the many efforts of the town to get help from the

60

territory and county, in vain. There was a small story about the recent robbery of an innocent traveler. There was a general review of other unavenged pieces of criminal impudence in the last two lawless months, which could be put to rights only by the hiring of a special town marshal.

But most of the page was filled with a stirring account of the early life and exploits of Jacob "Dutch" Hollander, in all the splendid dime-novel language Clement Hand could muster.

Jake ran his eye over it rapidly, making several false starts on a common obscenity under his breath. The article concluded with the League's offer of the post of town marshal to the renowned Mr. Hollander, who had consented to take the job on a temporary basis while the League furthered its efforts to find a permanent solution to the town's problems.

"You are trying to shanghai me, aren't you, you four-eyed penpusher?" he accused Clem when he had read it.

"I was counting on you to change your mind."

"Why?"

"Because you have nothing else to do for a month, and because you'll surely want to stay until you find your money. The search would be easier if you had legal sanction, wouldn't it?" Jake looked at him stonily. "Then, you'll need money to live on, money to travel on. You might win enough at gambling to take you out of here, but you'd need some money even to do that, wouldn't you? The job pays well, remember."

"Did you sit up all night thinking this out, or did it just come to you in a flash, like you were Moses?"

"Naturally, if you want to quit at the end of the month, you can, and have enough money to take you on to El Paso. You might well find your own money before that time."

"But you wouldn't bet on it, until you get the town papers or another deputy, right?"

"I simply felt you'd want to occupy yourself until you found your belt. I hope you'll stay on after that because you want to. The town needs your experience, and you might

61

come to like having the respect and admiration of a lot of people again, Jake."

"Who says I haven't been respected?"

"You know what I mean."

"I know what you mean, all right. I see you didn't mention in your paper that the 'innocent traveler' who got himself plucked was me. That wouldn't go very well with this malarky about the big gun who was the terror of the Kansas clod kickers, would it? No, you have to build me up to get some attention from Santa Fe. Make it seem like things must be pretty bad down here if you have to hire a professional gun to watch out for you. What I want to know is, who am I supposed to scare? That bunch of rube miners who were out in the street yesterday dressed up like mick politicians?"

Clem turned a little pink, Jake noticed. The reaction brought an enlightened smile to Jake's thin mouth.

"Wait a minute—that's it, isn't it? That's really it. All this talk about the town needing law and order is just a cover. *You* need a bodyguard! Yes, and you thought it would be nice if the rest of the town paid his salary. What did you do to get the muckers pissed off with you? Print the facts about their mothers? Catch them in the hay with each other?"

Carrie came in with the coffee. She handed a cup to the grinning, triumphant Jake, examining first his face, then her brother's.

"I think we made a mistake, printing the special edition, Clem," she said in a cool little voice. "Mr. Hollander doesn't want our help, and he doesn't want to be of help, either. And who's to say he isn't being wise? After all, he isn't a young man any more. It may be that he's lost whatever small skill he had in the past. Who would know that better than he? Perhaps that's why he had to turn to gambling to make a living. Did you ever consider that? If he can't protect himself—as he certainly couldn't last night—what good would he be to the town? We already have enough drunks here who do their drinking at their own expense. Why import one and pay him to perform? The only talent he seems to have left—"

She stopped because Jake was holding the muzzle of a small gun up under her brother's chin. His other hand still held the coffee cup, but some of the coffee had slopped over on the floor. He and Clem exchanged looks of mutual understanding. Clem looked almost triumphant. Jake put away the gun and Carrie reached out to clutch her brother's arm.

"That wasn't good," Jake apologized. "Besides being a dumb, showoff thing to do, it just wasn't very fast, but it was the best I could do in my drunken condition. Thanks for the coffee. I'll take your goddamned job for one month. Come on, Paco."

Paco tore out from behind the press with a whoop and ran out the door in front of Jake, dragging the silent Urraca by the hand.

When the door had slammed behind them, Clem turned and looked at his sister. She released his arm suddenly, as if just aware of how she was gripping it, and started for the kitchen door.

"Carrie, do you think that was wise?"

"What? You mean to dig at his stupid male pride? It made him agree to do what you wanted, didn't it?"

"He'd already made up his mind to do that a moment before."

"Out of the goodness of his heart or his friendship with us? No! Only because he needs money now. Well, you've got him. But if you want to get any use out of him, you'd better not pay him in advance. If you do, he'll be gone."

Clem sighed and smiled faintly at her. "Yes, I'm afraid you're right about that. The thief who robbed him was more persuasive than all my arguments."

Carrie burst into tears and fled to the kitchen.

Clem wisely let Jake alone for a few hours before approaching him with the badge of office and the keys to the cells.

He naturally looked for him in several of the saloons first, but, not finding him there, he tried the jail. Jake was sitting alone polishing an ancient Colt. His long legs were propped on the jail's only table. Clem was astonished at the size of the old gun.

"My God, I haven't seen one of those for fifteen years. Is that the same one you used to carry?" Jake nodded. "I'm surprised you'd keep it all this time, traveling as light as you seem to do."

"Kept it to pawn when I needed the money," said Jake. "Gunsmiths are crazy about them. What are you down here for? Got somebody you want arrested?"

"No, I want you to come down to Red Front with me to meet some of the town people. We don't have anybody with the authority to swear you in, but meeting them will make it seem a bit more official. Anyway, you'll want to know some of them and get off to a friendly start."

"Will I?" Jake stood up and strapped the heavy gun belt around his hips. "Have you got a badge to go with this job, or do I just wear a sign on my back?"

"Oh. Yes, here it is. And the keys." Jake took them without looking at either and pinned the tin circle on his vest. Clem opened the door again and made a slight, inviting gesture, like a man trying to put a surly dog out on a rainy night.

The Red Front Tavern was a two-story shed that smelled of beer, sawdust, and burning coal oil. Its clientele seemed to be gathered there to mourn some common loss. They turned their heads to watch Jake and Clem walk the length of the narrow room to the stairs in the back, but no one spoke to them. The bartender wiped his hands on his vest and followed them, leaving the care of the business to his fat wife.

The saloon's upper room was filled with Jake's employers, sitting on a congregation of rough benches and chairs. Clem presented Jake to them with a short speech, then made the social introductions as they rose and came forward.

"Jake, this is Bert Kelly, our host, so to speak. He owns the Red Front."

Bert Kelly was two hundred and fifty pounds of Irish gloom with a drooping mustache, and a hardshell black derby that he never removed in public.

"I'm from Chicago," said Bert. "You ever been to Chicago, marshal?"

"Once," said Jake. "It was raining."

"Ezra French, and Mrs. French," said Clem, hurrying on. "Ezra has the General Mercantile Store down the street. He was one of our first citizens, weren't you, Ezra?"

"Brought two wagonloads of goods in here from Santa Fe," Ezra said briskly. "Sold out my stock, sold the wagons, sold the mules. Had to fight to keep one to get back home to Emmy with. Saw it was going to be a dandy little place to do business." He was the essence of the Yankee trader; spare, sharp eyed, with a goat's beard like Uncle Sam's. His wife was a tiny, toothless crone, wrinkled like a dried peach. She smiled and worked her tightly closed mouth vigorously, but no words came out as she pumped Jake's hand.

He saw Carrie standing at the back of the crowd. She actually smiled at him and pointed down to something out of sight by her side. A moment later Paco and Urraca broke through the forest of trousered legs and stepped on his boot toes.

"We been eating all day at Angelina's, and we're gonna get to eat some more at Carrie's later. You can come, too, she says," Paco croaked.

"Get off my foot, damn it."

He endured the rest of the crowd's frank curiosity and their awkward attempts to draw him out. Jesse Dugan, of the Miners Supply House, asked him if he thought he could handle somebody up in Lincoln County called Billy the Kid the way he'd handled the McNaughton gang. Jake didn't answer.

W. C. Clay, of the Silver Man Saloon, asked if he'd fought

in the late War, and on which side. Patchy Murdoch, a country sharp with a piebald face, asked if he liked to play poker sometimes, but was elbowed away by the town barber, Zeke Patterson, who told Jake he'd give him a shave and a haircut for fifteen cents any time, because they were both Kansas men.

There were others, whose names he forgot as soon as they were spoken. The women in the group were the last to come forward. As Carrie inched nearer, still looking surprisingly benign, a stout, redfaced woman with a commanding jaw got in front of her and grabbed his hand. Behind them both he saw Delia Moon, wearing a bird of paradise hat and a wicked grin.

He heard the stout woman say, "Marshal, I'm Annie Cuddeback. My husband is d' foreman by d' big mines out here. When Carrie told me your name I said, I bet he must be a Cherman, chust like me. *Ja?* So! How long hass it been since you hat a big piece of home-baked kuchen? You come by my haus und I give you some, *ja?*"

Delia took her place immediately, cutting in front of Carrie. Her eyes were sparkling. She seized both his hands and leaned forward to give him a good look down her dress. In a guttural parody of the Cuddeback woman, she murmured, "Und my name iss Zzatin-Ass Alice from Crrib-haus Corners. How long hass it been zince you hat a liddle piece of nookie, marshal? Vell, you come on by my haus und I gif you some, *ja?*"

Jake tried to swallow his snort, but it burst out of him, bringing the other conversations to a stop. Delia simpered past him and out the door.

When he remembered to look for Carrie he found she was gone, too.

7

Jake made his first official tour of duty that evening. As he came out of the jail the shrieks and bellows erupting from the cantina drew his attention first, but he didn't hurry to get there, in spite of the slaughterhouse pitch of the noise.

One of the washtub whores was being chased in and out among the tables by a customer cheered on by the rest of the house.

"Hold 'er, Newt, she's headin' for the barn!"

"You're gainin' on her, Reb. Put some salt on her tail!"

The woman showed surprising reluctance to be caught. Bottles and glasses smashed to the floor wherever she or her pursuer failed to take a sharp corner.

Sánchez saw Jake standing in the door. "Hey, *patrón!* You are medicine for sore eyes. See what that burro is doing."

Jake came to lean over the bar. He shouted, "Has anybody been in here spending a lot of money today? More than usual?"

"Eh? *Patrón!* Prudencia! Stop this games."

"Or did anybody leave town since yesterday? Not to go to work. I mean, pack up and leave."

"I can hardly hear what you say, *patrón*. This son of a donkey will put me out of business. Stop him! Prudencia! To the back and shut the door."

Jake twisted about in irritation just as Prudencia made another lap around the floor and passed him. He put his foot out behind her and tripped her lover into a belly slide that ended with stunning suddenness against the far end of the bar. Before the man could get off his hands and knees Jake jerked his gun out and hit him across the back of the head with the long barrel of it.

Two of the victim's friends jumped up to fight for him, but stumbled to a halt when the gun barrel swung around to them.

"He wants to go home," said Jake. "You take him there." To Sánchez he said, "If he owes you something for tonight you'd better get it now."

The two miners lifted their dazed friend as Sánchez hurried around the bar to pick his pockets under their critical eyes. When they were gone out the door with their burden and Sánchez was fondling the five dollars he had collected, Jake plucked one of the dollars from his fingers and stuffed it into his vest pocket.

"His fine for disturbing the peace," he said. "Now. Has anybody been in here today spending a lot of money, or has anybody left town suddenly, that you know about?"

Across the stage road from the cantina was Dugan's Miners Supply. He found the doors there properly locked and went on to the next saloon. It had a dead Indian painted on the window: The Happy Apache.

"Who's the biggest spender in here tonight?" he asked the bartender.

"Jesse Dugan. He's been buying for everybody."

"How much has he spent?" Jake saw Dugan coming toward him, arms upraised in recognition.

"Two dollars and thirty cents."

"What?"

"He never buys anything but beer."

Dugan reached Jake and threw his arms around him.

68

"Here's our new marshal! Howdy, Dutch! Have a beer on me." He put his face up close to Jake's and whispered, "Let's you and me ride up to Lincoln County and catch ol' Billy the Kid. Make you famous again." He put his head on Jake's shoulder and belched.

"Two dollars and thirty cents?" Jake asked the bartender.

"Dugan gets drunk eating sourdough biscuits."

Jake shifted the drowsing Dugan until he got him balanced. "All right, Dugan. Let's go."

"Wait a minute!" cried the bartender. "He'll be all right in a little while. Leave him here."

But Jake had felt a bulge around Dugan's waist. He hauled him down the street to the jail, dumped him onto one of the cell bunks, and pulled open his clothes.

He didn't find his chamois money belt. The bulge was a lumpy canvas contraption with copper bands clasping it at intervals. Dugan's belly was striped with green corrosion from the metal. On the copper belt buckle Jake read: DR. WELL-MAN'S GALVANIC ENVIGORATOR.

"It works pretty good, too," murmured Dugan, grinning at him beerily. "Wanna see my cock?"

Jake slammed the cell door on his first prisoner and strode out.

The pool hall was a retreat of quiet minds. He passed it after looking in the door. The rest of the block was quiet, too, until he reached the Golden Moon. There was a fight in progress on the porch.

"Hey, you! Break it up!" he said from the boardwalk. They wheezed and grunted, paying no heed to him as they locked arms around each other's neck. As he started up the steps for them, one broke free and shoved the other one back. The man stumbled off balance and fell on Jake, sending them both to the ground.

Jake struggled to his feet cursing and ran up the steps,

butting into the second man's stomach and bowling him over on the porch floor.

The front door swung open as Delia and three of her girls came to investigate.

"What in hell is going on out here?"

Jake hauled the man up by the shirt and prepared to throw him down the steps.

"Augie! Jake! What are you doing?" Delia snapped.

"I'm stopping a fight," Jake gasped, and shoved his captive down the steps, where he fell on the first man. He stopped, out of breath, and wiped his wet face while Delia glared at him, her fists on her hips. From the heap of bodies at the bottom of the steps he heard groans and laughter.

"Hell, we wasn't fightin', Deel. We was just funnin'. I told Rance I was gonna get his girl tonight. He's sweet on Big Irma."

"I ain't no such of a thing!" Rance brayed with guilty laughter.

Jake, still panting, watched them pick themselves up and climb the stairs again, grinning at him like a pair of china apes. They were burly blonds in their twenties, with a family resemblance that they now confirmed.

"Marshal, you don't need to pay us no mind. We're the Gebhardts. I'm Augie—and this is my brother, Rance. We was just playin' the fool with each other. Deel can tell you. God A'mighty, Rance, you like to tore off one of my ears there."

"I was just funnin', Aug," his brother wheezed.

Jake looked at Delia. She shrugged.

"They were just funnin'," she said. "Come on inside, boys. Big Irma's been waiting for you. Are you coming in, too, marshal?"

Jake picked up his crushed hat from the porch floor and descended the steps without answering.

The other side of the street was no different, except that it had more saloons. In the Schooner he left two brawlers staggering from the weight of his long gun barrel. They had been locked together like rutting elks when he came up behind them. After estimating their dead weight on him for a two-block journey to the jail, he left them to the jurisdiction of the Schooner's owner instead.

The Silver Man yielded him another drunk. The Red Front Tavern was still in mourning. He paused there for a drink and watched for a while, suspiciously, but no one stirred or spoke above a mutter. He left and returned to the jail, where he found Paco and Urraca waiting for him.

"Go to bed," he said briefly, and when they had he locked them in the cell. He sat down exhausted and waited, doing nothing, until it was time to make a second patrol.

On the second sweep he arrested a marksman who was using the Apache's lamp chimneys for targets. He waited patiently in the door until the man had emptied his gun before moving in on him.

"How about this one?" he asked the bartender. "Do you think he'll be all right in a little while? I don't want to take away all your business."

"Get him out of here."

"Better get what he owes you for the broken glass first."

And when the fine had been exacted, Jake took a dollar of it.

"For disturbing the peace."

He found Patterson, the barber, on the boardwalk outside the Silver Man, crawling on hands and knees.

"Lose something?" Jake asked, standing in his way.

"This is my anniversary," Patterson said indistinctly.

Jake helped him to his feet. "Is your wife still in the Silver Man?"

"Oh, no, Edna's at home. She was always a woman who liked to stay at home. I bet she's back there right now, celebrating my anniversary by waxing the front steps."

"Yeah. Well, you better get on home to her. Where do you live?"

"In Kansas. I'm a Kansas man just like you, marshal. I always say my heart's in Kansas, no matter where I roam."

"Come on, Patterson. Your wife's waiting up for you. Where do you live?"

"I live in a damn barbershop, marshal. Sleep in one of the damn chairs," Patterson said in sorrow, beginning to ooze drunken tears. *"Edna* lives in Kansas—waxing the damn steps so you can't put your foot on 'em without breaking your ass! She don't hold with liquor, so she threw me out, ten years ago tonight. It's my anniversary."

Jake wheeled him around in a one-hundred-and-eighty-degree turn to face the jail.

He found he had collected too many drunks. Paco and Urraca had to come into the tiny room to sleep with him for the night. Patterson sang and wept for hours. Urraca wet the pallet again, and Paco woke him a little after dawn to ask about breakfast.

He was careful thereafter not to arrest too many people at one time. He fined his prisoners two dollars apiece for the inconvenience of harboring them, then released them. He made eleven dollars in fines the first day.

The women and other milder citizens of Arredondo were pleased with his diligence, because the incidence of broken windows and shot-out lamp chimneys declined sharply after the first few days. Quarrels were taken outside the town limits to be settled, and drunks tried to balance themselves with greater care as they traveled the streets. But he hadn't found his money belt or any clue to the theft of it. Though he probed and questioned relentlessly, he could still find no better suspects to his own mind than Clement Hand and his hulking assistant, Judd.

To some of the Citizens' Government League, Jake's method of peace keeping smacked more of vengeance than of diligence. The saloonkeepers complained about the justice of the gun barrel at the next League meeting, where Jake was an indifferent guest.

"Hollander, if you don't ease up with that God—with that hog leg of yours, half the population of this town is going to be addlebrained."

"That's right! Damn it, Jake, there ain't hardly a boy big enough to wean that isn't wearing his hair parted with a dent from that thing. And after some of them get their heads cleared they're meaner than a snake with the shingles, too."

Jake was sitting on a chair beside Clem's presiding table with his legs stretched and crossed before him, while the rest of the League perched on their benches watching him. Arms folded and insolently at ease, he studied Delia Moon's wonderful bodice as it shook with suppressed laughter. Carrie sat with Clem at the table, taking notes and watching Jake.

Smitty, of the Schooner, was testifying. "Lord Almighty, man, you take the wrong people off to jail, it seems to me! The only ones *you* bother with are harmless. The fix they're in when you grab 'em, they can't do any more damage than to piss down their own legs—excuse me, ladies. No offense. Now, where's the sense in that?

"And then when we collect from them for damages, you take a dollar of it away from us for a *fine.* You're fining *us,* not them, when you do that. Why don't you take them down to the jail and fine 'em double, like you do the drunks?"

"Fines?" Carrie asked, puzzled. "What's this about fines?" Clem frowned, and there was a muted murmur from the few other people in the room who hadn't heard about the fines. Delia snickered, attracting Jake's eyes to her face for a moment.

"Marshal Hollander." Carrie's voice was sweet and cool. "I'm sorry to interrupt your meditations, but what is Mr. Smith talking about? We've never discussed fines."

"I fine them a dollar for disturbing the peace and two dollars for public drunkenness," said Jake.

"But you don't have the authority to do that."

"I'm afraid Carrie's right, Dutch," said Clem uneasily.

"Nobody has any authority around here," Jake said. "What am I supposed to do with the people I arrest? Take them to court? Where's your judge? Do the town people want to be tried by the miners' court out at the Hassayampa? The nearest real court is fifty miles away, so you told me."

"I'm afraid Dutch is right, Carrie."

"But he can't just take it entirely upon himself to collect fines, and even set the amount, without at least mentioning it to us."

"That is a point, Dutch. We—"

"It's illegal!" said Smitty, justified and pleased.

"No, it isn't," said Jake.

"I think it is," said Carrie warmly, her eyes beginning to glow. "Nobody gave you permission to do it."

"Is there a law *against* collecting fines from the drunk and disorderly in this town?" Jake asked her.

"Of course not!"

"Then it isn't *illegal* for me to do it, is it?"

"But—well, just because there isn't a law against it doesn't mean it isn't illegal, anyway." She appealed to Clem. "Does it?" But Clem was studying an ink smudge on his thumb.

The rest of the meeting was a confusion of voices. When it was over and the rest were scattered to their homes or businesses, Delia Moon lingered on the street with Jake until the Hands had disappeared into the *Arrow* office.

To Jake's surprise, when he started to leave her Delia walked along with him.

"Aren't you a little turned around?" he asked her. "Your place is back that way."

Delia put a hand to her lungs delicately. "Oh, mister, that smooth charm of yours just turns my heart right over. Say no more or I'll be led astray."

Jake snorted. "What do you want?"

"I want to see where you live. You're so unsociable, I want to see what you've got down here that keeps you at home all

74

the time." She grinned at his guarded look. "And you could give me a drink when we get there. Civic duty is pretty dry work."

"Why in the hell do you go to these tea parties?"

"For laughs. And to see what they're up to. Besides, Mr. Hand himself asked me to come. How could a girl say no?"

When Jake opened the door to the jail office, Paco and Urraca were in the midst of some charade, dressed in Rosie's underwear and shawl and Jake's coat. "Get out of my coat! Take that stuff off and get into bed." After a week in town, he was still saddled with them. The eager adopters of children that Carrie had promised him had not materialized. He grabbed his coat as Paco shucked out of it, and gathered up the heap of cotton skirts and shawl as he followed the children into the cell area. There were no other prisoners that night.

As Jake locked them in, Delia made her inspection of his quarters, letting forth girlish cries of mock astonishment at what she saw.

"Fresh sheets! And a clean shirt, too. My, my, my. Somebody is taking good care of you. Can I guess who it is?"

Jake brushed past her going into his room. "Miss Hand cleans up a little and feeds the kids, sometimes," he said without enthusiasm. "I've got a bottle in here. Get those two glasses off the shelf in the other room and close the door when you come back, will you?"

"*Miss Hand?* Is that all you call her, when the poor bony little thing is working so hard to make it homey for you here?"

He wished she'd stop spreading the marmalade. It wasn't her style. She appeared waving the two glasses as he bent over the old carpetbag.

"Why, I'd think that the least you could do for her would be to— What's that?" The slight change of tone made him glance up.

"My liquor supply." He took a bottle out of the bag and threw the bag back in the corner, where it landed with a solid thump in its own cloud of dust.

75

"Is that thing yours?" she asked, staring at it.

"It belongs to the kids. Carrie—Miss Hand—thinks it's empty, so a bottle is safe in it. As you see, she ransacks my own stuff when she feels like it. Hold out the glasses."

Delia did so absently. "Then it was really Rosie's, wasn't it?"

Jake swallowed his drink. "I guess so. She was carrying it. Why?" He put the bottle and his glass on a small table.

Delia continued to gaze at the leprous thing. "Oh—I don't know. It's just funny, seeing it. It sort of brings her back to me all at once." She sighed. "Poor kid."

"Yeah. Poor kid. Are you going to drink that or not?"

She sipped it, barely, then handed the rest to him. He put it down and reached for her.

She clung to him with that quick, professional passion of whores that always put him off a bit, but for which he was now prepared to make allowances.

But a few moments later, when he let her mouth go and was nuzzling her perfumed ear, she said, "I guess she died broke, too, huh?"

"Who?"

"Rosie."

Jake sighed. "I told you last week, the law in Tucson took whatever money she must have had before they gave me the kids. Is there anything else you'd like to talk about now? The cattle market? Free silver?" He *was* a little put off, and it irritated him that she was frittering away a promising moment. He kissed her again and got the same mechanical response. But her eyes were open, distractingly; watching him.

They parted the second time with a mutual sigh, Jake's a bit sharper. She pulled away with a friendly pat on the arm.

"Listen, Hollander. I hate to break up a good set, but I better go."

"What the hell's the matter with you? You invited yourself down here."

"I know, honey, but I've got half my mind on business and the better half doesn't stand a chance. I've got a new dealer, and I really ought to get back and see how he's doing. You know how it is. Listen, you come down later and we'll—talk some more, huh?"

Jake let her go with both hands as if he were dropping a sackful of cats in the river. "Sure. Run along. Don't catch your bustle in the door."

She smiled with maddening inattention, and left.

He lit a cigar and stalked slowly through the jail sipping her rejected drink, rankled by his own rejection; disturbed even more by his strong reaction to it. Anger made his ears feel hot. What in hell had she been up to? Did she just want to let him know she wasn't going to have to spend any more time buttering him up because she'd found herself a dealer? What a crazy damned way to go about saying so. Nature wasn't wrong when it gave women small heads and big asses. Even so, there was wasted space at the top.

Paco broke into his thoughts as he stood in the front door brooding.

"*Tío*, is that lady gone?"

"Yeah, she's gone. What do *you* want?"

"Urraca needs the pot. You didn't put it in here."

"Oh, for Christ's sake," Jake whispered in despair.

8

Every evening now when he made his patrols of the town Paco walked with him. Urraca, too, when Carrie didn't have her in hand for scrubbing, currying, or measuring for dress patterns.

They visited the saloons one by one, and Paco cadged sips of beer or puffs of cigars from the men while Jake surveyed the place for trouble. His income from the fines fell off in the second week, though he still collected them by the same methods, having discovered that the Citizens' Government League wasn't going to pay him until the end of the month. What money he did collect Paco and Urraca managed to eat up at an appalling rate, even with frequent handouts from Carrie and the cook at the Moon.

Urraca was an object of pity and curiosity wherever she went, but Paco was a universal favorite. Young children were so rare in the community that even the most anti-Mexican sentiments were softened by his gap-toothed cheerfulness. It was a phenomenon that Jake noticed and pretended he didn't.

While they walked the street, Paco talked. He saw or heard everything that happened in Arredondo. Jake never invited his reports, but he listened to them because Paco's information often proved sound, if biased.

"There is a strange man up at the Golden Moon now, *tío.*"
Jake didn't respond. "He is a *bandido,* too."

"How do you get that?"

"Angelina says. He is very mean and ugly, like a *bandido.*"

"A lot of people are mean and ugly who aren't *bandidos.*"

"She says he's got a big scar on his face where another *bandido* cut him with a knife."

Silence from Jake.

"Man, he sure must be an ugly-looking sonofabitch," Paco said pensively.

"Listen, you better cut out that kind of talk or Carrie's going to stomp the hell out of you. She thinks you learned all that stuff from me."

Paco was puzzled. "But I learned it all by myself. Good American. Don't I talk good American, Chake?"

Jake laughed and threw in that hand.

"Angelina says the *bandido* is hiding from somebody up there."

Jake looked slantways down at him. "Hiding," he echoed without inflection.

"Angelina says he's been up there for three days now and he don't go outside in the daytime, even to take a leak. She has to bring him all of his meals and drinks upstairs. Tía Deel don't like it, but he won't go away. Angelina says she's scared of him."

Jake slowed his pace as they neared the Golden Moon. Every window was ablaze with light behind the red-and-yellow curtains. That, and the amount of fancy jigsaw work that Delia had incorporated into the porch and gables, made it look like a Turkish lighthouse.

"You gonna go in and see him, Chake?"

Jake considered doing just that. But, after another moment spent listening to the harsh glee ringing inside the place, he turned on his heel and started across the street.

"If she wants any help she knows how to ask for it."

They made the rest of the tour, from the Schooner to the

Silver Man; through the raucous cantina, with its cages of canaries trilling and parrots squawking and its languid, scrub-weary whores dragging their round heels; across the street to the sullen Red Front; and back to the jail.

Carrie was waiting inside. Urraca sat beside her on the bench in self-conscious splendor, newly outfitted in clothes of Carrie's making. Her dress was a grim tan-and-black tartan, her stockings were black, and the high-buttoned shoes that completed the ensemble were cast on the floor in front of her. Neither she nor Carrie looked happy.

"She won't even try them on," Carrie said. "I've tried to make her understand they're for her, but she acts as if I'm punishing her for something instead."

Carrie had sailed into the task of civilizing Urraca with such low respect for Jake's efforts that Jake couldn't help feeling a quirk of satisfaction at her defeat.

"Maybe she likes going barefooted," he said.

"Well, she shouldn't. It's ruining her feet."

"Anyway, you're putting her off, the way you're frowning. Remember what you've been preaching to me—smile, look pleasant."

"Oh, Jacob, I have smiled. I have smiled and pleaded and cajoled for an hour, but she won't even look at them. And she curls her toes under when I try to put them on her myself."

"I can make her put them on," said Paco. He sat down by his sister and began a delicate pantomime of approval of her new dress and its funereal trimmings, the petticoat, and the stockings. Urraca's frown began to fade. She fingered her own finery doubtfully, watching him. Finally he noticed the boots. He picked them up as if laying hands on a treasure, poring over their every detail with avid hands and eyes. Urraca scowled again. He held them out to her inquiringly. She shook her head.

Satisfied with a first refusal, he began to remove his own old boots. When she saw his intention she snatched at her property indignantly. Jake had to go outside to laugh. Carrie followed him, restraining her own smile.

"He's very persuasive, isn't he? I almost began to covet them myself, watching him," she said.

"He's a smart kid." Jake took out one of the short, thin cigars currently in favor among indigent stage drivers, bit off the end, and lit it. The brief explosion of the match etched his long face, with its narrow bent nose, which gave him the look of a shabby ascetic. She remembered thinking once before that he looked like a shopworn Richelieu out of place in the drab world he inhabited. It was a look entirely at odds with his real personality, she thought with regret.

She saw he was watching her, wondering why she was lingering. She looked away, then took a breath for what she had come to say.

"Jacob, I've wanted to tell you this almost from the first day you came, but somehow I haven't had—I mean we haven't had the privacy to discuss it." She faltered, seeing that he was still looking down at her in the same cool way. She squared her shoulders. "What I mean to say is, I know you've been uncomfortable here with us, and if it's because of me, you have no cause to be." She looked away again. "Whatever we said, or thought, or felt about each other when we were younger is gone and forgotten. At least by me. It was so long ago, it just couldn't matter to either of us now. I've thought lately that you might be avoiding Clem because of me, and that would be wrong. Besides, I don't think he ever knew that we were—close. At least, I've never mentioned it."

Her face felt hot. She glanced at him again.

"How much do I owe you?" he asked, around the cigar.

"Owe me? For what?"

"For the kid's clothes."

"Why, nothing," she said indignantly. "I told you, they were a present. Urraca had to have something to wear besides Paco's hand-me-downs. He needs new things, too—"

81

She stopped as Jake brought out a quarter-sized ten-dollar gold piece.

"That cover it?"

"Jacob Hollander," she began. He put the coin in her palm and folded her fingers over it. "I don't want that!"

"I'll bring her little stuff back in the morning, then," Jake said unfeelingly.

"Why? Will you tell me that? Why are you like this? I was trying to make—peace with you, and you just ignore my efforts. You don't spend a penny on those children, except for the little it costs you to feed them and to try to make drunkards out of them. Oh yes, I've heard about the beer that Paco is allowed to lap up when he goes with you. You don't care a snap of your fingers for them, or for anybody. If it were up to you, they'd never have a bath or a change of clothes. You treat them like a pair of hunting dogs! But if I try to do one decent thing for them, out of pity, you throw it back in my face."

"They don't need pity."

"I'd like to know why they don't! Look at them—no family, no home. Sleeping in a jailhouse, locked in a cell by you. Living on beans and beer three times a day unless I give them something else. Hanging around saloons, picking up all kinds of filthy language and habits."

"It's better than going hungry."

"Well, children need more than just food! They need some security and love and attention from someone who thinks they're more than just little animals."

"I still haven't heard your bid," he said. "Have you got some better place in mind for them?"

"I'll find one," she said, tight lipped. "Anyplace would be better than here with you."

"I won't argue about that. You find the place and we've got a deal."

"Do you mean that?" she asked warily.

"Sure! What place did you have in mind, the workhouse or the county orphanage, if there is one?"

She whirled around and stalked away from him, arms straight at her sides, the gold piece still clenched in her fist.

He had expected her to throw it back at him. He sighed for it, and wondered what pleasure he had expected to get out of baiting Carrie. It was true that anger warmed her face to youth again and brought a deeper color to her icy blue eyes.

He examined the remains of his cigar with sudden distaste. It was going to be a bad night, when Carrie started looking good to him again. Especially since she had just made it clear she had washed his name off her blackboard years ago. He threw away the cigar and went in to chase the brats to their cell.

Urraca, having first resisted wearing her new shoes, was now just as adamant about removing them.

"All right, sleep in 'em," said Jake. "But take your dress off. And remember what that thing in the corner is for. I'm not running a hotel here, with clean sheets every day."

Though she was deaf, he always spoke to her directly, leaving it to Paco to make the necessary interpretations. But now, as she started to unbutton her dress, he wondered if she could hear after all. She could cry and shriek; she wasn't mute. He sat down on the bunk and watched her struggle with the buttons.

"Come here, Urraca." Paco turned to look at him questioningly, but she continued to fumble with the dress.

"I can do it for her, *tío*," Paco said, but Jake stopped him with a gesture.

"Urraca, come here." But she had seen his hand move, so he couldn't be sure. She came, solemnly, and he inexpertly unfastened her dress. The buttons were small jet rosettes that closed with heavy thread loops, more for decoration than use. He wondered at the craziness of women who put such

83

traps in a kid's clothes and expected her to get out of them alone.

"Sonofabitch," he whispered in exasperation when one of the little black balls broke off and bounced away. He saw the corners of Urraca's mouth turn up in a little cat smile.

He abandoned the rest of the job to Paco and went out to sit with his feet up on the table that served as a desk in the front room. He had nothing to do until his second patrol, sometime after ten.

On the table was a brown bundle of mail with a scribbled note from Clem. He started to toss it on the floor with the other mail, which he hadn't bothered to open since he took the job, when he saw that some of it consisted of "wanted man" flyers. He glanced at the note. It stated the obvious. Clem must want him to start hunting bounty now, to make another story for his seedy journal.

Opening the bundle without enthusiasm, he thumbed the uninteresting catalogue of horse thieves and offhand killers. Only the last one deserved more than a cursory glance. The man in that picture had such a look of country innocence and utter astonishment at being included in the rogues' gallery that Jake paused to snort at the popeyed wonder of him. Below the picture was a doggedly thorough Pinkerton description of his person and habits.

WANTED. FRANCIS RAWLS BECKER, ALIAS FRANK BECKER, ETC.

Escaped from the Territorial Prison in Yuma, Arizona, where he was serving a ten-year term for robbery, having on the 22nd of December, 1873, robbed the Wells Fargo Express Co. of $10,000 while posing as an employee, wounding in the commission of the crime the Express Office Clerk, James T. Bray. Becker escaped from Prison on the night of March 6, 1880.

Frank Becker is twenty-five years old, five feet ten inches in height, weight about 150 pounds. He has prominent blue

*eyes, short, pug-shaped nose, pale blond or tow-colored hair,
and a ruddy complexion. He bears a recent scar on his face
from the corner of his right eye to near the corner of his mouth
from a wound inflicted on him with a trowel by another prisoner.*

*His occupations are known to have been wagon driver,
farm laborer. His criminal occupations are robber, pimp,
and confidence man. He is a known gambler and may be
found in the company of gamblers, tricksters, and prostitutes.*

*He has no known relatives in the territory, but he is said
to have had a common-law wife before his imprisonment, a
Mexican woman known as Gringo Rosie . . .*

Jake let the front legs of his chair down flat on the floor
with a thump. He read that paragraph a second time.

*. . . They may be traveling together. The governor of the
territory of Arizona has authorized the payment of a reward
of two hundred dollars for his capture, dead or alive.*

THIS MAN IS DANGEROUS

P.N.D.A.——————Agency

Jake read the circular a second time, then folded it slowly
and put it in his inside vest pocket. He sat motionless until
Paco put his head around the door to say good night. Then
he gave a short bark of a laugh and took his long legs down
from the table.

"Hit the bunk, Paco. I'm going to take the second turn
around town."

"It ain't time yet, Chake."

"What are you, a Swiss watch? I may play a little poker
first, okay?"

But once out in the street he passed Patchy Murdoch without recognition, because Gringo Rosie had once had a scar-
faced lover who had just escaped from jail, and Delia Moon
had a scar-faced unwelcome visitor. Jake was eager to see if
he was worth two hundred dollars to anybody, dead or alive.

9

He went into the Golden Moon, stiff legged as a dog exploring an unfamiliar alley, but after the first minute standing in the hall checking the crowd he began to relax. The air was thick with smoke, the house was packed, the noise was abrasive. To Jake's senses it felt like home.

Paco's scarred *bandido* was working the box at the faro table. His scar was a disappointment.

It wasn't a fresh pink two-hundred-dollar gash from eye to mouth. It was an old, well-healed indentation across the man's brow, possibly from a saber cut honestly earned in some distant battle. Also, he was too old. He looked as if he had used up the first twenty-five years of his life twice.

But the kid was right about one thing. He didn't look as if he'd used them making friends.

Delia saw Jake just as he had about decided to leave as quietly as he came in. If she was surprised or relieved to see him there, she hid it well, beckoning to a pockmarked man in richly gartered shirt sleeves to take her place at the blackjack table while she rose to greet him.

Her face was powdered whiter than the last time he'd seen her, making her carroty hair more flamboyant. Her eyes and cheeks were heavily painted, and she wore a purple-and-gold satin gown so loud it seemed to hum. It occurred to him that she might be color blind.

She gave him an ivory smile and held out both hands. "I thought you were mad at me, Highpockets. Did you finally come down to see how it's done?"

Heads turned in the room to see who she was speaking to, and there was a fleeting silence before the play resumed. The town at large had watched his movements, and everybody knew he had both avoided the Moon and given the cantina girls a cold eye. Some people even approved of this unnatural celibacy in a public figure, but most of them were skeptical about it. Now it seemed that he was not only human, but also amusingly slow to admit it.

Delia took his arm when he would have turned away. She had a good grip, he noticed. She was nervous, after all.

"Let me show you around the place, marshal. You left in such a rush the last couple of times, I didn't get a chance. I think it's the best-looking house in New Mexico."

She pulled him back into the hall and up the front stairs. He smiled a little at her nerves. That faro dealer had been giving her some kind of trouble, just as Paco said. Jake was in no hurry to relieve her mind. Let her enjoy her drifter's unwelcome company for a week or more while he checked out his identity with the Pinkertons. Meanwhile she'd have to take the matter up with Clem at the next League meeting, since he wasn't authorized to do anything more violent than twist doorknobs.

He slowed his pace deliberately in the upstairs hall, viewing the writhing wallpaper pattern with feigned approval.

"Very nice. How many girls do you have?"

"Twelve. Come on down this way. There's a back stairs that leads down to my room. We can talk better there."

"Twelve girls. Does that include you?"

"Would you swim to China if you could ride in a boat?"

They went down the back stairs into the kitchen, then along a hall to her room, which seemed to be just behind the down-

87

stairs game room. It was surprisingly plain, comfortable, and businesslike. A large desk stood in one corner, littered with papers that were lightly weighted by a pair of gold-rimmed glasses. She saw them at the same moment he did and hurried to roll down the desk top over the clutter.

"What's the rush?" he asked, smiling.

"No rush. I just wanted to talk to you, and I knew we'd get a big laugh out there if I brought you in here by the direct route, that's all." She motioned him to a seat. "Sit down, Jake. Want a drink? I owe you one."

He shrugged agreeably, and from a cut-glass decanter she poured a generous amount of what looked like brandy into a heavy glass tumbler and handed it to him. For herself she chose a sticky red liquid in a thimble-sized glass. At her repeated gesture he sat down in her easy chair and tasted her brandy, waiting for her to come to the point.

"What did you want to see me about?" he prompted, when she didn't begin at once.

"Oh, nothing serious. Not to me, I mean. It's about Angelina, my cook." Jake looked blank. "You see, she's sweet on those two kids of Rosie's. They come up here all the time and let her feed them and make over them." She twiddled with her glass and looked as sentimental as her face paint would let her.

"Poor Angie. You know, she's Sánchez's mother-in-law. At least, her daughter had a batch of kids by Sánchez before she ran off to Sonora with a smuggler. Angie hasn't seen her own grandchildren for four or five years. I guess these two kids make her homesick for them, or something." Her warm brown eyes made an appeal to him as she laughed in embarrassment.

"So it looks like I made a couple of mistakes when I turned down those little brown babies. I made you mad at me, and now I stand to lose Angelina. She's beginning to talk about quitting me so she can go down to Mexico and see her daughter's kids. I can't let her do that. Why, she's the only decent cook in town. And she can wash out a lady's unmentionables without rubbing the lace to rags, and make peace between the girls when they get touchy better than I can." She shrugged in helpless surrender to the fact. "I can't run the place without her.

"So, I thought, why not make it easy on both of us? You shouldn't be saddled with a stranger's kids. Just throw their clothes together in something and send them down to me. Poor little things, if Rosie wanted me to have them it's the least I can do for her now. There's plenty of room here. They wouldn't be in anybody's way except Angie's, and she'd be tickled to have the extra trouble. I know she wouldn't leave me once she had them to look after, and you'd have them off your neck. What do you say, Jake?"

Jake finished his brandy first, because it was very good brandy and he wasn't going to be offered seconds.

"I say you tell rotten lies," he told her pleasantly. "It's almost embarrassing."

Her eyes opened in disbelief. "What?"

"You didn't run me up and down two flights of stairs and hide me out back here just to ask for the loan of a couple of wet-nosed kids."

"I don't know what else you think I'd—"

"Want with me? I don't know, but I've already seen this pitch worked before. Clem Hand took a big interest in the kids' welfare the minute he saw them. But what he was really interested in was getting me for a bodyguard against the muckers. Like you said the first time I met you, just tell me the catch and save us both some time. What do you really want, a bouncer for your new faro dealer?"

Something flickered across her face mingled with real surprise. It vanished before he could read it, but sudden understanding hit him like a wagonload of coal, and he jumped up and made for the bedroom door. She tried to get in his way, but he set her firmly aside.

The door at the end of the hall led to the game room. He

made it in four long strides. It was locked, but the key was in the door.

"Wait a minute, Jake!" Delia whispered sharply. "What are you going to do?"

"Get out of my way, you damned she-mick! You didn't want anything out of me. You just decoyed me in here so he could run out the front door, didn't you?" He jerked the door open, startling the players on the other side.

The scar-faced man was gone, his place taken by a placid brown whore with gold hoops in her ears. She and Jake exchanged stares for a second, then he shut the door and wheeled around Delia to get to the kitchen at the other end of the hall.

That door was locked, too, and when he wrenched at the knob it came off in his hand. "Goddamnit!"

Then his spurt of anger with Delia ran out as suddenly as it had flared. The whole thing was ridiculous: *he* was ridiculous. Every time he got anywhere near the damned woman he found himself playing the rube comic in her private show. He ought to be wearing balloon pants and a checkered coat. He peered out the window, but he could see nothing. Glancing back, he saw she was out of sight, too.

When he opened the door to her room she was standing by the desk with the decanter in her hand, watching him with the narrow-eyed scrutiny of a veteran cattle buyer.

"All right, who is he?" he demanded.

"His name's George Ramey. Do you want another drink?"

"Where did he come from? I haven't seen him around, and there hasn't been a stage in since I came."

"Say, that's right," she said in mock wonder. "I bet he must have used one of those things everybody has around here. What do they call 'em—horses! I know you don't have one, but you must have seen them around." She held out his second drink with a wicked grin.

Jake took it. He was feeling like a fool, but he asked

stolidly, "You've been keeping him under cover pretty carefully, haven't you?"

"Under cover? Why, honey, he's been sitting out there dealing for the past two nights. You're the one who's been under cover. You just don't get around to the good places." She was still watching him in that peculiar way.

"What the hell is he doing out here fifty miles from nowhere looking for a damned job?" he snarled.

"Well, how the hell should I know?" she yelled in outrage. "What's anybody doing out here? I didn't ask him. He said he needed a job, and I said I needed a dealer. We had a drink on it and I gave him a deck of cards." Then her eyes glinted with amusement again.

"You know, honey, you aren't the smartest man I ever met. I bet if it wasn't for your sweet disposition you wouldn't have any friends at all." She pushed his glass with her finger. "Drink it and get out," she told him without heat. "Let me worry about my help. Ramey is honest enough to suit me. And if he isn't, I can handle that, too. Is there paper on him? No. Then you just run along and roust drunks. And rest up, so you'll be in shape to chaperone all the little brides when they get here." She bit her lip, but the grin escaped her anyway.

"The what?"

Delia brayed with laughter. "The brides, honey. The mail-order virgins—they hope! That's what Clem really wants you here for—a chaperone, not a bodyguard. You're supposed to see that nobody gets a cherry till the pie's been cut. Didn't you know anything about this?" She gave the Belfast bray again. "I can see you didn't."

Jake frowned. "What's Clem Hand got to do with a bunch of mail-order brides?" He reached for the decanter absently, but she held on to it.

"You don't need any more. You smell like a bar towel now."

"And you smell like the whore of Babylon—any relation?"

91

"Oh, touchy, touchy—"

"I said, what's Hand got to do with—"

"He sent for them. They were his idea! You don't believe me? I thought you knew him. He whooped it up in his paper almost from the moment he got to town. I hear he's even mentioned it to God a few times in that Sunday school that he and Careful Carrie organized. It's going to be a—what was that line of his?—'a civilizing influence on the whole town.' And you can bet your balls it will be, because he's some little persuader when he gets wound up, let me tell you." She took a Clemlike stance for a second. "Why, when he starts telling you how great it's going to be here, you get up the next morning expecting to find manna on the streets instead of horseshit. Oh, God, I love to hear him talk!" She turned such an ecstatic face up to the ceiling Jake thought she must be getting ready to speak in tongues, but she only chuckled and shot him another one of those odd, sharp, amused glances.

"He got the poor lonely bachelors so hot thinking about 'con-*nub*-ial bliss,' as he put it, that they put up two hundred dollars apiece to get some." She dropped back into a normal voice and finished off the rest of the details in a businesslike clip. "He sent the money off to some New York agency. They're supposed to find some pure-hearted little pioneers who want to come out west and help shovel rocks for their supper. They have to put up some kind of money of their own or they don't eat on the way, I guess; because they're sure as hell going to be shipped out in a cattle car at that price.

"There's just been one little thing go wrong with our boy's plan. The girls are late, and the grooms are getting nervous." She looked at his face. "Oh, hell, go on and have another drink. I guess you need it."

He needed it. "How many women are coming?" he asked, while his mind tried to imagine how to organize the ground rules for a community rape.

"Fifty. Oh, there's going to be so much sanctified tail

92

around here soon I'll have to start making hats and baking pies for a living. And, you know, when he tells me about all this, he gets such a light in his eye that—damn! I almost think he planned the thing as a special favor to me." She laughed again, like an adolescent boy.

Jake was getting numb. The three hastily swallowed brandies were vaporizing in his brain. He had almost forgotten what they'd been talking about before. No, he hadn't. She'd made some kind of phony offer for Paco and Urraca, whom she needed and wanted like an extra tit. He didn't buy her offer, but her behavior baffled him. What did she want? She was still giving him that look, as if she had expected to hear something from him; had been watching and probing until she saw she was drawing blanks.

He didn't like to feel he was missing a point, but he knew he was. His only consolation was that she must be as puzzled as he was. She couldn't know how far out of the game he really was at the moment. He was worth something to her. How? The interest women took in life was mainly confined to matters of love, hate, and money. Love and hate had nothing to do with the two of them. It had to be money. But that was just as farfetched. What, then?

She was standing with her head to one side, eyes narrowed thoughtfully. "Did you go to sleep?" she asked softly.

He smiled slightly. "No. I was just thinking about you baking pies and running a home for Mexican orphans. I'll get you a big checkered apron before I leave town. It's going to give me a lot of peace of mind, knowing you'll be here taking care of Rosie's kids—while I'm down in El Paso spending money."

It was a crude shot in the dark, but it was right on target. He saw two little spider gleams of greed light up her eyes. He smiled at them warmly as he returned her decanter and glass.

"Thank you for the hospitality, sweetheart. And for the education. It's time I made another patrol."

It was Delia's turn to be left behind, he was happy to see. He let himself out into the hall and started for the kitchen door. She came trotting after him.

"Wait a minute, Jake—" She stopped. In the kitchen George Ramey was getting himself a dipper of water from the pump. He didn't act like somebody who was trying to evade Jake. But Delia looked unhappy to see him there anyway.

"Ramey, what are you doing away from the game?"

"I just stepped outside for a minute."

"What for?" she demanded in a haughty voice.

Ramey looked from her to Jake and back, then grinned. "Why, ma'am, I had to take a leak."

Jake busied himself with fixing the doorknob.

"Well, that's all right, George, but you better get back to work now."

"Yes, ma'am." Ramey moved away at his leisure. By the time he was gone Jake had the knob fixed and the door open. Delia put a restraining hand on his arm.

"Listen, Jake. We keep getting interrupted. About those kids—"

"I'll think it over and let you know."

She gave him the ivory smile again. "Sure. And, Jake, just because we've butted heads once or twice doesn't mean I'm not glad to see you come down here. You're welcome any time, for a drink or a talk, or—anything. So don't be a stranger, huh?"

He let his gaze drop slowly from her big cow-brown eyes to her smiling mouth, her white throat, and her deliciously overstuffed gown. The ghosts of a tree full of dead magnolias were emanating from between those firmly packed breasts.

He let himself have one more breath of her before he said, "Sweetheart, we've never been strangers."

She shut the door with more energy than necessary, and he heard the key turn in the lock.

10

Coming out from behind Delia's house in the dark, he heard the confrontation across the street before he saw who it was.

Clement Hand was in front of the Schooner Tavern, surrounded by his creditors. Jake stopped in the shadows beside the Moon to listen to them. They had apparently just caught Clem.

"Damn it, Reb, you got to watch them big feet of yours! A little feller like Mr. Hand cain't step over both of them without trippin' himself."

Clem was adjusting his spectacles. "That's all right. No harm done."

"Well, now, we cain't be sure of that. Why, you like to've busted your specs there when you fell down. Let me see 'em."

"No, no. They're fine—" But the glasses were removed from his nose by a massive thumb and forefinger and turned over to a second pair of hands when Clem reached for them.

"God A'mighty, look through them, will you? I don't see how a man could be so blind! If you was to break 'em, I bet that pretty sister of yours'd have to take you around town by hand."

"They'd be goin' Hand in Hand!" This piece of rare wit

drew a round of laughs that drowned out whatever Clem was saying. But somehow he managed to recover the glasses and took out his handkerchief to clean the smeared lenses.

"Look there now, Gowdy, you greased 'em up so much Mr. Hand cain't see out of 'em. We better take him home before he gets turned around and stumbles into that hurdy-gurdy house across the street."

"He wouldn't go to no hurdy-gurdy house even if he was blind. He come right out foursquare agin 'em when he took our money and sent off for all them sweet little girls. Didn't you, *Mr*. Hand?"

"Maybe he was foolin' us."

"What're you talkin'—"

"Maybe he didn't send off for no sweet little girls at all."

"You got a suspicious mind, Reb." They had begun to take Clem down the street toward the *Arrow* office, jostling him, elbow to elbow, while they played at their mock quarrel. Jake drifted along on the opposite side of the street after them.

"Maybe he took our money and put it in the bank some-wheres."

"That's a bad thing to think of a man—"

"Maybe he bought himself a sweet little woman in some other town."

"He wouldn't do that with our money. No, sir!"

"If somebody was to give me ten thousand dollars to buy a bunch of women and I didn't get one myself, I might take some peculiar notions."

"Well, you got crooked ways about you—I always know'd that. But Mr. Hand here is a gentleman."

At the mention of ten thousand dollars Jake stopped auditing their talk to do some rapid calculations. Two hundred dollars times fifty disgruntled miners was—ten thousand dollars. But not even Clement Hand would be dumb enough to swindle the muckers out of their money and then stick around town to be found out.

But suppose he had lost it. Suppose the women weren't

96

coming, and the money was down the drain, and Clem knew it. What would he do then? Pick somebody's pocket? The little bastard wouldn't have the nerve! Or would he? He was holding up pretty well under the rough joshing he was getting across the street. Jake had half expected to see him break away from Reb and Gowdy and run for home like a terrier pup.

He stopped on the corner by Dugan's store and let Clem's escort deliver him to his front door. They wanted to go in with him, but were shut out somehow without a struggle. They began to beat on the door and call him. Jake strolled into the street. He wanted Clem to himself for a few minutes.

Gowdy's mule was tied up in front of the Silver Man. The animal had a homing instinct that surpassed bad pennies and United States Army pigeons. Gowdy was proud of her talent and depended on it after a night at leisure in Arredondo. Jake turned her loose from the hitching rail, then fanned his hat at her nose.

She backed away from the rail and started down the street at a weary walk. Jake was just bending over for a pebble to throw at her flanks when Urraca, a nocturnal truant, came out from between the Red Front and the Arredondo *Arrow* and was startled by the sight of Reb and Gowdy. She had a large white cat in her arms. She dropped it, and it streaked across the street just under the sleepy mule's front feet.

The mule, spooked by a darting white phantom, gave a scream of terror and a kick in the air, then bolted up Hassayampa Street, stirrups flapping. Jake dropped the pebble.

"That's Annabel!" Gowdy shouted. "How'd she get loose? Come back here, mule. Help me catch her, Reb. Annabel! Damn it, mule, it's me—Gowdy! Annabel!"

They were gone, and Urraca had disappeared, too. Jake let her go for the moment. When he reached the *Arrow*'s door he beat on it several times without getting any response.

He followed Urraca's path around the building, but she was nowhere in sight. The *Arrow* had a back door, and he saw lights burning in the small windows on either side of it. He rapped on that door and waited.

Clem's voice was cautious until Jake identified himself. When the door opened he was surprised to see a small pistol in Clem's hand. Carrie stood behind her brother, a dark robe pulled over her plain muslin nightgown, her pale, thick hair twisted into a single plait that was already coming undone.

"What is it, Dutch? Was that you at the front door just now? I thought it was the usual party of drunks." He sounded relieved.

Jake took his eyes off Carrie. "Do you keep a pistol handy for just the 'usual party of drunks'?"

Clem shrugged and put the little gun away.

"He isn't afraid of drunks," Carrie began, but Clem stopped her with a brief look.

"What is it you want, Dutch?"

Jake was looking at Carrie again. "I was down at the Irish Riding Academy just now, and I heard a funny story. I thought you might like to hear it, too."

Carrie took fire at once. "You mean you came over here at this time of night and fri—got us out of bed to tell some bawdy joke? Close that door this minute, Clement Hand, or I will!" She tried to push past her brother, but he balked, looking at Jake.

"A funny story, Dutch?"

"Yeah, if you take it the right way. It's about a sort of con man; an arranger, a fixer—you know. He's not in it for money —I think. He just likes to fix things up for people. Reminds me of you. You're even in the same business: nose sharpening.

"Well, this typesetting Jesus wants to settle down, because he isn't getting any younger and his gospel box isn't getting any lighter as he humps it from one place to another. But the place he's in is terrible. It's too poor to grow warts. Anybody else would get out quick, but not him. No, he knows just how to fix things so the place will be perfect. He opens up his gospel box and starts right in to turn it into a nose sharpener's paradise. A town where he can run the government, preach the sermons, tell everybody how to live. But first he needs some breeding stock—"

Clem stepped back and motioned him in. "I should have told you at the beginning," he sighed. "Frankly, I'm surprised it's taken you this long to hear about it."

"He was too busy thinking about himself and his money," said Carrie.

"Please, Carrie. Hell, Jake, you're right to feel I haven't been fair with you. I should have told you the whole thing at the beginning, but I thought you'd laugh. And it wasn't the only reason the town needed you. I really thought it was a piece of luck for both of us when you missed that stage."

"Luck!" Jake scoffed. "Luck, hell! You didn't depend on luck. I never saw a stage driver who wouldn't wait two minutes for a paid-up passenger. You stepped out the door as soon as I was gone and told that Charlie I wasn't coming back. Then you rolled me so I couldn't leave any other way but on foot! And then you bigheartedly offered me a chance to make eating money by standing between you and a bunch of pissed-off miners if your shipment of women doesn't come— and refereeing a riot if it does. Well, it's been a profitable experience. I wouldn't throw it in for a pair of jacks. But I've had all the education I can take now. Just hand over my money belt and I'll be getting along."

"Jake, I don't have your money!"

"You were the only man in town who knew what I had on me that night. The man who rolled me didn't even bother to go through my pockets, he was so sure of what he was after." A thought occurred to him that made him smile nastily. "You were the one who made me the local law here, too. I'm dutybound to investigate all crimes committed inside the town limits, right?

"So I'm going to search you for that belt of mine. If you don't have it you don't have a thing to worry about. But if you do have it I'm going to haul you up to the county seat and see to it that you get about ten years to play in the Territorial Rock Garden!"

"No!" Carrie cried, her eyes black with shock. "You can't do that. You don't have any right to break in and search us without a warrant."

But Clem took her by the arm and held her back while Jake walked past them, as puzzled as he was suspicious. Because if Clem was so willing to let him come in and search, there wasn't likely to be anything there to find.

He looked, anyway. There was little to see. Clem's room contained a bed, a trunk, a table, chair, and lamp. There was a rag rug on the floor and a row of hooks on the wall. Nothing else. Clem turned back the mattress for him, opened the trunk, and even picked up the rug, while Carrie stood clutching the doorframe with a face like a Fury.

"That's it," Clem said finally. Jake stood still, burning with anger and embarrassment. Carrie suddenly sobbed and went back to her room, slamming the door.

"I could look in her room for you, Dutch, but I really don't think you expect it to be in there, do you? Meanwhile, there's the kitchen, just beyond that curtain. I'll get the key for the office."

"Never mind," Jake muttered.

Clem held the back door open for him. "Sorry," he said softly. He even looked sorry.

"Sorry to have bothered you," Jake growled.

He stalked the streets in a rage with himself and Clement Hand, who was so meek he'd roll over on his back like a feist hound at anyone's bark. Who'd let Jake walk into his house in the middle of the night, accuse him of theft, and search him without making a protest. What the hell kind of man would be so spineless, and still have the nerve to rob Jake on a public street?

That was the unreasonable part. The more evidence Clem gave that he was unable to do such a thing, the more certain

Jake felt that he had. He must have! He'd sent ten thousand dollars off to some thimblerig marriage agency, and it was lost. There weren't going to be any mail-order women. And he had Jake's money hidden to use as a refund when the miners found out they'd been gypped. He didn't have to keep it in the house. It could be buried in a tin can in the yard. But if it was, how was Jake going to find it?

He stood on the corner listening to the dreary cheer from the cantina before deciding to skip the rest of the patrol. All he would get for the work was Patterson and a couple of other drunks to fill the jail and keep him awake all night with their talking, singing, puking, snoring racket.

It wasn't worth six dollars in fines to harbor them. Tonight he needed something pleasant, like a dumb-struck woman in a soft bed. Or a piece of good news, such as that the Apaches were coming tomorrow to burn Arredondo to the ground. He turned back to the jail.

There was a light burning in the front that he thought he'd blown out before he left. Paco must still be up, peckering at the mud walls with a nail, his favorite afterhours pastime in the cell.

Jake strode in, ready to take a swipe at the brat's tail for letting Urraca out to wander around in the dark—and found Carrie waiting up for him in the office.

She was dressed again, though her hair was loose down her back. It was straw blond and straight. Her eyes were the blue of a thundercloud. He sighed with impatience when he saw her there. She'd come to lay him out for intimidating her milksop brother, of course. Let her say her piece, then, and get out, so he could go to bed.

She had a knitting bag at her feet. She bent over it silently and brought out a yellow, sweat-stained chamois belt sewed all around with firmly packed, snapped-down pockets. She stood up and offered it to him. He took it, too surprised to speak.

"It's all there," she said. "Though of course you'll want to count it to be sure. And while I'm here—" She fished a small purse out of the bag and took a fold of bills from it.

"Twenty-five dollars. Half a month's pay. Now we're even. Except for my apologies, naturally. You have them. Now you're through here. You may go any time you like, any way you like. Tonight, if you choose. Don't worry about the children. Not that you would. I'll take care of them."

He snorted. "You mean you're firing me?"

"I'm firing you."

"Where did he have the money belt hidden? In your room?"

"He didn't have it anywhere. He never had it. I did." Her chin lifted. "I stole it from you. If you want to have me arrested for it, go ahead."

He smiled at her effort, but shook his head. "No, Carrie, that just won't hold water."

"Jacob Hollander, I have only recently become a thief. I haven't had time to make myself a liar for you! I stole your wretched money. Don't you even want to know why? I guess not. The money is everything, isn't it? Well, there it is, all of it. I didn't even look to see how much there was until after you told me." She was getting stiff lipped and tearful, not full of the brassy confidence of a good thief.

He had a sudden recollection of a time long gone when he had seen her stand so, her hair loose on her shoulders and her eyes brimming with hard-fought tears. He had found her behind that stand of sunflowers in her back yard that were as high as her head: her private place. It must have been the night her father died. He hadn't thought of that in years.

"All right," he said. "Tell me why you took it, then."

11

She looked down at the knitting bag she was twisting between her hands.

"Because he needed you. I thought you'd be gone before he could tell you all of it. I knew I wasn't the person who could make you stay, just by asking. But I thought that if—something should happen to keep you here—I asked Judd to help me. That was wrong, too, but I didn't know who else to ask. He's like a child, you know. They torment him here, and I've tried to be his friend to make up for it. He'll do almost anything for me, but I shouldn't have asked him.

"Because he misunderstood, or he was too nervous—I don't know. He was scared to death afterward. He even cried." She looked at him somberly. "I was afraid, too. When I first touched you to turn you over, I thought you were dead.

"Then, when I was making sure you were all right, I felt the belt under your shirt. I knew what it had to be. I wasn't thinking very clearly, but I thought something like 'This will make it seem more serious,' or something stupid like that. I meant to give it back to you the next night, but you ignored me and went off with that Moon woman." She blinked rapidly at her tears. "That's no excuse either, is it?

"It was only because he needed you! Those wretched women are nearly three months overdue. We haven't heard from them; the agency hasn't heard from them. And the men here are beginning to think just what you think: that Clem has swindled them in some inconceivable way, that the women are never coming and their money is lost. And God help us if they're right!

"He says not to worry. But they've shot out our windows every time a stage comes in without their women. They shoot high, but bullets ricochet. He says not to worry, but they come around at night and seem to be trying to break in. He says they won't, really. But how can he be sure? How could he forget how it was the last time?"

"What last time?"

But she didn't hear him. "If they do fumble the door open some night, and they're drunk enough, or just feeling mean, what else will they do to him? It happened like that before, and you weren't there. You should have been there for him then. You owe him something now. You owe him—" She stopped, looking up at him slowly, as if she had just heard her own voice.

"I owe him what?" Jake asked, frowning.

Carrie wiped at her wet cheeks suddenly, blinking away the tears that blurred her vision. "Nothing. Nothing, now. I fixed that. I'm sorry, I really am. Take your money and go. And let me go now, too, please." She tried to get past him to the door, but he stepped back and leaned against it.

"Not yet. What do you mean, I owe him?"

"Never mind. I'm sorry I spoke. Let me by, please. It's too late to talk sensibly."

"No. It may be that I'm a glutton for punishment, because I've already been scoured like army brass twice tonight. But I'm tired of little mysteries.

"Now, you wanted me to stick around town and help your brother, so you knocked me over the head and robbed me to make sure I did. That makes perfect sense. Who couldn't understand it? And now you're sorry. Fine! My head's still a little sore, and I've probably missed out on a business deal

I've waited years for. But you gave me back my property and said you were sorry.

"I forgive you. Okay? But here's the tough part. This is what I don't understand. If you wanted me here so much, why are you trying to run me out of town in the middle of the night now? The cat's out of the bag, you've confessed your sins. I don't want to tell you how to play your hand, but isn't this the time for a little diplomacy? Or have you hired Judd for a bodyguard now?"

Carrie looked at him in despair and began to cry again, putting one hand up blindly to shield her face from him. He was more moved by that defensive gesture than by anything she had said, but he continued.

"The second thing: you say I owe your brother something, dating back to Kansas. Just what that could be, besides the pleasure of being set up for a target by him for the sake of a good headline, I don't know, but try me—"

"Oh, Jake, you fool! Do you really believe that? Do you really believe that Clem tried to provoke people into killing you just to make good copy? You knew us for four years there. Was he ever so bloodthirsty? Was he ever anything but on your side and against people like Ben McNaughton?"

"Let's say he had a colorful imagination when it came to politics, or increasing the circulation of his paper, and his imagination about me made it difficult for me to stay alive there."

"So you ran away before the job was finished and left him to face them. You coward!"

"I'm sorry I disappointed you. Maybe I was just a good-for-nothing sonofabitch, but I didn't like killing half-wit kids who thought they were faster than me. Kick 'em in the ass maybe, but not kill them. It was a little weakness of mine. What happened, did some ten-year-old get the drop on him with a slingshot?"

Her face was bloodless with rage; her voice was a whisper. "No, you miserable, selfish, callous travesty of a man. Ben

McNaughton hired four men to revenge himself on you for killing his sons. And when they couldn't find you they came and did everything to Clem they were supposed to do to you! Do I have to tell you what they did? Ben McNaughton was a cattleman. He wanted some kind of—physical proof that they'd found you. Do I have to tell you what that was?" Her voice broke. "I've never told—anyone. But I want you to know!"

Jake was motionless.

"They came late at night, after looking for you. You were gone, but we didn't know that! They tore up the office, poured ink on the paper, threw the type into the stove, turned over the press. They insisted Clem knew where you were. They told him what they'd—but he didn't know!

"They took us out to Ben McNaughton's place. *He* wasn't there, of course. He was going to look innocent, whatever happened.

"They put me in the barn and—and they took Clem outside to the place where they branded and—did things to the cattle. They beat him, and told him— I screamed to him to tell them anything. I would have told them, if I'd known. I'd have turned you over to them, then, to save him, and I loved you! I thought I loved you. You knew that. Is that why you left without telling me? Did Clem know and keep it from me? He shouldn't have, because he was worth more as a man than you ever could be."

Tears choked her. She made for the door again.

"Did they do anything to you?" Jake demanded, trying to catch her arm. But she jerked away from him.

"No!" The door banged shut, and he heard her swift feet on the planks until they left them for the softer ground between the buildings.

He didn't follow her, or even feel inclined to do so. She had left him shaken and incoherently angry. She had accused him of sins of omission he couldn't even define. What was she mad at him about? But his mind recoiled from reviewing the last few minutes and the pictures she had conjured for him there.

All her tears and accusations were only meant to make him feel guilty, and he had nothing to feel guilty about! He hadn't done anything, then or now, except what anyone had a right to do: leave a place when he chose to go. He had never deserted anybody, because that implied ties, and no one had any claim on him. He wasn't Clement Hand's keeper, or hers. They knew nothing about him.

The whole business had been nothing but the hysterics of a crazy old maid who had seen a man she thought had once deserted her and decided to work her revenge on him. It was female foolishness beneath his notice, now that his money had been returned.

He went to bed.

But she was not easily dismissed. He lay quietly, breathed evenly; body commanded to stillness, mind instructed to think of nothing—or of something else. At the end of an hour he was still awake and the room was an airless tomb, haunted by howling women and bloodied little bastards who couldn't keep their noses out of other people's business.

Defeated, he got up and took his chair outside, tipping it back against the adobe wall where the air was dry and cool and he could smoke and think.

He had to admit the woman had got to him. How, he didn't know. She had set on him every chance she got from the moment he landed in this hole. She had planned an attack on him and had him brained; had rolled him herself, like a Barbary Coast tough. Then she'd come in here tonight and made him feel like a criminal. God, what tongues women had! She'd managed to make him feel as if he not only owed her an apology, but even owed her damned interfering brother a pound of flesh.

In a pig's eye! He owed them nothing. He had his own back again, and he was free to go; she'd said so.

Free to go was an unexpectedly long thought. Nothing followed it for a while.

A slight noise in the doorway disturbed him. Paco was watching him with one wet eye just visible around the frame. Jake started to order him back to bed, then relented.

"You got a bellyache?" he asked.

Paco sniffed and inched farther out the door until both eyes were fixed on Jake.

"I thought you was gone," he said.

"I thought you were locked up for the night."

"You forgot. Chake?"

"What?"

"You gotta go away tomorrow?"

"Where'd you get that?"

"She said. She kick you out, Chake? Can she do that to us?"

Jake pulled on his cigar, considering. "I don't know. I guess she thinks she can. Maybe she can. What do you mean, us? She didn't say anything about you going."

"If you don't stay, I don't stay neither," Paco said fiercely. "The hell with her!"

Jake twisted around to look at him. "What's the matter with you? She likes you! She wants you to stay, and she treats you pretty good. I guess you wouldn't even be sleeping in the jail if I wasn't here. She'd probably make Clem come over here and put you up in his bed."

"I don't want to! I like to sleep in a jail with you, Chake."

"I'll be a son of a— Here—you look like you need a smoke. Don't puddle up like that."

He handed over his cigar to Paco, who took a suffocating pull on it, then coughed explosively as some of the smoke went in the wrong way. He leaned on Jake's knee, choking and tearful, while Jake beat him on the back. A moment later, somehow, he was sitting on Jake's lap wiping his nose and eyes on an unusually clean shirt sleeve. After a brief stiffening, Jake relaxed and let him stay there.

108

They shared the cigar in silence for a time.

"You gonna go now, like she said?"

"Well, I'm out of a job here. What do you think?"

"Don't do it! She can't boss us around. She ain't even got married yet."

Jake grinned at him. "Where'd we go? We'd still have to move out of the jailhouse, and you know how you feel about sleeping in jail. Why, you'd have to get arrested to find a bed like that anywhere else."

Paco began to chortle as he saw the joke. "Hey, Chake, if you ain't the marshal no more, then there ain't nobody that can arrest people. There ain't nobody that can arrest us if we want to keep on sleeping in the jail. We can do what we want and nobody can arrest us." He nearly upset himself from his perch laughing at this sudden revelation.

Jake grunted to himself because he had a vision of Carrie Hand heading a vigilante mob to get him thrown *out* of jail.

"You're a pretty smart kid," he acknowledged for the second time that night. "But you hang around with the wrong bunch of people."

"I don't hang around with nobody but you, Chake."

"Yeah. That's what I mean."

"I don't want to hang around with nobody else. I like you better."

Jake put the cigar between his teeth again, thoughtfully. "Why?" he asked around it.

But Paco was at a loss to say why. He shrugged, studying Jake's stained vest for a clue.

"Since I know you, you just hit me one time," he murmured. "And you don't make fun of Urraca 'cause she can't talk, like some of the other *tíos* did. And you show me how to play cards good so I can get rich like you when I grow up." He fingered his nose.

Jake looked at him in silence for a few seconds. Then he tipped his chair forward and dumped Paco easily back on his own feet. "It's time you went back to bed, cardsharp. Me, too. Get going." Paco obeyed him, unruffled by the sudden end of their communion.

Jake did not follow. He heard the cell door clang shut and the bunk creak slightly under Paco's body. After that the harpy festival down the street at the cantina was the only sound, and it was growing fainter.

He continued to sit motionless against the adobe wall, watching the empty street where his discarded cigar's tiny ember made the only light.

12

Dreams didn't often trouble Jake. When he had them they were anxious shadow struggles involving the loss of something: a heavy jackpot, his hotel room, or even his place at a bar. But when he woke they always vanished like smoke, leaving no more than a faint stain of apprehension on his mind.

This one was different. He remembered it vividly, as if seen by the light of a large fire in the night, the image a chiaroscuro of orange on black. The memory was tinged with a furtive excitement, too, and a clammy sense of shame he hadn't felt since he was sixteen years old.

He sat on the edge of his bed, rubbing his face awake and disliking the sensation. His mouth tasted as if he had been eating worms, and he ached like a rejected bridegroom.

He had slept in his clothes, but he didn't take time to change shirts or shave. He needed to get outside and see if strong New Mexico sun and sand-dry New Mexico wind could do anything to banish the damp-cellar depression he felt. He paroled the kids and took them toward the cantina for breakfast.

When they passed the window of the newspaper office Clem scrambled out from behind his desk and opened the door.

"Jake, have you got a minute?"

Jake paused unwillingly, finding it difficult to look at Clem this morning. "They haven't had breakfast yet," he parried feebly.

"Going over to Sánchez's? Good, I'll come with you."

Jake shrugged agreement, and Clem fell into step beside him.

"Carrie told me about last night, Dutch. I ought to try to explain—"

"Never mind. It's all been explained."

"Well, my apologies are in order, somehow. She only did it to help me. That doesn't excuse her, of course. Or me, for not insisting she return your money as soon as I suspected what she'd done." He sighed. "She's not easy to deal with, as I suppose you know by now. She's been an angel of a sister to me, and I love her, but when she takes it into her head to do something for my own good— Well, I had no choice but to keep silent, did I?"

"Would you really have gone to jail for her, if she'd hidden it where I'd have found it?"

Clem blinked at him. "Why, I don't know, Dutch. Would you really have sent me there?"

Jake answered that with a snort.

"There's another thing," Clem said after a moment. "She said she fired you."

"That she did."

"Well, she certainly exceeded her authority there. The League hired you, and only the League could dismiss you. I know they want you to stay on. You will, won't you?"

"Damn it, Clem, I don't know what I'm going to do. Just say I'm paid up to the present and let it go at that." He finished gloomily. "I don't know how I'd get out, anyway, unless I rode one of Sánchez's ice wagons down to Sonora."

The almost boyish grin of relief that flooded Clem's face didn't make Jake feel any better. He looked away from it

112

quickly to the street beyond, and stopped. "What the hell is that?"

In the open lot behind the cantina's laundry yard a small army of men and women were wrestling with a large tent.

He recognized Ramón from the livery stable and a half-dozen other Sánchez cousins, as well as the full contingent of laundresses, led by Prudencia. Sánchez stood in the middle of the stage road directing the work.

"*Arranque! Arranque!*" He saw the two men approaching and smiled. "*Señores, buenos días.* How do you like her? Is she not beautiful? It will make a fine thing for your paper to tell about, Señor Clem."

"Where did you get it?" Jake asked, as the canvas began to expand into shape like a huge dirty muffin, trailing strings of tattered bunting flags from its peak.

"From the *bruja, patrón;* the red one. Hey, *burros,* what are you doing there? Pull the ropes! Manuel—Prudencia, stop this tickling!"

"He bought it from Delia last month," Clem said. "But I didn't think he was supposed to get it until he paid—here she comes now."

Delia, clad in a dragon-infested kimono hastily pulled on over a corset and underdrawers, came sailing into the street trailing an admiring crowd pulled out of the saloons and stores she had passed. Her hair was wild and her face was stern.

"All right, you little sneak, put it back or pay for it!"

Sánchez looked startled, then began to swell into a defensive posture. "It is mine! We made an agreement."

"And you broke it!" She saw Jake. "What are you standing around for? Make him put it back, or put him in jail. That's my tent until he pays me what he said he would!"

"Deel, you shouldn't be outside like that. Take my coat or something," said Clem, preparing to cover her where she least needed it. She shoved him out of the way, advancing on Sánchez.

113

"Keep your own clothes on, Shorty. Listen, you chiseling little greaser, I've been waiting for that shipment for a month. I'm down to the dregs!" She turned on Jake again. "He agreed to pay me six barrels of whiskey and twelve barrels of beer for that thing four weeks ago. His wagons have been down to Agua Prieta and back three times since then, and I still don't have any of it. Until I get it, that tent is mine. Make him put it back!"

"This woman is telling lies! I told her the whiskey was hers the moment my tent was in place. *Her* whiskey is on its way. Ramón's sons are bringing it. *My* tent is in place. It was a gentleman's agreement, Señor Hollander, and she is not a gentleman now."

"You bet your ass I'm not a gentleman, and I'm not a fool either. No whiskey, no tent, and that's flat!"

"Deel—" said Clem.

"Later. Listen, Jake, I'm a practical woman and I've got a pretty thick skin, but I'm fed up with this little crook trying to cheat me and put me out of business. Have you heard the kind of stuff he's been telling people about me and my girls? I can't even get my house painted since he told all his relatives I'd put the evil eye on them! And all because he couldn't get a free lay while his wife's out of town." She stabbed a long finger at Sánchez. "Something for nothing, that's his motto. He's got it tattooed on his prick!"

"She is putting a curse on me!" shrieked Sánchez, covering his crotch with both hands.

"Deel, for God's sake—" Clem begged, seeing that the town's women were beginning to join the crowd.

"Now, just calm down," Jake began, but Prudencia rushed into the group suddenly to defend Sánchez from the harmful finger.

"*Cochina! Perra! Ramera!*" she screamed.

"Calling your three sisters?" Delia asked her. "Mind your own business, you nickel dose of clap."

Prudencia swung her arm back for a skull-cracking blow,

114

but Delia calmly pushed her in the face before it unwound and sent her sprawling back into Sánchez's arms.

"All right, that's enough now!" Jake said, but Prudencia threw herself at Delia with another scream, grabbing two handfuls of red hair for an anchor. Delia's fingernails raked her, and the two of them fell to the ground.

The tent fell, too, as the men dropped their ropes and came running to see the fight.

Jake made several attempts to reach into the struggle, got his hat knocked off and his shins kicked, but managed to seize Delia's waist as she came up on top again, and dragged her off Prudencia. There were cheers and applause from the crowd as she fought to get away from him.

"Just let me brain this bitch, and then I'll take an ax and chop the damned thing down myself!"

"It's down, for Christ's sake! It's down! Look!" He grabbed her jaw and twisted her head around. "There, are you happy? Now, cool off. Aaa!" he warned Prudencia, just getting to her feet again with murder in her eye. "The fight's over. Take her inside, Sánchez. Paco, you go with him and order some food." His arm still full of Delia, he swung around to look for Paco and found Carrie standing behind him.

"I'll see that they have a proper breakfast," she said coolly. "You seem to have your hands full. Clem, Mr. French wants to see you about his Easter advertisement." She captured a child with each hand and wheeled them away from the cantina.

Jake released Delia. Clem didn't stir.

Delia seemed to regain her good humor immediately. Her breasts still heaving, her eyes glowing with victory, she began to preen herself, running her fingers through her hair to claw it into a rough order. Her robe hung open, showing off her splendid body. There were whistles from the men in the street. The town's women left the group.

"Free show, boys," Delia crowed, watching the women leave. "Just to let you know what you've been missing if any

115

of you are still throwing your money away in that cockroach club across the street!" She held up both arms like a winning prize fighter. Then her eyes came to rest on Clement Hand, tight-faced and silent, still holding his proffered coat. She let her hands drop to her hips.

"What do you want done with your damned tent, now that you've got it down again?" Jake asked her. "Who's going to haul it back up the street for you?"

Delia licked her lips, watching Clem. "Let the little bull thrower keep it. I just wanted to show him he couldn't get away with anything behind my back. But tell him if I don't get my whiskey by this weekend I'll put a hex on him that'll set his britches on fire." She laughed happily. "You should have seen those little runts sneaking that tent out of my yard this morning. Like a bunch of ants kidnapping a snake!

"Your sister's calling you," she told Clem.

"If you're ready to go home now, Delia, take my coat and cover yourself up," Clem said quietly.

To Jake's surprise, Delia sighed and began to wrap her kimono around her waist, letting Clem drape his coat over her shoulders and take her arm. They were almost the same height and still looking at each other steadily.

Without turning her head she nudged Jake with her free elbow and said, "Keep an eye on that Mex for me, honey, will you?"

Jake watched them go, frowning, until he realized he was the last man left in the middle of the street.

He walked into the cantina still looking thoughtful and ordered his usual breakfast of tortillas and chorizos. He favored the hot country sausage that Sánchez's old mother made, because he supposed that the amount of chili she put into the pork was more than enough to overcome any disease lurking in the body of a Mexican pig. With the food, he had beer. Sánchez had no respect for coffee, so there was no use ordering it in his place.

116

Sánchez examined him shrewdly as he ate. "Señor Hollander, you are not well."

"I'm fine."

"No, no. I am seldom deceived. As the son of the best *curandera* anywhere, I see things others would not notice, perhaps. You are pale and silent. Your face does not have the rudiment complexion of good health this morning."

Jake shifted his attention to Sánchez, unwillingly snagged on this latest shard of speech.

"It is the *bruja,* is it not? I saw you coming from her house last night. You need have no fear. If she has poisoned you or put a love spell on you, my little queen will cure you. She knows all herbs, roots, remedies. Tell me what food or drink the *bruja* gave you and my mother will do the rest."

"You've got your English twisted, Sánchez. Delia may be a bitch, but she's no witch."

Sánchez laughed indulgently. "Bitch—witch. That is very comical, *patrón*. But I understand all English very well, and it is witch that I mean. Do not cross her, *patrón,* or you will see what she can do, even without her evil eye. Now, she has other help. That scarred man who is in her house is worse than a *brujo*."

"Ramey? What do you know about him?" Jake asked, suddenly interested.

"Come into my office and I will show you something."

Sánchez's office was a pantry-sized room smaller than Jake's quarters. It was furnished with a heavy table and chair, a strongbox that must have come to the New World with Cortes, and a ten-year supply of wanted posters and express bills furnished by the stage line. Jake stood in wonder at the montage of ugly faces and assorted charges that papered the four walls.

It took Sánchez a moment to find his man, but the face was unmistakably George Ramey's. Army deserter, renegade, slaver.

"Slaver? This poster is ten years old, but that's still pretty

117

late for slave trading. Who was he supposed to be selling to who?"

"Indians, *señor*. Indians to the Indians, and Indians to any rancher or *hacendado* on either side of the border who wants them. It still goes on. I myself have known cases."

Jake had a sudden recollection of his first meeting with Delia, when she refused the kids. "Sell them to Sánchez," she'd said. "He'll buy anything." But he didn't quote her to the *cantinero*.

"What's Ramey doing in town now?" he asked.

Sánchez shrugged. "Who knows? But it is sure to be something very bad, and very profitable for him, I think."

Remembering that he had a wanted poster of his own, Jake felt for it to see if Sánchez knew anything about Frank Becker. But the paper was no longer in his vest pocket. He thanked Sánchez for the information and started to leave, then paused.

"By the way, Delia says you can keep the tent, as long as she gets her whiskey by the weekend."

"But of course she will get her whiskey. She has the word of a Sánchez on that. Unless"—he smiled blandly—"something should happen to it on the way. It would be a great pity if those cursed Apaches should take it into their heads to raid the wagons and steal her whiskey. Because, as I told you, it was *her* whiskey, as soon as we made the bargain of gentlemen."

He flicked a bar towel at the swarm of flies settling on the remains of Jake's breakfast. "But the Apaches also are not gentlemen. Who can say what they will do?"

Jake strolled the streets aimlessly, feeling disconnected and ill at ease. He wasn't happy with the feeble way he had resigned himself to spending the rest of the month in Arredondo at Clem's first plea this morning. He could say he had little choice, but that was a blushing lie because he hadn't even made an attempt to get away before he gave in.

118

And for a man who was so universally needed last night, he sure as hell was unpopular today. Where was everybody? Neither Carrie nor the kids were in the *Arrow* office. Delia and Clem—he still hadn't come out of the Golden Moon.

What went on in Delia Moon's head? She gave him funny looks and told him bad lies; led him on— It had occurred to him late last night that when she offered to take the kids she might have been working around to inviting him to move in with her, and then only turned peculiar because of his own thickheadedness.

Would she behave like that? Women didn't like to do the asking, he knew. But plenty of them did, anyway, and he was usually disposed to let them. It saved a lot of time and money.

He hadn't turned her down last night, and she had still been trying when he left. But this morning she looked right through him and walked off with Clement Hand, who couldn't buy five cents' worth if Delia was selling at a dollar a ton. Was she egging Clem on just to spite Carrie, or to make Jake jealous?

The raw vanity in that thought made him snort. That woman didn't have any more use for him than she did for Rosie Robles's kids.

He loitered in front of French's, frowning at his own reflection in the window, and that of the Golden Moon behind him. He needed a shave. He usually shaved first thing in the morning because his beard was beginning to show a lot of gray. He saw Clement Hand in the glass, coming out of the Moon with some sort of ledger under his arm.

By God, he wouldn't give the kids to that whore across the street if she paid him in gold. She might sell them to Ramey.

He ought to go over there and arrest Ramey and collect that two-hundred-dollar reward.

But he'd have to take him fifty miles to court by himself. And then wait six months to a year to collect the money.

If the money was still being offered.

Ramey wasn't worth six months of Jake's time.

119

It beat the hell out of him what Delia would want with those kids. She *must* want to sell them to Ramey. Well, she'd play hell. They must have some relatives, somewhere, however strange the word might be to Paco. All Mexicans had relatives by the dozens. If Carrie couldn't find a good place for them here, as she'd promised, he'd wire Yuma before he left town and see what else he could find out about Rosie Robles.

There was bound to be somebody who would claim them, and he wouldn't refuse to pay their fare, or even make a little side trip on his way to El Paso to drop them off.

He stopped on the corner by the Silver Man, searching for a cigar. In the field behind the cantina the tent had blossomed again. Its blue and red pennants fluttered frantically in a strong northern breeze. There was some sort of lettering on the canvas walls that the men were blotting out with a coat of yellow paint.

Rosie Robles did have somebody back in Yuma, Jake remembered suddenly. Frank Becker. That fact was what had sent him down to Delia's last night to begin with.

The poster had described Rosie as Becker's common-law wife. A fancy title for a pimp's property. But if he was Rosie's man six years ago, what else might he be? Paco once said his papa was with the devils in hell.

Frank Becker had been shut up for all Paco's life in a place they called "Hell on the Colorado"; Jake had read that term in the *Police Gazette*. He must be back there again by now, unless he was lying dead out in the Yuma desert. Nobody had ever really escaped from Yuma penitentiary.

As he was staring at the tent a match flared under his nostrils, startling him. Remembering the cigar in his mouth, he bent to get it lighted from Patchy Murdoch's match.

"Want to play some cards, Dutch?"

"That's the first good word I've heard today." Jake grinned, relieved to give up thinking. "I hope you've got plenty of money."

13

He was sitting in the Silver Man, cradling a full house in one hand—aces and ladies—and a stack of silver dollars in the other, wondering if Patchy Murdoch was going to try to bluff him twice in a row, when he heard Paco coming down the street yelling for him. He didn't move. Neither did Patchy or any of the others.

"Chake! Chake! Hey, *tío!*" Hoarse and out of breath, Paco fell through the door of the bar, followed by a chorus of "Hey, boy. What's the matter, boy? You lost somethin'?" and imitative "Hey, Chakes." Paco rushed up to him, flapping a loose shoe sole.

"What's the matter with you?" Jake asked with massive indifference.

"Hey, *tío,* Urraca's stuck under the house at Gebhardt's store and she's cryin' like hell!"

"Well, drag her out. Patchy, are you going to play your hand or keep it for a souvenir?"

"They won't let me get her out, *tío.* And she's really scared, man!"

"Who won't?" He saw Patchy's bid and raised it five more.

"Them damn *hombres* down at the feed store. They think it's funny when she yells."

121

"All right, just a minute. What are you going to do, Patchy?" It had come around to him again.

Patchy, his blotched face working between concentration on his hand and Jake's face and attention to Paco's tale, grinned slyly. "Why don't you go on and see to your little girl, Dutch? We can finish this when you get back."

"The hell! Finish it now."

"Well, now—"

Paco began to sniffle beside him. "Come on, Chake. She don't like little dark places, ever since Mama lock her up in a closet once. Anyway, you ain't got nothing but a bunch of ones there."

"I guess I'm out," said Patchy.

"Goddamn it to hell!" snarled Jake, throwing the hand down. "If you ever do that again, I'm going to—" He looked at Paco's face. "Oh, all right. Come on, let's get her out. Get your laugh out, too, Murdoch," he growled at Patchy. "I'll be right back." He scooped up eleven silver dollars, too many of which had been his to begin with, and followed the boy down the street.

As they drew near the feed store he could hear Urraca's toneless shrieks under the laughter of the men tormenting her.

"What's the matter, girlie? You stuck? Why don't you holler for help?" Augie Gebhardt sang as Jake approached them. When Augie saw him he switched to "Oh, looky here! Here comes Uncle Jake to git you out. Here he comes, bogeyman! Don't snatch that chile down in that great big hole yet."

The group of four or five rubes fell back to let Jake through. He dropped to his knees and elbows, then to his belly, to inspect the hole in the foundation through which she'd crawled. There was something dim and white inside, but it was more than an arm's length away.

He struck a match on one of the sandstone blocks and put it through the opening, then tried to squeeze through after it. The white spot was Urraca's drawers, now filthy wet. She was facing away from him, the way she had gone in. There was plenty of room for her in there and very little for him. Coming back out had been the cause of her trouble. Her skirts had caught on a protruding spike in a floor joist and pulled her dress and petticoat backward over her head as she retreated. She was not only stuck; she was also blinded because her own rump cut off the light, and she was stifled in her own clothes.

He wedged himself into the hole as far as his shoulders would let him and reached for her skirt, hearing something about himself tear as he did so. When he touched her she began to scream again, and one of her bare feet caught him in the face, hard.

"Stop that, damn it," he grunted, trying to fend off her feet with the same hand that was trying to free her. He smacked the dimly seen drawers as hard as he could in such a position and made an additional discovery. "Oh, shit, Urraca," he snarled.

When he had torn her skirts free, he locked her ankles together in one hand and began to inch backward, pulling her out after him. A boisterous cheer went up for his success.

Urraca, mouth stretched into a square, wailed her outrage and terror into his ear, her arms choking him as he tried to get to his feet with her. They were both filthy. His shirt was torn at the arm seam; her dress was unrecognizable.

Paco was jubilant, dancing around Jake like some savage around an idol. The half-wits surrounding them were grinning and patting him on the back, too heartily; particularly Augie, the older Gebhardt brother. While Augie was still chortling and brushing off the back of Urraca's tattered dress, he made the same discovery that Jake had a moment before.

"Hey, there, Uncle Jake, I think you just struck the mother lode. Little something in her britches for a bonus."

"You were wasting your wit teasing her, Gebhardt. She's deaf."

"Oh, I know that, marshal. I was just having a little fun."

123

Jake's hand snaked into his pocket and made a fist around the roll of silver dollars. Shifting Urraca to the left side, he threw all the force of that silver-weighted fist into Augie's grinning face. He felt his knuckles pop as Gebhardt's nose crunched under them. The spurt of blood that followed and the sight of Jake's business face reduced the levity of the others to a murmur.

"The next sonofabitch I ever catch making fun of this kid is going to be wearing his face inside out!" He turned away without waiting to see if Augie could get up or not.

"Get my hat, Paco."

He hoped to hell he hadn't broken his hand.

They were both such a mess he halfway hoped Carrie would see them, be rightfully outraged, and carry the kids off for a bath, so he could clean himself up and get back to Patchy. But she didn't come. She wasn't in the office. She hadn't even brought the usual bucket of water over to the jail that morning. The bucket was there, but it was less than half full. It wouldn't begin to clean him, let alone Urraca.

"What in blazes were you doing under there?" he asked her in exasperation.

"She was trying to catch that cat that's going to have babies, Chake," Paco answered for her.

Jake exhaled a hot word as he went into the cell room. He came out immediately, searching the corners.

"Where's that carpetbag with your other stuff in it?"

"You got it, *tío*, remember? But it don't have nothing good in it now. You smoked all the cigars." He trotted into Jake's room and brought it out, opening it.

"Hey, Chake, somebody left a bottle of whiskey in here and it got empty."

Jake snatched the bottle from him, then took the carpetbag. It was indeed empty now. He stood looking down at it, not moving. Paco waited for it to be tossed back to him. Urraca sat on the tabletop, wiping her nose.

"All right," Jake said after that silent moment. "Down to

124

French's for some more clothes, then off to the barbershop for a bath. I could keep a string of Chinese fan dancers cheaper than you two." His words were still rough, but the tone was muted and his face was benign enough to make Urraca smile her cat smile at him. He put the carpetbag back in his room himself and closed the door when he came out.

"Come on, Urraca. You smell like— Jesus, so do I!" He picked her up again, gingerly putting his arm with the already ruined shirt sleeve under her bottom.

They lingered in the dry-goods store until Ezra French had to light up his pipe in self-defense, while his old wife picked out a change of clothes for each of the children and a shirt for Jake.

From there they went to Patterson's bathhouse, where Jake drove out two earlier arrivals so he could bathe Urraca. Paco took care of himself. When they were both clean, with their black hair clinging to their skulls like wet seal fur, he made them dress in the corner with their backs to him while he bathed.

"You still got soap in your hair," Paco told him as he was dressing. Jake didn't answer the charge. His fingers briefly brushed the hair at his temples, where the shoe blacking he'd been using to cover the gray had washed away in the bath.

When he was ready they marched in file to the *lavandería* and left the filthy clothes, then back to the cantina for an early supper. Sánchez smiled paternally at the children as he slid bowls of hot stew onto the table before them.

"Well, my little *mineros*. How is it with that mine you got behind the jail? Did you strike silver today?"

"They sure as hell did," Jake muttered, watching the last of his poker winnings disappear into Sánchez's pocket. "About eleven dollars' worth."

Nevertheless, after supper he bought them each a sack of horehound drops, and they began a slow stroll around town.

"That's nasty," Paco said, taking the first several drops out of his mouth to examine them.

"Yeah, I know," Jake answered absently. Paco returned the candy to his mouth and licked his palm clean.

They stopped to look at the tent. More flags were aloft now, and there were candles set out on either side of the entrance path in paper sacks weighted with sand.

Jake ducked into the opening and glanced around. All the canaries and parrots had been transferred to the tent. Their stridence, added to the torrid heat trapped under the canvas, gave it an exotic, tropical air. Most of the girls were busy primping because the miners would be coming in from outside town by seven o'clock. It seemed that most of the contents of the cantina's second floor had been emptied into the tent, too. Blankets and ropes formed modest partitions between the cots.

He declined Prudencia's offer to let him be their first customer and whistled to the kids, who were already at the canary cages trying to let the birds out. They continued their stroll.

As they approached the Golden Moon, two of Delia's girls came out on the porch, very demure in summer dresses and carrying parasols, to take their semiregular walk before they went to work.

When they saw Jake and the children they turned and fell in step with them instead, giggling with Paco, flirting with Jake.

They were both young and had passable bodies, but their faces were pitted and coarsened with smallpox or acne, and their teeth were so bad they both covered their mouths with their fingers when they laughed. But Jake was feeling indulgent if not attracted, and in a short time had one of them hanging on each arm, while the children ran in front.

They left the borders of the town and took to the desert road for half a mile; farther than either Jake or the girls had been from town since arriving. The sun was a solid-looking orange ball swathed in purple haze, just settling on the upper peaks of the western Hassayampas. The girls exclaimed over its beauty in loud voices, as if they had never seen it set before. Jake was watching a wagon approaching at a fast clip from the direction of the mines.

It held Carrie and another of the League women. Her frozen face went by him as he and the girls moved to the side of the road. He had the forethought to remove his hat and place it over his heart, which brought gales of laughter from the young whores and not so much as a backward look from the straight-backed women in the wagon.

Dust from the passing wagon billowed up over their heads and spoiled the girls' taste for desert exploration, so they turned away from the rough scrub.

By the time they returned to Arredondo, twilight had begun to soften its raw ugliness with a mellow gloom. After their brief retreat into the desert air the familiar town smells of coal-oil fumes, wood smoke, kitchen grease, and boiling coffee seemed especially pungent. The street, seldom filled until after dark, was quiet now at the supper hour.

The girls hurried away up the steps into the Golden Moon. Old Mrs. French nodded to Jake and the children as she sat in her yard working a dip of snuff up under her upper lip with a dexterous matchstick.

The tap-click and murmur from the pool hall were as academic as ever. The Happy Apache glowed with hospitality through oilpapered windows. Dugan was still open for business at the Miners Supply.

They paused on the corner of Hassayampa and the Mesilla stage road and Jake sighed, savoring a secret peace, his chamois belt once more tight against his belly, his morning doubts allayed by a chance discovery with comic implications that only he would ever be allowed to appreciate fully.

He glanced in the direction of the tent and found it so illuminated with lanterns from within that the lettering on its side stood out clearly in spite of the hasty paint job.

It said MOONEY'S MARVEL SHOW. He laughed out loud at that, and Paco laughed with him without even asking what was funny.

Carrie and Clem were waiting for them outside the jail. Clem seemed to be trying to persuade Carrie of something.

"Good evening, Jake," said Clem. "We were just out here to tell you there's a League meeting in a little while, if you can come. And Carrie has something to say to you, too." There was more metal than usual in his voice when he prompted her. "Carrie?"

Her chin rose. "Mr. Hollander, it seems I exceeded my authority last night when I asked you to resign. I'm told I'm very much in the minority in the wish, so I hope you will reconsider, for the sake of the rest of the League, and stay the rest of the month."

It was a touching recantation. Jake almost felt sorry for her as she stood there stiff as a gatepost, her hands squeezed together in front of her, making her enforced apology. But he could see that her fuse was burning pretty short and that anything he said in reply might be taken ill; so he said nothing, only nodded to her and tried to pass by. But that wasn't going to be allowed either.

"There!" she told Clem. "I hope that makes you happy. You see how much good it does to try to be civil to him. He's too liquored up to even answer." Jake, who hadn't had a drink in hours, turned in surprise.

"Oh, I've been following your exploits today," she said. "You've certainly been giving the town something to be proud of, haven't you? Brawling behind the feed store. Dragging that little girl into the bathhouse with all those men in there to see her. Letting Paco run in and out of saloons and bawdy-houses looking for you, while you sit and gamble."

"Carrie, that will be enough," said Clem firmly, taking her by the elbow.

"Wrestling with that woman until she was nearly naked in the middle of the street, while everybody laughed."

128

"Carrie!" She was being dragged away.

"And then strutting around town with those two tarts, like one big happy family."

"The second one was for the kid!" Jake called after her. "Delia's going to let him move in and shill for her. I thought he ought to get acquainted with the staff." He grinned at the last sight of her face as Clem jerked her through the *Arrow* office door.

Paco tugged at Jake's coat, worried. "We ain't really gonna move in with Deel, huh, Chake? That's a joke, huh, Chake?"

"What's that?"

"You gonna keep us, ain't you, *tío?*"

"Sure, kid. I was just lathering up Carrie. Not that she needs any help." Her jealous outburst not only had failed to rouse him to anger; it had even had the reverse effect of making him feel better. He was freed from some cobweb emotion that had stretched between them last night.

He entertained the kids with three-card monte until it was time to go on his rounds. He performed saloon inspections lightly; ignored loud disputes, and even smiled absently on an eye gouging until he saw the bartender reach under the bar for an ax handle. Jake took it away from him and tapped the near winner behind the ear just hard enough to stun him and allow the loser to crawl out from under. After that he played poker again with Patchy Murdoch in the Silver Man.

When he came out of the game it was late. There were few people in any of the saloons that night. Most of the action was in Sánchez's canvas cathouse.

As he crossed the stage road, heading back to the jail, he heard a single rider coming in from the west. He stopped to watch as the man dismounted in front of the cantina and stood looking around until he became aware of Jake. For a second the figure seemed about to retreat, then approached into the deeper darkness in the middle of the road.

"Say, friend. What's the name of this place?"

"Arredondo," Jake answered from the boardwalk.

The newcomer chuckled. "Well, now. That old daddy I found knew his stuff after all. I've been head fo'most and bewildered for better than a week. This evening I called to mind an old granny story I once heard. I caught me a daddy longlegs and asked him how to go. When I put him down he lit a shuck for this direction. That's pretty smart for a bug that ain't even got a head. Is there a *ho*tel here?"

"No. Try the cantina there."

"I'll be damn," said the stranger softly. "Looks homey. Got a stable?" Jake pointed it out. "Much obliged. Oh, one more favor, if you'd be so kind. Might be there's a friend of mine here, name of Ramey. You ever hear of him?"

"Try the Golden Moon." Jake started to walk on. He didn't like conversation at twenty paces in the dark.

"Golden Moon? Fancy house?"

"That's right. Up the street the other way."

"That'd be where old George is, then. He likes a soft bed. Obliged again. Expensive, I guess?"

"Well, it's no mission house."

"Yeah. Well, I guess this cantina is plenty good enough for me."

Jake decided to close the meeting.

"If you can't find a room there, come on over to the jail and I'll give you a bunk for the night."

There was no answer from across the street.

Jake went into the jail quietly, checked the kids, locked their cell, bolted the front door, and took the lantern from the table into his room. He closed that door, too. Then he reached under his cot for Rosie Robles's peculiarly heavy, apparently empty carpetbag, which, he had finally realized that afternoon, must have some kind of false bottom. The key to the bag's mystery opened a couple of other doors, too. Why Delia had gotten so interested in the kids, for instance. And the tent had given him a clue to the bag itself.

He hadn't had the opportunity to look, but he felt a pleasant certainty of what he was going to see when he did, and he had been treasuring the moment all evening, like a secret sweet put away in a kid's pocket for a future treat.

But there was nothing under the cot except his own valise. He made a thorough search of the room and then of the whole jail. The carpetbag wasn't there.

14

"What did you do with the old carpetbag?" he asked Paco the next morning.

"You got it, Chake."

"If I had it, I wouldn't be asking about it, would I? How about Urraca?"

But Urraca looked at them both with maddening incomprehension when they tried to pantomime the taking of the bag, until Jake gave up in disgust.

"Was there anybody in here last night while I was gone? Anyone at all? Carrie? Clem?"

"No, *tío*. What you want with that old bag?"

"Nothing. I just wondered what happened to it. Forget it."

Urraca had made off with it, he was certain. But there was no use trying to pry its whereabouts out of her. He would just have to watch where she played until he found it. If he made any more fuss about it now, Paco would be telling everybody. Besides, he could be wrong about the whole thing.

Nevertheless, he thought he would go down to the Golden Moon and drop a line into Delia's pool to test his suspicions.

It was still early enough that he expected he would be rousting her out of the bed again, but when he tapped on the door Delia opened it instead of Angelina.

She was dressed in the green silk kimono with the dragons again, and not much else. Her hair was wild, and there were peculiar red streaks across her face above and below her mouth. Something had happened, and she glared at him as if she thought he were to blame for it.

"Well! Speak of the devil," she said.

"Maybe another time," Jake murmured, turning to go.

"No, come in here, Hollander! You're just the man I need to see." She looked at him darkly as he passed her. "I've been robbed!"

"Money or virtue?"

"Oh, you're so funny! That's what I needed—a good laugh," she said furiously. "I just spent half the night tied up hand and foot. Rolled up in a quilt so I nearly smothered, and everybody in the house as deaf as that damn kid of yours—"

He held up his hands in surrender. "Did you see who it was who robbed you?"

"You bet your sweet life I saw—" She stopped, considering how he was going to receive the revelation. "It was George Ramey."

"Honest George Ramey?"

"Listen, Hollander, I've had about enough!"

He could see that she had. Her eyes were like coals.

"All right. Give us both a drink and tell me what happened."

"Come back to my room and I'll show you."

Angelina, who was straightening up the mess when they entered, left at a gesture from Delia. A table and lamp had been overturned; the lamp broken. Kerosene stained the carpet.

"You put up quite a fight," Jake said in admiration.

"Oh, I did that after the bastard left, trying to get somebody's attention." She poured two stiff drinks and drank her own immediately, pouring out another while he was still sipping his. "Alcohol makes me belch," she complained, demonstrating.

"You shouldn't take it so fast."

He settled himself in her chair while she paced the room jerking at the sash of her wrapper.

"Slim—that's my blackjack dealer—always takes care of my money. I mean, I send him over to the express office every morning with yesterday's take, and they put it in their safe for me. I just keep enough in the house for my expenses. Last night Slim wasn't feeling well, so I took his spot, and when we closed Ramey helped me wind things up and count the take." She clouded up again, remembering. "I feel like a gully, telling you this." Then she shrugged. "Anyway, we sat and talked and had a drink. I had a stiff neck from sitting so long, and he offered to rub it for me. The next thing I knew, he had his hand over my mouth and nose and was dragging me back here! I thought he was going to kill me, right then. I tried to get loose, but after a few seconds all I wanted to do was breathe, and he just let me fight while he held on, until I passed out. God! When I came to, he had a gag in my mouth and my arms tied. He thought he'd grab a free one while he was at it, but my feet weren't tied, so I changed his mind about that, the bastard. I guess he really could have killed me, then. I must have been out of my mind—but I was so damned mad! Well, after he slapped me around for a while, he tied my feet, then wrapped me up in a quilt and put me in the chair and tied me to *that!* Tore up my best sheet to do it. When he was finished he took the money and left. I spent the night beating my bare feet on the floor and trying to wiggle loose. I got turned around enough to kick over the table, but nobody paid any attention until this morning when Angelina came in with the coffee."

She sniffed angrily and threw the second drink down her throat, laid one hand on the decanter again, but changed her mind with a shudder.

"I don't suppose any of your girls would know where he might have gone?" Jake asked.

"You think he'd go upstairs afterward and say, 'Hey, girls,

134

I just robbed the house. If anybody asks for me, I'll be down the road'?"

"I just wondered. Did he sleep alone?"

She gave a magnificent shrug. "Who knows where he slept? He was supposed to share a room with Slim, but I never checked to see if he did."

"Did he leave anything behind up there?"

She looked at him with new respect. "Say, maybe you're not so dumb after all. I never thought of that. Let's look."

Slim didn't seem to be seriously indisposed. The room was unoccupied. There wasn't much in it, and what there was Delia identified unhesitatingly as Slim's. While they were looking, Slim arrived with one of the girls from yesterday's walk.

"Hey, Deel, Bea just told me something you might want to hear."

Bea preened herself at the sight of Jake, but sobered under Delia's hard stare.

"Somebody came here last night asking for Georgie, Deel."

"Who was it?"

"I don't know. I never saw him before. He wouldn't come inside, either." She smiled at Jake.

"Well?" Delia prompted impatiently.

"Well, he came about midnight and knocked on the door. When I opened it—first thing—he asked for some girl named Rosie. I told him there wasn't nobody here named Rosie, but would I do—you know? But he said, 'You mean there ain't a pretty little Mex here named Rosana?' And I said, 'You mean Chica? With a gold tooth?' And he said—"

"For Christ's sake, get on with it, Bea!" Delia's voice cut across the other woman's, hard and high, with a note of fear in it.

"Well, honey, that's about all. Except then he asked if George Ramey was in here, and I said he was in the middle of a game. I asked him to come on in and have a drink with me, but he wouldn't. He just said to tell Ramey he'd be over

135

at the cantina waiting to talk to him, and to tell him he was much obliged. Then he left."

"What did Ramey do when you told him?" Jake asked her when Delia didn't.

"Nothing. He didn't even act like he heard me at first. Then, when I was just starting to tell him again, he laughed, sort of, and said, 'Okay. Thanks for the message.' It didn't seem to be any big thing to him, so that's why I forgot it until now."

Delia was looking pale. "Thanks, Bea. Slim, will you go downstairs and give Angelina a hand dragging my rug out of the bedroom? That coal oil's going to have to be scrubbed out and let dry in the back yard."

"Bea," said Jake. "One more thing. What did the man at the door look like? How was he dressed?"

"Well, listen to old Bill Pinkerton!" Delia scoffed, but even her sarcasm was muted for once.

"Now that you mention it, that was kind of interesting," Bea told him. "He was a white man, I'm sure. But he was dressed like a Mexican. You know—white pants and one of those blanket things they stick their heads through. But he took off his hat real polite when he talked to me, so I could see he was American."

"Light, dark; old or young?"

"Oh, light and young. He had blond hair, lighter than mine. He was real sweet spoken and good looking, except for a kind of long scratch on his face that pulled his eye down at the corner."

"You sure as hell saw a lot on a dark porch!" snapped Delia.

"Well, it's never too dark to see some things," Bea said indignantly.

Jake smiled and made himself comfortable on Slim's bed. "Thanks, Bea. You can go now."

Delia shut the door after her and turned to pace the room, not looking at Jake.

"Who was he?" he asked her after a moment.

"How should I know who he was? Ramey's partner, I guess," she said irritably, flipping the sash back and forth across her hips with one hand, as if lashing herself.

Jake sighed and sat up from the bed. "Yeah, I guess. Well, I'd better be getting along. I'll send their descriptions out on the wire and see what turns up. It may be a week or more, though."

"Wait a minute! Is that all you're going to do?"

"Well, sweetheart, there isn't much else I can do, is there? I'll ask around town to see if anybody saw them ride out last night. It doesn't seem like they'd stick around, does it? In fact, if they aren't halfway to the Mexican border right now there must be something pretty big holding them back."

She stood perfectly still staring at him, her eyes and mouth the only spots of color in her face.

"Is there something?" he asked her.

"You know damn well there is, don't you?" she said through her teeth. Then she hurried over to sit on the bed beside him, since he had leaned back again smiling at her. He could see the paddles churning inside her head. But she got something settled with herself in a moment and managed to smile back at him, though her eyes were still scanning him.

"Listen, Highpockets, can you really do anything like they say, except deal funny poker?"

"Like what?"

"Like use that gun? Is it true what Clem says about you, that you're really pretty good with it?"

"I don't know. What's good?"

"Goddamn it, can you shoot somebody with it if you try?"

"Who do you want shot, sweetheart?"

"You know who I want—oh, hell, I should have known better than to expect any help from you! After all, what do you owe me?" She looked as if she might be close to tears. She also looked genuinely worried.

Jake reached out and took her arm. "Hey, you throw in

137

too soon. How'd you ever learn to play blackjack? Try me again. I never said I hated redheads."

She eyed him. "What do you want to hear?"

"Try the truth. Only act like you're still lying. It'll make it come out easier." He waited. "Who's the man?"

"A friend of Rosie's. Maybe. I don't know."

"But you think. Who?"

"A kid—a man—called Frank Becker. He used to work for us as a shill in the tent show. A rube come-on for the shell game or monte."

Jake stroked her arm. "There, that didn't hurt too much, did it? What else did he do?"

"He robbed the express office in Yuma when we were there once! Got away with ten thousand dollars—almost. They caught him just before he would have hopped over the Mexican border, but they didn't find the money with him." Her eyebrows took wing. "If that's any big surprise to you. They put him in the Yuma pen for it."

"Then why are you worried? Maybe he's still there."

"And maybe he's here, looking for Rosie, who maybe had the money he stole all this time! Isn't it time you had something to say to me?"

"Rosie didn't look very rich when she died."

"No? Well, she was carrying fancy luggage!"

Jake laughed happily. Delia continued to glare at him for another second. Then she softened, even began to chuckle herself. She put her hands around his throat, as if to strangle him, and shook him.

"Damn you, you Dutchman! You've known about all this from the start, haven't you? And you've enjoyed watching me try to hustle you!"

"I like to see a pro work." Still smiling, he drew her down to him. The change in her attitude was gratifying. Her mouth was absolutely pliant; her firm, heavy breast was as pleasant as gold in his hand. When she drew away after a long moment she had a look of feline smugness about her.

138

"You like me?" she purred.

"You're very nice." She was.

At the next opportunity he asked, "Why are you scared of Rosie's boyfriend? In jail or out, what's he got against you?"

"I put the law on him. Gave them his description and everything. He stole Pop's magic bag out of the wagon and fifty dollars out of our money box when we were broke down and stranded in Yuma. The little sonofabitch tried to make it look like Pop was in on the steal, too, when they caught him. They put Pop in jail—on Becker's say-so—when he was coughing up blood, and the old guy died before they could even have a trial. He had rotten lungs, but Frank Becker killed him as much as they did! So I testified against him. I don't think we'd be friends any more."

Jake smoothed back her hair. "Rough," he murmured. She was accepting sympathy, too. They grappled softly for a time. He began to think the next two weeks in Arredondo weren't going to be so bad after all.

"Did you lock that door?"

"No, but nobody will come in while it's shut."

"Mn. Who's Ramey? Did he work for your old man, too?"

"I never saw him before he came here. And I swear I never knew he had anything to do with Becker or Rosie, or I wouldn't have let him in the door."

He thought that made sense. If she was on the track of the missing money she wouldn't have stuck Rosie's kids under the nose of somebody who might know them. "You were pretty anxious to keep him away from me, though," he reminded her.

"The way you acted, I thought there was paper out on him. I didn't want you arresting him and having to take him up to the county seat and not come back with—"

"With the money," he supplied. But his opinion of her was improving by the minute.

"Listen, Jake. I did you some good, didn't I? I mean, I

139

told you about Becker so you'd know what to do when he comes back."

"Maybe he won't come back."

"Why shouldn't he?"

"Why should he? He didn't find Rosie here, and neither did his partner. I don't know what they had agreed between them. Maybe this wasn't the place they were supposed to meet after all. It would have been somewhere below the border, and they're on the way there now."

"But when he doesn't find her there, he's bound to come looking for her!"

"You're supposing a lot. He's a wanted man. He didn't like to show his face to you last night. You think he'll come back and make a house-to-house search later? He'd be smarter to forget about the money and enjoy Mexico."

He saw she wanted to believe that, but that there was something else just as urgent with her. She wasn't about to forget the money, whatever Becker did.

"But what I told you meant something, didn't it?" she urged.

"I never forget a favor." He began to kiss her throat.

"I could do you another favor. No, we could do each other a favor, couldn't we? You could quit that chicken-feed job and come in here with me. We could get along with each other now, couldn't we?" She was half on top of him, her kimono open while he nuzzled her breasts.

"It seems like it. But Sánchez says you're pretty expensive. I don't know if I could pay the board for all three of us down here." He expected a laugh for that, and then he was going to tell her about the bag. But she pulled back.

"All three of us—who?"

"Me and the kids."

"What do you want with those greaser brats now? You've got the money. Get rid of them. I don't know why you've kept them this long!"

"I'm not sure myself." Something in her reaction made

140

him say, "But I thought you wanted them down here to keep the old woman happy." Then he added with a straight face, "They don't eat much. And they hardly drink at all."

"Jesus Christ, Jake! You know why I said that! And you ought to know that if Becker does come back looking for Rosie and that bag, having them around would be like putting up a sign: 'Here it is.' And anyway," she said with a ritual shudder of distaste, "I can't stand kids, especially half-breeds. Give them to Carrie Hand. She's got a big yen for you, only she's too prissy to show it. She'd bust up with gratitude if you made her a present of them. Better than that, sell them to Sánchez. He—" She looked at him in sudden exasperation. "You're kidding me, aren't you?" She laughed. "My God, you take me in every time! How am I ever going to know when you're serious, when you're so good at playing dumb?"

She leaned forward again, but he was somehow less ardent. He fixed a strand of her hair behind her ear and gave her a thin smile.

"Better yet—I could tie them in a bag and drop them down a mine shaft."

"Well, I don't think the world would lose much if you did. But I didn't mean anything like that. What's the matter? Did you go soft on those dingy little spicks? Do they make you think about what you might have left behind in somebody else's bed, somewhere? I guess there could be a little Jake or two running around the country that you don't know about, huh?" She laughed at Jake's eyes, grown suddenly darker, like those of a surprised cat. "Haven't you ever thought about that? I guess men don't, damn 'em.

"Never mind, honey. I'll tell you what to do. You tell Sánchez that you can't keep them any longer. He'll find somebody who'll buy them for—oh—twenty or thirty dollars apiece. He keeps that. Then you give him a few dollars extra and tell him, if anybody comes looking for them, to say they and their mama stopped here with him and rode one of his wagons down to Sonora. Easy. And the kids won't come to any harm, if you're worried about that. The people who buy them don't hurt them. They just train them to be useful, like house servants or farm workers. What else would they ever be anyway?"

She beamed at him. "How's that? Can't Delia fix things? Sure she can, because, honey, you can put your boots under my bed any time. But I can't run a charity house for you or anyone else, even if some of the damned men around here seem to think so, like that lousy Sánchez! And some of the other cheapskates—they're so poor, I ought to have holiday sales, like Ezra French!"

She chortled at the notion. She was beginning to sound confident of him, though she kept her eyes on the small, cold smile that had set on Jake's mouth.

She began to run one hand down his lean body with deliberate slowness, but before she had satisfied her curiosity he caught the hand, kissed its palm, and got up, pulling her along with him. She came smiling but puzzled. He untied the belt of her robe and drew her against him, his mouth on hers like a thirsty man at a spring. With a deft motion he slipped the robe from her shoulders and let it drop, smoothing her back and buttocks with a firm hand. She purred her triumph.

Into her mouth he asked, "How much?"

"Wha—"

"Everybody pays. How much?"

"Honey, I don't—"

"Ten dollars?"

"Jake—"

"Eight?"

"I don't know what the hell you—"

"Or maybe just for love, or because we're so much alike." He scooped her off her feet and swung her around to the bed. A certain doubt had been growing on her face, but now she sighed and closed her eyes, reassured.

142

Then he dropped her on the bed so suddenly she squealed and bounced.

"That's not a bad idea about having a sale," he said in a matter-of-fact voice. "You need something to compete with that tent. I'll mention it around town if you like." She stared up at him, unblinking. "Unless you'd rather run an ad in Hand's paper, or put a poster on the porch."

"Jake!"

"It'd be cheaper to just put signs on the girls' asses." He was going out the door before she could scramble off the creaking bed. She made a grab for her robe as she staggered up, but missed it. The door slammed shut in her face; she jerked it open again as he reached the top of the stairs at the far end of the hall.

"Jake Hollander, you dirty sonofabitch!"

He descended the front stairs to the landing at an easy lope. She ran to the railing and hung over it, gripping it with white fingers. Her eyes were like a mad horse's.

"You lousy, cheapskate Dutch bastard! Don't you ever show your face in here again! Do you hear me? Or send those dirty brats here, either! Stick to the cantina! That herd of sheep is more your style!"

He stopped halfway down the second flight of steps. Doors were flying open all over the house as the girls rallied to the sound of her voice. Slim and Bea appeared behind her with astonished faces and tried to lay soothing hands on her. She shook them off furiously.

"You two-bit, stinking, penny-ante card shuffler!" she yelled. "You're going to get what's coming to you! I hope to God somebody catches you cheating and shoots off both your thumbs. They're worth more than your balls!"

He reached into his vest pocket and fished out a coin. It was a ten-dollar gold piece. He winced, but it was the necessary final point to the lesson he was giving her. He flipped it up as she hung over him, screeching. It went between the banister spindles and fell at her feet. She swooped down on

143

it and flung it back at him, cracking her hand painfully on the newel post in the backswing.

"Take it back, *tío,* and buy yourself a tonic! I don't make any charge for old men who can't get it up!"

He strode past a frozen Angelina in the front hall and slammed the door behind him. Inside, it sounded like a barnyard gone mad. He stalked toward the jail, a hard elation stiffening his legs so that they moved jerkily.

Paco and Urraca weren't in the jail when he got back. He called them several times with the sharp whistle that could bring them in from the other end of town, then went out back and looked over the litter of boxes and barrels that Paco had dragged from other lots to build a miniature Arredondo of his own around his pretended silver mine.

"Paco!" he shouted.

Carrie came out of her back door at his call, fixing paper sleeve guards around her wrists to protect her spotless white shirtwaist.

"They're gone, Jacob."

"Gone? What do you mean, gone?"

"Mrs. Cuddeback came in a little while ago and took them home with her. She's agreed to keep them for a while, to see how they all get along together, but I'm sure they'll be fine. She's had ten children of her own. She'll know how to care for them properly." She saw that he hadn't moved. "I must say, you don't look very pleased. I thought you'd be jubilant. Now you'll be free to do as you like, and they'll have some sort of normal home. Or did you particularly want them to go live with Miss Moon?"

"Who took them?"

"Mrs. Cuddeback. The Hassayampa Mine foreman's wife."

"You mean that woman with the iron jaw who looks like she used to recruit mule skinners for the army?"

Carrie flushed. "We are all as God saw fit to make us. Annie Cuddeback is a good wife and mother, and a good Christian woman. She'll see that the children get proper food

144

and rest, and begin to learn decent speech and manners, which is more than you— What *is* the matter with you? You know you told me that if I could find someone who would take them you'd be glad to let them go! Now you look as if I'd thrown them to the wolves. Surely you're not sorry to have them out of your way?"

"Hell, no! Why should I be? They're not my kids." He was still feeling the aftereffects of his encounter with Delia. She had stirred him more than he let her know.

"What's wrong then?" Carrie asked, coming forward a few more steps, frowning at him. "You look pale. Are you sick?"

"Sick?" He did feel a strange emptiness in the pit of his stomach. "No. I haven't had any breakfast yet. I'm hungry."

He looked at the welter of trash that was strewn across the back lots, from the jail down to the stage road beyond the Red Front. Somewhere in all that mess was Rosie Robles's carpetbag with its false bottom, hiding—unless both he and Delia were wrong—ten thousand dollars. Without Urraca to guide him, how was he ever going to find it now?

15

The carpetbag remained hidden from him. His break with Delia was complete enough to make him swerve to the other side of the street right after checking the Happy Apache and avoid her end of the block entirely. With the kids gone and his belt returned to him, he should have known peace for the remainder of his time in town, but it was not so.

The two westbound stages, from Mesilla and El Paso, came in the following two days. He saw their dusty, travel-dazed passengers totter into the cantina, gorge themselves on Sánchez's risky stew, and climb aboard again, while he nursed a solitary drink at the bar. Jake felt a hopeless envy for them, like that of a pauper watching the wealthy disport themselves in some wasteful, tiring game with rules he can't follow. Only when they were gone toward Fort Bowie fifty miles away did he ask himself why he hadn't gone with them.

The only answer that occurred—that they were headed the wrong way—did nothing to stifle the anxiety and doubt growing in him. He asked himself what was so special about El Paso that he would be confined in this voluntary hell to get to it, now. El Paso, for God's sake!

He could have returned to Tucson, then gone northeast to Santa Fe, or up to Denver. He could even have returned to California. There wasn't a spot in that state, from the worst mining camp in the north to the army-dampered Presidio of San Diego, where he couldn't find more money being spent in a better climate.

The damned wind here blew seven days a week! You had to guide yourself around with one hand while you pawed grit out of your eyes with the other. It was already hot as a California July in the daytime, but still colder than a San Francisco winter at night, and this was only the middle of March.

And if anybody was getting rich from the silver in the ground out here it was being kept a secret from him.

He sat in the cantina, hating himself for doing nothing. Then, when he finally moved, pushing himself listlessly from the chair he said, "Come on, P—" The word died on his tongue. He looked at the other customers to see if he had been heard. He felt as if he had just stopped short of summoning the dead.

And that was nonsense, because he'd spoken out of mere habit. They had followed him like the echo of his own footsteps for two weeks. They were like that fly that had buzzed so insanely in the jail the night before and dodged all his attempts to kill it. When its tiny scream finally stopped, because of exhaustion or death or escape, he could still half hear the sound.

When he returned to the jail to waste the rest of the afternoon, Carrie was inside, busy with a broom and dustcloth.

Her intrusion was welcome by that time, though he felt obliged to frown at her activity. "You don't have to do that."

She raised her eyebrows diffidently.

"I know I don't. But I thought I might as well take the children's bedclothes away and look around for anything they may have left behind. I couldn't find that carpetbag their things were in. I bundled up what they had in a box for Mrs. Cuddeback. Do you know where the bag is?"

Jake took his breath in slowly, then let it out with a shrug.

147

"I guess they dragged it off to play with. I'll look around for it later."

"It really doesn't make any difference now. I just wondered."

He lounged in the inner doorway, watching her sweep out the cells. Several apple cores, an empty wadded paper sack, and a thing that looked like a pressed mouse corpse came from under Paco's bunk. She leaned forward to look and gave a little cry of disgust—because that's what it was—then swept it out of the cell to his feet. He took it by the tail and tossed it into the street.

It was a good thing she'd asked about the bag. Now he'd be able to look for it openly without seeming odd, raking through the litter that was tumbled around everyone's back door.

"Did Paco give you any trouble over going?" he asked, for something to say. "He claimed to be crazy about sleeping in jailhouses."

She looked at him soberly. "What he meant, of course, was that he liked being here with you, Jacob. That was what made me feel almost guilty about sending them away. And knowing that I was going to miss them myself, even though it's all for the best that they're gone, as I'm sure you'll agree. But I hated to deceive him. I told him that they were just going out there for a visit, to see the mine and the mill and get acquainted with Mrs. Cuddeback's youngest children. If he'd known they were meant to stay, I'm sure he would have refused to go. As it was, he went happily. He didn't see me give Mrs. Cuddeback their clothes."

Jake smiled faintly. "You always know how to handle things, don't you?"

She stiffened. "I tried not to upset them more than was necessary, in order to do what was best for them, if that's what you mean. But I don't think it is. What is it, Jacob? You looked so strange that morning. Do you resent my finding a

148

home for them, even if you don't want them yourself? Do you think I'm just an interfering busybody?"

"No, not at all," he said hastily. "You did the right thing. That's all I meant."

"It isn't what you said."

"Well, it's what I meant. Why do you always get so cockle-burred whenever I say anything to you? You took care of them like you said you would. You take care of Clem. You even take care of me. You help run the paper and the Sunday school and the League. You cook and sew and wash. You help deliver the paper and write up the news. You do it all very well."

She continued to look at him as if he were accusing her. "Well?" She pushed a pale thread of hair back in place.

"Nothing! It was meant to be a compliment. But—"

"I thought there would be a 'but,'" she said, vindicated.

"You're as touchy as a cat. I was only going to say—hell, I don't know what I was going to say! You work too hard! Don't you ever think about taking a little time off now and then? Let somebody else take care of you for a change?"

"Who? Why?"

Jake sighed, wondering how he'd got into such a bind.

"Why? For pleasure; for fun. It wouldn't hurt you to have a little pleasure out of life, would it? You ought to. As for who, I don't know. I guess there are enough men around here who would like to. I see them watch you when you go down the street, but you never give them more than half a nod. Don't you want a husband? Most pretty women do. Most ugly ones, too." He came to a lame and sorry halt. Whatever it was that his inner mind had tried to unfold to her, that couldn't have been it.

She turned pink slowly. "Your compliments and concern overwhelm me, Jacob. I didn't know you'd paid that much attention to my plight. Are you about to play the part of John Alden now?" She saw that he didn't know about John Alden. Her mouth quirked. "Let's try to clarify this. Are you urging

149

me to get married in order to have more 'pleasure' and 'fun' out of life? Do you have any prospects in mind for me who could offer me a life of such ease? I'd be fascinated to hear about them. I, myself, know only *one* person here who has a good deal of money but no house to keep, no children to raise, no clothes to be mended, and no work that needs an extra hand."

"Sounds pretty good. Who is he?"

"You. Move your feet, please."

She swept Paco's litter past him and out the door, then came back to pick up the bedding. Her eyes were glowing, but whether from amusement or pique he couldn't tell.

"Ordinary women have to work hard all their lives out here, wherever they live and whatever their circumstances. It isn't a soft country. I count myself luckier than most of them. I'm not tied to a man who despises me while he uses me for a slavey and a brood animal. My brother needs me and he respects me, so I'm glad to help him all I can."

The closing door ended their exchange before Jake had to think of a suitable reply to that.

The woman was like an armadillo. Anything you said to her made her bunch up. It was a good thing her brother needed her. He had the skin for it. Anybody else would need body armor, too.

He saw that the circular on Frank Becker was just where he had dropped it days before. He snorted, reading it again, and put it in his pocket. He'd have to ask Sánchez if the man had really been in the cantina. But not now. He had just come from there himself.

An hour later he was still idle, sitting with his feet up on the table, staring into the middle distance. With one hand he toyed with a silver dollar, rolling it over and between his fingers, side over side. It was a juggling trick he'd picked up from a magician with a weakness for inside straights. He used it as an exercise to keep his fingers nimble.

Thinking about the Great Orloff brought him around to

150

Mooney's Marvel Show, carpetbags that did disappearing tricks, and Delia.

He'd handled her wrong, like everything else lately. Something she'd said had got to him. If it was about selling the kids, he'd wasted his anger, because while she was saying it Carrie was taking them off his hands anyway, if he had known it.

Even if he hadn't known it, why did if affect him that way? Women were always saying things that were stupid, or cruel, or ignorant. He didn't recall ever postponing his pleasure in them because of their mouths. Delia was only saying what she thought he wanted to hear. But it wasn't what she said about selling Paco and Urraca that had cooled him. It was the remark about his leaving little replicas of himself to grow up hungry without his knowledge.

It was crazy, but he felt a cold horror of the idea. Some piece of him, some reincarnation without his death, might be alive somewhere; living without his consent; feeling without his control. It made his flesh crawl.

He caught the coin in his palm and put it in his pocket again. Delia had called him an old man who needed a tonic. She'd been right enough about that. He left the jail, looking for some kind of action.

But it was the wrong time of day.

The industrious Anglos were all hard at work. Patchy Murdoch was making a water haul from his source of supply in the mountains. The other regular card players were gone, too. Patterson, the barber, was out of his shop. The pool hall was deserted.

He had a drink at the Happy Apache, then went over to the shooting gallery. The proprietor, a gunsmith of limited talents named "Reamer" Farney, was dismantling an elderly Springfield for cleaning. Jake put money on the counter and picked up a rifle and cartridges.

He fired steadily at the standing targets until he was out of

151

ammunition. Reamer put down his work and examined the results. "Looks like you get a free game, marshal."

He set the revolving targets in motion. Jake knocked them over remorselessly. The sound of his rifle made a one-to-four counterrhythm to the racket of a carpenter's hammer on the roof of a new house down the street.

He began to attract a small crowd. He paid little attention to them. The minor destructiveness of the shooting and the ease with which he was hitting the targets were balm to his soul. He hadn't done any shooting for several years, but he had always had a natural eye for it and a steady hand, in spite of his sedentary habits. At least that hadn't changed, he thought, and was surprised at the relief the discovery was to him.

Augie Gebhardt and his brother, Rance, joined the crowd. Patterson, the barber, came with several girls from the cantina. Sánchez and Clement Hand stood on the fringe.

"Hollander, why don't you stop massacreein' tin ducks with a popgun and show us what you can do with that old hog leg you wear?" Augie called to him.

"Not in here you don't!" said Reamer. "That damn cannon is big enough to blow the back end out of my stall. Get some bottles from the saloon and do your shooting out in the street."

Jake shook his head.

"Maybe it don't shoot no more, Rance," said Augie. "I never see him do anything with it but brain the poor drunk muckers." He worked his way through the girls to Jake's side, grinning.

Jake began to reload.

"I heard he killed seven men in one week with it once. 'Course, that was a while back. Maybe something got a little rusty since, hey, marshal?"

"Don't start up on me, squarehead," Jake said evenly. "I was just beginning to forget about you. How's your nose?"

Augie's grin soured as the girls and his brother laughed.

152

"Hollander, I bet if I was to throw a brick up in the air in front of you, you couldn't hit it for five dollars." There was a chorus of support for Jake from the girls and Reamer, to which Clement Hand added his voice.

"That's pretty easy money, Dutch. Why don't you take him up on it?"

Jake looked around and saw him: bright eyed and flushed, hands in his pockets; cocky as a terrier pup. The little bastard was drunk! He'd been siphoned out of the cantina by the noise.

"Maybe you'd like to put an apple up on your head and stand out there," Jake suggested. Clem batted his eyes twice, then nodded.

"All right," he said.

Jake swore under his breath and turned back to his targets, but the rest of the crowd cheered Clem and sent up cries for an apple. "Get an apple!"

"Here's one!"

"That's a horse apple! Goddamn it, Reb, we want a Kentucky redstreak. What's the matter with you?"

"I got somethin' better—a bottle of redeye!"

Jake turned to look, because he recognized Gowdy's voice in the chorus.

"Hey, that's my bottle, Gowdy-y!" Augie bawled in anguish. "I just bought that bottle. Get you an empty one, for mercy's sakes! Jake!"

Clem was standing in the middle of the street with Augie's bottle balanced on his head and a sheep eater's grin dying on his face. His eyes searched for Jake, but he didn't move as Gowdy danced back from him and pulled a battered pistol out of his belt.

"Old Jake's scared to try it! I'll show you how it's done. Stand up there, Mr. Hand—don't teeter!" The crowd drew back to a safe distance, their anticipation only slightly dampened with apprehension. Gowdy took careful aim, resting the short barrel of the pistol on his other wrist.

"Gowdy—shit!" Jake drew and fired from the back of the crowd before Gowdy could. The bottle on Clem's head vanished in a glittering shower of whiskey and broken glass that rained down over his tight-squeezed eyes and mouth. Smoke from the black powder threw a white pall over Jake, but he emerged from it, gun leveled at Gowdy. Everybody whooped and applauded.

Gowdy hastily put his gun away. When Jake was close to him he said in a dangerously friendly voice, "How would you like to be the first man in town with two ass holes?"

"He was just funnin', Jake," Augie said. His own face still showed traces of anguish for his lost bottle, but he clapped Jake on the shoulder in spite of it.

"The second man in town, then," Jake amended instantly. "Not much of a distinction. But how about it?"

"No, sir," Gowdy said earnestly.

"Then you better back up every time you see me on the street, starting right now!"

Gowdy backed all the way to the Schooner, guided by his friend Reb. There were a few requests from the remaining crowd to "Do it again" and "Get an apple," but it was evident that the show wasn't going to be repeated, and they began to drift away under his watchful eye. When he turned to glance back at Clem he saw him still standing in place, wiping whiskey and broken glass off his coat carefully with a handkerchief.

"If you were looking for a filler for the dunce column I guess you've got it now: 'Hollander Gets the Drop on Half-wit Mucker.' Is that what you wanted?"

"No," said Clem, beginning to laugh weakly. "I just wanted to see you do it, too."

"So much that you'd bet your own head on it? That was pretty chancy, considering that we aren't exactly blood brothers!"

Clem continued to laugh as he took off his stained glasses and tried to clean them with the sodden handkerchief.

"I couldn't help it."

"You crazy bastard, you're drunk as a cider-maker's sow! Gowdy couldn't hit the ground with his hat, and you just stood there and let him take aim!"

"Well, he did have me worried for a second, until I saw you come out." Clem's eyes squeezed shut again with the memory, and his shoulders shook helplessly. Tears ran down his face.

"Me? Goddamn it, I was forty feet away!"

"But I knew you wouldn't miss. You're still Dutch Hollander, Jake—whether you like it or not." He peered at Jake nearsightedly before adjusting his glasses, then snorted again at what he saw on Jake's face.

Jake groaned. "Christ, you're worse than Paco!" He didn't know what to make of such a person as Clem. "If you knew I wouldn't miss, you knew a hell of a lot more than I did! The ammunition in this piece is so old, I didn't know if it was going to misfire or blow up in my hand!"

Clem was instantly sober. "I'm sorry, Dutch. I didn't think about there being any danger to you. You shouldn't have taken the risk."

"Oh, for— Come on—get your ass back into the cantina before Carrie catches you, and I'll buy you something to settle your nerves."

Before the day ended, the ridiculous story had gone around town, and a dozen locals came trotting to beg Jake to repeat it for their benefit with their own bottles or an apple. Clem's head was still the most popular choice for a target base. When he made his rounds he was greeted everywhere with pats on the back and offers of free drinks. In the eyes of the Arredondans the incident had made him neither a hero nor the fool that he feared, but simply one of them. They were ready for friendly roughhouse and a personal recounting of the Mc-Naughton slaughter from the man who had seemed too cold, dry, and colorless until now, whatever his ancient fame.

155

Jake, as always, withdrew from camaraderie the more it advanced on him. But he tried to endure it, because there was nowhere to escape it but back in the empty jail office.

As he expected, plans were drawn up for a re-enactment of the event. Without his participation, target bearers as game as Clem were hard to find. Bottles were tossed instead, and were either blown apart in midair or smashed on the street. There was a massive destruction of liquor and glass at the intersection of Hassayampa and the stage road. The more sober residents began to complain because he wasn't doing anything to stop it, either.

"You are the cause of this, Jacob Hollander," Carrie said. "Go out there and do something!"

"They'll cool off in a while. Meantime, they're not killing anything but their own whiskey."

"You mean you just intend to loaf here and watch?"

"What do you want me to do? I can't arrest them all. If I pull a gun out now, everybody is likely to get killed. Besides, your brother is as much to blame for this as anybody. Look at him right now—happy as a firebug in hell." Clem was standing in the office door absorbed in the street scene. Carrie looked at him doubtfully, but rallied at once.

"That's a shoddy way to avoid your own responsibility, Mr. Hollander. Anyone here knows how hard Clem has worked to bring some kind of civilized order to this town, even to the point of hiring you, useless as that was. He detests this sort of irresponsibility; he always has. And he's been willing to stand up against it with every edition of his paper."

Jake snorted. "I know what he prints. But he's what you might call a sunshine peace lover. Every now and then he likes a little violence to sweeten the pot."

She looked grim. "If you aren't man enough to stop this, perhaps I can," she said, and swept around him to the corner, where Bert Kelly, the gloomy owner of the Red Front, stood in his own door. He was cradling a double-barreled shotgun in the crook of one arm to protect his property from any further raids on its stock. Jake saw her snatch the gun from Kelly. He uncoiled himself from his lounging position as rapidly as he could, to reach her and take it from her while she was still fending off Bert.

"Bert! Carrie! Damn it, what do you think you're going to do?"

"Get their attention!" she shouted. He put her back with one hand, cocking both hammers of the gun with the other, then let it off at the sky. The roar brought a startled pause to the play in the streets.

"Is that what you had in mind?" he asked. Then, to the crowd: "I've got an announcement to make! Mr. Clement Hand of the Arredondo *Arrow* has offered to sponsor a shoot next Sunday afternoon, outside of town. He'll get up some prizes for marksmanship with pistol or rifle. He doesn't know just what yet, but he'll think of something.

"You'll have to supply your own ammunition, so you better start saving it now. Also, this hell-raising is disturbing the ladies and children! Cut it out; you're wasting good whiskey. If you keep shooting up the supply, you're going to run up the price to where we'll all have to drink beer!"

The grumbling that had begun dissolved into laughter. Jake grinned at them, relaxed deliberately against a post.

"Miss Hand, here, says she'll have to clean up this mess you made if you don't do it first. I don't think she ought to have to cut her pretty little fingers on all that glass when some of you are so horn-handed you could scoop it up like feathers. But I'm sure she'll be glad to supply a box to dump it in so it won't lame the mules when you pull out for home tonight."

His last appeal brought out all the drunken valor and bare-handed foolishness he thought it would. He returned the shot-gun to Bert and met Carrie's eyes briefly. He couldn't read her face at all.

. . .

157

Later, she came to the door of the jail to look in on him, hands clutching her upper arms as if she were cold.

"Did they get it all cleaned up?" he asked without much interest.

"Yes. Then I had to use up all the iodine and bandages I had. Some of them will hardly be able to hold a pick tomorrow, thanks to you."

"Or a gun?"

"Yes. That's what I came about. I want to apologize for saying what I did. You—you handled them very well, and you weren't afraid of them. I could see that. I'm sorry I said you were."

"Don't be too sure everything you see is so. If I'd come out sounding like John Law they'd have made a sieve out of me. They might have anyway. I was lucky, like this afternoon."

She winced, looking from him to his feet on the table between them. "Yes, Clem told me he had something to do with that, too. I'm also sorry for that. I know he sometimes drinks, more than he should, and then he tries to find some way to—prove himself, I suppose."

"Prove himself?"

She looked uncomfortable. "Prove that he's the same as —other men. I don't say anything to him about it, because he has enough to bear." He was silent before her embarrassment. She got herself in hand and looked at him again. "Well, I am sorry for putting all the blame on you. That's what I came to say. We're all weaker than we'd like to be. I suppose when we're denied the indulgence in one human frailty we tend to overindulge in another. My brother sometimes drinks too much, and I—talk too much. Good night, Jacob."

The day had seemed eternal. He had accepted too many free drinks and had not had enough to eat. He had a dull headache. Paco's chatter would have driven him crazy if he had been forced to endure it, but without it there was no proper period to the day. He fell asleep with difficulty, then

158

woke sometime in the night, oppressed by the same sad, dreaming lust that had waked him that morning and the morning before.

He got up and lit a cigar to put things back into perspective and went outside, in spite of the chill air, to smoke it.

When night came in Arredondo it was absolute. There wasn't a sound or a light anywhere except at the cantina, where there was always a light. The moon was down.

He was going to have to make peace with Delia pretty soon, or lower his standards and find comfort at the cantina. If he hadn't been so thin skinned he'd be up at the Moon now, in that big soft bed of hers, with her making little sleepy protests maybe, but—Christ! Stop that, he thought, before you start acting like some pimple-faced boy.

Still, he looked toward Delia's, wondering what she'd do if he went down and tapped on her door now. Laugh her head off, then slam the door in his face, he supposed. He sighed.

A shadowy figure emerged from the larger darkness of the Golden Moon, walking carefully. It stopped once to look back, then hurried across the street in Jake's direction. Jake froze, cigar in mouth, watching it. Before it passed the light from the cantina he had identified the walk.

It was Clement Hand.

16

Clem saw the glow of Jake's cigar as he was about to turn into the walkway beside the *Arrow* building. He faltered, then walked forward more slowly until he reached the jail.

"You're up late, Jake."

"Couldn't sleep. Like you." Jake made a bitter sound between a cough and a laugh at the silent figure. "You really are some kind of miracle man, Hand. You ought to write yourself up."

"Why is that?"

"Well, it's news, unless I'm as dumb as Carrie. I never knew they could grow *back* again—like tonsils."

Clem sagged against a post of the corrugated-tin sun roof. "Oh," he said softly. "She told you what she—I—didn't think she would—could." He sat down on the edge of the board-walk.

"She left something to my imagination, but she wanted to make sure I'd know how much I owed it to you to stay here."

"Oh my God. I'm sorry, Dutch."

"I'll bet you are! You know, the longer I'm in this flapjack town, the more like a boy from the country I feel. I thought I'd heard every con, gull, rook, and bluff that could be played on a poor sucker, but you people can pull off some of the damnedest things! How in the name of hell could you let a woman think a thing like that about you for eighteen years? It's impossible! No, it isn't, because I can tell she believes it. But why? What for? What do you get? It doesn't make any damned sense at all!"

"I guess not. It's—complicated." Clem seemed to want more prodding from Jake, but didn't get it. The end of Jake's cigar burned furiously, and a ghost smoke drifted on the moving air. Clem cleared his throat.

"I don't know where to start, except to say that it never really had anything to do with you, whatever Carrie thought. Oh, it's true that Ben McNaughton hired four saddle tramps to cut you up, and they came to me when they couldn't find you. That chicken-livered sheriff told them I'd be the one to ask. I guess he had a little hankering for revenge against me after what I said about his conspicuous absence during the whole McNaughton trouble.

"So they came to scare your whereabouts out of me. But the rest of our own particular grief—Carrie's and mine—was my fault, and I can't explain it any more than I can tell you why I let Gowdy put a bottle on my head and start to shoot it off.

"Maybe it's got something to do with my size. I'm short, I'm half blind, I can't fight and never could. When I was a boy, every other boy in town, and two or three girls, could and did beat me up whenever they took the notion. I never won. But, Dutch, I never backed down, either! Never! I can't, to this day. It isn't that I'm not afraid. It's that something happens in my head when I'm threatened and I—" He ran his hand over his face and through his hair. "This sounds stupid," he muttered. "What it boils down to is, they broke in on us that night, demanding to know where you'd run off to, terrifying Carrie with their talk about what they were going to do to you when they caught you, tearing up the office. They were ignorant tramps. I should have given them a direction to go looking in, and cleaned up the mess.

"But I couldn't do that. When they started to push me

161

around I turned stubborn. I wasn't afraid of them for the moment. In my great, fatheaded certainty I thought they wouldn't have the guts to hurt us if I faced them down, because I was on the side of righteousness—and because I thought you were coming back." He laughed softly. "I really thought you were on your way to get about a dozen U.S. marshals to come down and arrest Sheriff Cobb and clean out the whole McNaughton family. It's what I would have done myself if I'd had your chance." He sighed. "That isn't funny. None of it was funny. Not even the part where I was mentally composing the blistering editorial I was going to write the next day, while McNaughton's men were pitching my type into the stove. They took us out to McNaughton's place and worked me over like I was a bag full of snakes. McNaughton wasn't there. That was his defense at the trial, that he didn't know; they were drunk and I'd provoked them. He testified against them. Everybody in town knew he'd hired them and for what, but he got fined and they got a year in jail."

"A year? For trying to kill you?"

"No, for assault and battery, breaking and entering, destruction of private property."

"Nothing else?"

"No."

"Then how did Carrie get the idea they'd cut you?"

After a pause Clem said, "She was there. They put her in the barn while they were busy with me. They threatened to do it; she heard them. She'd heard before, in the office. They took enough hide off me, I guess they'd have finally made good on their threat, but I passed out, and they left me for her."

Jake set the front legs of his chair on the ground.

"She said nothing happened to her."

"I know. She's always said that. That's why I let her believe what she does. Jesus Christ, Jake, if it would have helped her in the least I would have killed them all later, somehow!

162

I would've! But when I understood how desperate she was to deny it, how frightened and alone she was with her shame, I couldn't do anything! I didn't charge them with rape, for her sake, and I let her think what she thought—when I found out what that was—for her sake, too. Or for my own punishment. She wouldn't have suffered if I'd used any sense. If I'd cared about anything in the damned world but feeding my own peculiar vanity by keeping stone silent while they knocked me down. God! I didn't understand what she thought had happened to me until much later. I believed all her tears and secrecy and agony were for herself, as they should have been. When I realized"—he almost laughed—"I didn't know what to say! And then I knew I couldn't say anything to her, ever. I was the stupid young prig who had let his sister be ruined for a lie he had told just by refusing to open his mouth. She was eighteen—a baby; my sister. I couldn't talk to her. I was ashamed to tell her I was all right, that she was the only one damaged. And she couldn't talk to me about such a thing, naturally. We never have, to this day. Never. It was all just sealed up."

He got up and leaned against the post again, facing away from Jake even in the darkness.

"I fixed my own punishment for hurting her. I decided I would have to live as if what she thought were true. We left Willow Bend for a place where no one knew us. I took care of her and she took care of me. I thought when she was a bit older and stronger, when the memory had healed, she'd find someone to marry and I'd be free. You see, at the time I wasn't planning to make it a lifetime sacrifice." One by one he began to toss a handful of pebbles he'd gathered from the street. "But it didn't work out that way. She didn't intend to marry, because she thought she had to devote her life to *me*, you see. I'd been the cause of her pain, I'd spoiled her hope for a normal life, but I was going to be served and shielded and cherished for it forever. She thinks I deserve that, for my suffering.

"And if that wasn't hell enough for me, I made it hotter year by year. Because I cheated her again and again. You see, I found I couldn't live the pure, monastic life I owed her and meant to give her." He let the rest of the stones fall from his fingers. "You'd think that as scarce as women are out here, a three-quarter-sized man with poor eyesight and damned little money would have trouble adding fornication to his list of sins, wouldn't you?" He snorted. "Jake, I've never had any trouble at all, wherever we lived. Most of the time when we moved it was because I was afraid Carrie was going to find out about a particular woman. Letting her find out and be done with it has been one of my worst temptations. But it's the only one I've been able to resist. So we've moved a lot. And I've always found another woman."

"Like Delia?"

"Like Delia." He turned his head after a second. "You don't seem much surprised. Didn't you believe what Carrie said about me?"

Jake sucked a tooth. "I'm not much in the habit of believing or not believing. But I saw how you rushed Delia off home that day after she'd been rolling around in the street with that other punk. I guess I thought you looked like a man who figured he had one coming and was in a hurry to collect it. I had other things on my mind then. I do wonder about something now."

"What can I keep from you after this?"

"Yeah. Well, when you decided to grab me off the stage, was it really for a drunk tender, or did you want somebody who'd keep Carrie busy while you were in bed with Delia?"

Clem was silent for a while. "I don't know," he said finally. "I really needed you here, Jake. And I admired you. You used to be what I would have given my soul to be when I was twenty-two in Willow Bend. Didn't you ever see that? It wasn't opportunism that made me spread your name all through my paper; it was— I won't embarrass you with the callow word that comes to mind. About the other, I don't

164

know. I hope I didn't want to make a tool of you to use against Carrie, because I love her. But I usually have more reasons for anything I do than I like to discuss with myself." He pushed himself away from the post.

"As for whatever plans I might have had for myself and Delia, they're all off now. She's through with me, for some reason. I don't know what's the matter with her. Tonight she told me that I was the only man she'd ever known who had treated her like something other than a cow. Then she said I was an idiot. She told me that if I ever came down to the Moon again she'd tell Carrie about us. She doesn't know what the secrecy is all about, but she's sharp enough to see that it's the one thing I can't allow. So—that's that. I'll say good night. I have to be up again in a couple of hours."

Jake let him go in silence.

The next day a rider came in with news of a promising strike in the southeast, where the short-tailed Hassayampas declined into furrowed ridges and solitary mesas.

The nonminers reacted as if it were the first strike. There was a run on supplies at Dugan's store as the newly declared prospectors girded themselves for the hunt and started trailing out to the hills. The news had a deleterious effect on the merchants, Jake discovered.

"Damned amateurs," Bert Kelly grumbled. "Some of them pull up stakes if somebody flips a dime under their noses. Silver! Silver! Shit, that's the only kind of silver they know by sight, and yet there they go looking for ore. They'd all see a damn sight more silver if they stayed here and tended to their jobs. A good carpenter or a blacksmith is worth five times more here than another damned miner, unless he's one man in a thousand. But they've all got to be prospectors or they can't rest! One of them goes out there and sees piss stains on a rock and yells, 'I found color!' Then the rest of them think, 'Oh, hell, he's gonna get rich while I'm stuck here building chicken coops,' and off they go until you can't get

165

a nail drove or a shoe soled. I wish I was back home in Chicago and had never seen a mining town!"

Sánchez explained it further. "The town people want the silver to run, but they don't want it to run too far away. If it does, the *mineros* don't come into town so much. And then one day somebody takes a wagon full of whiskey, lamp oil, and frijoles out to them, and they don't come back at all. Instead, there is another town. It is very bad for the town people, but what can one do?"

"What will you do if the town runs dry?" Jake asked him.

"Me? Nothing. I do not worry. Sánchez was here first. He will be here last. There has been a Sánchez here since who can remember."

"I thought you told me your old man's family was very big down in Mexico?"

"Eh? Oh, that. Of course. The Arredondos had many holdings, very many. This place was my uncle's. It was once a holy place—a monastery he let the fathers build on our land. But they did not stay. The Apaches drove them out."

"I've wondered sometimes if you don't have some Apache blood in you, Sánchez." He watched the little man bridle at such a notion and added smoothly, "I hear they have a lot of respect for your wagon trains. That's something they don't give to many who aren't their own kind. *Muy machos*, those Apaches." He studied his beer while Sánchez considered this.

"*Patrón*, you have very sharp eyes," he said in a grave tone. "I have not said this to the others, because there are Anglos and there are Anglos, no? But I tell you, *en confianza*—for your own ears—that what you say is true. My mother, my little queen, is one of that people. A chief's daughter. Yes. She never speaks of it because, you see, they drove her out of the tribe because of her love for my father."

"Yeah. You told me the Arrendondos threw him out because of her, too. Seems like they had a rough time all around."

166

"True. Very true. Very hard for them, and for me. Who knows what I might be today instead of a poor *cantinero?* Except I would not want to be in my red cousins' skins now. Their time is past, *patrón.*" He sighed. "Such a brave people."

While he was still considering this newly discovered branch of the family, Jake unfolded the wanted poster on Frank Becker and showed it to him.

"Have you seen him in the last few days? He's got a long scar, here; dressed in Mexican clothes."

Sánchez shook his head.

"Are you sure? Think back about three days. The night you put the tent up."

"No, *patrón.* I have never seen this one. Faces of men stick in my eyes, always. I never forget them. But I have not seen this one."

For a time that afternoon Jake occupied himself with a casual-seeming search of the rubble for the missing carpet-bag, turning over boxes, looking into barrels; finding nothing.

He was going to have to rely on Mrs. Cuddeback's regular trips into town to bring Urraca back to find the bag for him. If she had any treasures hidden in it, or any game left unfinished to play with it, she'd make a beeline for its hiding place, and he'd just have to wait. Magpie that she was, she might enjoy a new treasure to hide away with the old.

The idea seemed like a good one, so he went down to French's before they closed to see what he could find for her.

He bought a jackknife for Paco so his offering wouldn't be lopsided, but finding something for a small girl was more difficult than he had supposed. French's didn't keep a stock of toys. There was no market for them. Another jackknife didn't seem suitable, and food would just go directly into her mouth.

He fingered buttons, thimbles, sewing boxes, and put them aside. He examined sunbonnets, net purses, and a heap of

Spanish shawls, embroidered and fringed. One of them, less garish than the rest, was of a cream-colored silk with fringe of the same hue, and pale pink flowers scattered on the field. He touched it a second time, then lifted it to see how the fringe swung almost like a woman's hair.

He had been giving tentative thought to how he could appease Delia, even before Clement Hand's revelations the night before. The shawl seemed a bit tame for Delia's taste.

He was on the point of giving up when he noticed a pile of oddly shaped lumps, like pillows, in a box on the floor. They were made of bright calico and they were hard as bales of hay, but there was an aroma about them that was familiar and pleasant. He picked one up and saw that it was meant to represent a cat. The face was embroidered on, with a button for a nose and two tiny peaks for ears.

"What are these?" he asked Ezra French.

"Cedar cats. The ladies like them, to put in their trunks or closets to keep out the moths. Emmy makes them in her spare time. Smell good, don't they?"

Jake bought a blue one for Urraca. Some obscure impulse made him buy the cream silk shawl, too, although when he got it back to the jail he wondered why he'd wasted the money. To interest Delia it needed to have a red-and-green dragon on it spouting money from its mouth. And nobody at the cantina would need bribing, provided he should sink to such desperation.

He rolled it back up in the newspaper and threw it under his bed.

Neither Clem nor Carrie came near him all day. He occupied his evening with a card game.

When he left the game to take his patrol, the cousin of Sánchez who kept the livery stable was making lonely music for himself on a homemade pipe. Jake started to pass him with no more than the usual upheld hand for a greeting, but turned back on second thought and sat down on a bench near

168

the tall, open doors of the stable to hear the rest of the song and inhale the not unpleasant smell of hay, mash, and horse manure that wafted out of the stalls.

When the music was finished they exchanged grave greetings and opinions about the weather, which never changed, and the new strike, which might change everything.

Ramón inquired about the children and was glad to hear they were well taken care of. He had a trio of jet-eyed sons himself, old enough to drive Sánchez's supply wagons over the border and back every week.

He accepted a cigar from Jake with much pleasure and paid for it with a measure of pulque that set Jake's hairline a half inch farther back on his head. When the formalities had been observed, Jake took the poster out of his vest and unfolded it on his knee. Ramón looked at it by the light of a match and nodded.

"*Sí, jefe*. This one was here for a time, but only to feed and rest his animal. He would not go to the cantina for himself. He ate food with me that María brought to us and paid me well for it, very well. I said nothing to my cousin about it because, you know, he thinks he is like the church here. Everything a man makes, he wants a part of it. Why is that? If God made the gold and silver, as He made everything else, surely He can have all of it He needs without the priests squeezing little coins through the fingers of the poor like soft mud? My cousin is the same way, the *chinche!* He swallows money, but he only shits out centavos!" He wheezed a rusty laugh and took another swallow of the pulque.

"Did this man spend the night with you?"

"No. He was only waiting to see a friend, the man called Ramey. He said they were treasure hunters, but they did not look like *mineros*. They had no tools, no pack animal. Yet every man thinks he is a *minero* today."

"Ramey came over here to meet him, then?"

"*Sí*. He was very much surprised. He did not expect his

169

friend to be here so soon, I think. But they took their animals and rode away together laughing."

"Laughing?"

"*Sí*. First, very much surprise, then a little smile, then the laughing. It made me think of how those paid *bandidos*, the *rurales*, laugh while they are making up their minds whether to take your bribe, or just shoot you in the back and take all you have."

"Which way did they ride?"

"South, away from the other mines. Maybe they heard of the new silver, too. If so they won't get much, I think. All that country is full of holes already. They say the *gachupines*, the Spaniards, made the poor Indians dig it all up hundreds of years ago."

Jake thanked him for the pulque and finished his patrol. The lights went out one by one along the street as the hard-laboring Anglos turned to their beds. He sat in his office, toying absently with the cedar cat. A light tap at the door brought him out of a bleak concentration on nothing. Carrie opened the door.

"I brought you a bucket of water for the morning."

"Thanks."

She put it down beside the bench. "What's that?" she asked, looking at the thing in his hands.

"A cat for Urraca. She likes cats." He held it up, then handed it over to her. She looked at him in sober wonder.

"They didn't have anything else for a girl kid. I got Paco a knife to whittle with."

"Why, that's very nice of you, Jacob, although I'm not sure Paco's old enough for a knife. Still, I know he'll be thrilled to have it. Especially since it comes from you. You do miss them a little, don't you?"

Jake shifted in his chair. "I miss them. About like I'd miss being in the army. I don't know why you're looking at me like that. The stuff didn't cost anything, and it doesn't mean anything. I won't be around much longer, and I thought I'd

170

buy them some kind of thing before I left. Call it a farewell present."

"I see." She put the cat to her face and inhaled. "I used to have one of these. The fragrance lasts for years." She put it down again; still lingered. Jake was growing tense without knowing why. He thought it was the longest time she'd ever been in his company without taking into him for something.

"Jacob," she said at last, "have you seen Clem this evening?"

"Now and then. Why?"

"He's been so strange all day. He's hardly spoken a word to me. He was out all evening at the cantina, I think. Now I don't know whether he's in his room or not. He doesn't answer. But then, sometimes he won't if he's in one of his moods, or if he's been drinking."

"Didn't you open the door and look in?"

"Oh, I couldn't do that! Besides"—she looked at the cat again—"he has a lock on the door. I'm worried about him."

"Let him alone."

"But he might be sick, or worse!"

"If he's sick from drinking whiskey, he's old enough to know the cure. Let him be, Carrie. He's a middle-aged man, not a boy. I saw him this evening, and he looked all right to me." That wasn't entirely true. Clem had spent the evening sitting in the cantina alone, looking like Saul after his chat with the witch of Endor.

"He's probably just worrying again about his shipment of petticoats." She nodded, but she wasn't convinced. "The trouble with you is that you miss the brats yourself. While they were around you didn't have time to wipe your brother's chin and tuck in his shirt, and now you want to make up for it." He thought that would spark her to action, but it only brought a smile.

"That's what Clem says, in a more delicate way."

"Well, then, you see? If he says so, I must be right. But, if you like, I'll brace him the first thing tomorrow and see what the trouble is. Maybe he's been trying to think what

171

kind of prizes to give away at the shooting match on Sunday."

Her tight little smile routed a dimple from hiding before it faded. "Yes, I'd forgotten about that. I suppose that must be your farewell gift to us. Well, thank you, anyway. I'll be grateful if you will talk to him tomorrow. Good night, Jacob."

"Wait a minute." He took his feet off the table and went into his room to feel for the paper bundle under the cot. "Here," he said when he returned. "This is for you. For taking care of the kids, and for putting up with me."

She let the paper drop and stood holding the heavy silk in her hands, shaking her head as if she'd been given a puzzle that wouldn't work out.

"Oh, Jake. It's very—beautiful. And very nice of you. But I can't take it."

"Why not?"

"Well, I can't. You shouldn't give me presents. I mean, you don't have to give me—a gift for anything. I—no, I mustn't take it, but thank you, thank you very much for the thought." She tried to put it back in his hands. He saw with surprise that she was confused and upset by the thing. She didn't look at him, but there seemed to be tears in her eyes.

He didn't take the shawl, but instead took a side step and put his hand on the door under the guise of resting against it.

"Now, what's wrong with me giving you a present, or you accepting it? And what in the hell am I supposed to do with it if you don't take it? You think French is going to give me my money back? If for no other reason, you ought to take it to keep me from looking like the kind of cheapskate you say I already am! Unless you think it's too gaudy to wear?"

She was flustered and genuinely contrite.

"Oh, no, it's beautiful. It really is. I didn't mean to sound like that."

"Then take it." She did, holding it close to her in an awkward bundle. "You sure make a fuss out of every little thing.

172

You know, when you get a present you're just supposed to make a curtsy, or something, and say thank you. Not take off in a circle like a bee stung you."

She was red with chagrin, but she laughed. "I suppose you're right. My manners weren't very good, were they? I don't often—get presents. I guess that's why. And then, I was thinking of what people might think."

"What people? What should they think?"

"Nothing. I'm sorry if I was rude to you."

"Apology accepted. Put it on."

"What?"

"Put it on." She unfolded the shawl and put it around her shoulders. The color of it was paler than her hair. It gave her an ivory look. He saw that it would never have suited Delia as it did her. She waited, still flushed, for his comment.

"You look good."

"Thank you, Jacob."

"You called me Jake a minute ago. I like that better. Jacob sounds like somebody with a wool tent and a string of camels. You look pretty." He touched the fringe. "The Mexican women wear theirs up over their heads, with a comb to hold it up in the back. Like this."

He took the material off her shoulders and put it over her hair, carefully. Then, without thinking what he was going to do until that moment, he kept her head in both hands and kissed her on the mouth.

The sudden realization of what he felt and what he wanted hit him like an electric shock. In an elastic second he seemed to see a dozen details: her dark-fringed eyes opening slowly, her soft mouth, her surprised face, the shawl slipping back from her hair with a whisper as his hands left it to take her shoulders and pull her to him.

17

For a moment she was like a warm honeycomb: sweet, compliant, open; like the lost imagined women of his distant adolescent daydreams; and he held her and kissed her with the same half-forgotten hunger.

Then she began to struggle like a trapped catamount, with sharp-nailed fingers and with knees and feet.

"Carrie . . . Carrie . . ."

"No! No, that isn't going to happen! You—"

"Carrie!" He might be mistaken about feminine ardor, but he knew panic when he saw it. He let her go, but as he did she caught him a lucky blow of the knee that sent him to the floor doubled over.

"I should have known—that was all you were up to! I won't have that happen—I won't let that happen again, do you hear? Let me out!"

He was slumped against the door. "Gladly, damn it! Just as soon as I can move."

She was trying to recover herself, but still backed away from him, fists clenched.

"What's the matter with you?" she demanded. "I didn't hurt you! You're just pretending I did, to keep me here."

"Oh, lady!" he groaned, and sat down on the floor trying to learn how to breathe again and diversify the pain.

174

"You're just sitting against the door so I can't get out," she said in a more uncertain voice. "If I hurt you I'm sorry, but I don't see what I could have done." Her chin began to quiver.

"Well, never mind! Just give me another minute. I can assure you, you'd be perfectly safe here now if you were Lola Montez!"

She turned a deep red and sat down on the bench to burst into tears. He looked at her in exasperation.

"My God, do you really believe I was planning to seduce you with a cheap Spanish shawl? Did you think I was just sitting over here with it, waiting for a chance to attack you? To whip it over your head and drag you into a jail cell?"

"No—yes! I don't know," she sobbed. "But I know you never had a disinterested thought in your whole life, and you don't have any respect for decent women or decent behavior."

"Oh, you know all that, do you? Where in the hell do you get all your information?"

"The way you talk to me, for one thing. Your language is straight out of the gutter! Nobody speaks to a woman that way if he respects her. And you make fun of Mrs. Cuddeback and anybody who's trying to do anything worth while here, and—and if you had any manners you'd know it isn't proper for a man to give presents to a woman unless she's a relative, or his—a—oh!"

"Are you looking for the word 'betrothed'?" asked Jake. She snatched a little handkerchief out of her cuff and put it to her mouth with a sob. "Well, why did you take it, then? And why, now that we come to it, do you come over here alone all the time if you're so damned proper and I'm so dangerous?"

"Are you accusing me of coming in here just to—"

"Oh, hell, Carrie!" he shouted, and she subsided into fresh tears.

He had begun to feel he might be able to get up, but he stayed where he was, watching her. He felt certain her panic had nothing to do with fear of assault. He was almost as certain that she was beginning to realize it, too. Her tears had taken on a different tone; less defensive, quieter. She was ashamed of herself, and it wasn't because she had broken the rules of deportment, or kneed him like a swamp fighter, or made a scene.

"I'm sorry if I upset you," he said. "I didn't have any base motives at the moment. If it doesn't make things worse to say so, I was a little surprised myself. I just saw a pretty face and kissed it, that's all."

"I'm not pretty," she mourned, mopping her eyes.

"You were a minute ago."

She shuddered a last sob and sighed. They sat looking at each other from opposite sides of the narrow room. Then she turned pink again.

"I—said something a moment ago, when I was upset, that I didn't mean to say. I hope you'll forget it."

He was puzzled, then remembered. He looked at her levelly.

"I guess I was too busy trying to defend myself. I didn't hear what you said."

She looked at him over her fingertips as she finished mopping her nose, then let her hands fall into her lap. "Thank you. May I go now?"

He got up, rescuing the shawl from the floor, and held it out to her again. After a slight hesitation, she stood and took it, folding it over her arm.

"Well," she whispered in a shaken voice that tried to make itself sound amused. "We both seem to have misunderstood each other pretty thoroughly, don't we? If the children were still here none of this would have happened." Her head drooped over the bundled shawl. "Then I wouldn't be feeling like such a stupid, foolish old maid." There was a loose strand of hair by her cheek that had escaped the rest in the struggle. For a brief second he felt all the sensations of touching her again to brush that pale straggler back into the fold, but he didn't move.

"You ought to get out of here," he said suddenly. "I don't mean the jail; I mean the town. There isn't anything for you here, and there never will be."

She sighed, fingering the shawl. "Thank you for your concern, but we've already been to so many other places. None of them were much different."

"I'm not talking about your brother, just you. Let him stay here and run his own life. He can do it. You get out and live yours."

She looked at him slowly. "Without Clem? Where would I go, what would I do, without him?"

"You've got brains and spirit. Teach school, keep books, run somebody else's paper. Make hats. Get married. Have kids. Live your own life before it's too late."

Her eyes clouded. "You said something like that once before. Did Clem ask you to make the suggestion?"

"Oh, my God, no. It just seems like the only sensible thing, for a woman like you."

"A woman like me." She smiled faintly. "I see. And where should I go to do all these wonderful things?"

"Anyplace you like. St. Louis, New Orleans, Denver, San Antonio—El Paso."

She studied him gravely now. "Have you been to all those places since you left Willow Bend, Jacob?"

"Most of them."

"But they weren't good enough to keep you."

"They were for a while. The thing is, you're free to do things there that you can't do here. And you're free to go if you don't want to stay any more. Nobody's hurt."

She nodded. "Freedom must be a fine thing for a man. For a woman it's different. I'm afraid I'd only be thinking about how lonely I'd be there, not how free. Or is it enough just to be there, even if you have no friends or family?" He was silent.

177

Her eyes held him. "Say it, Jake, why don't you? It's the only point this conversation has, isn't it?"

"If you went to El Paso, you'd know me."

"You do have truly generous instincts sometimes, don't you?" she said quietly. "I'm not being sarcastic. You've just been good enough to offer me the sort of gallant proposition you think every hopeless spinster needs to press to her heart, so she can say in after years, 'I was asked, though of course I couldn't accept.' Thank you for the shawl, Jacob." She slipped past him and out the door.

He let the latch fall and hit the closed door with his fist, doubling over clutching his bruised knuckles in the other hand a second later. "Oh, sweet Jesus!"

He felt as if he had been squeezed dry and sucked out hollow like one of Delia's breakfast oranges, and the only thing that rushed in to fill the void was contempt for himself for not seeing what had been so plain. He'd been conning himself all afternoon. He'd bought that damned shawl for her in the first place!

He paced the jail nursing his injured hand, then went out to walk the streets, trying to turn his anger with himself to some account. He needed a drink, but didn't buy one. The town was still awake and lively, but he was as blind to the activity as if he had been alone in Arredondo. Friendly greetings went unheard, and the look on his face was enough to quell any further approaches.

He returned to the jail determined to dismiss the whole memory of his self-betrayal and get some sleep. But he wasn't able to con himself into that. Sleep stayed at a safe distance while he lacerated his imagination with all the things he should have said or done in the last two or three days.

He should have told her about her sniveling, cheating brother, who had let her waste herself mothering and pitying him; who was out using what he wasn't supposed to have on Delia Moon while Carrie sat home lighting candles for the dear departed.

He should have balled Delia himself, first thing this morning. That was all that was wrong with him. All he would have needed for her forgiveness was a little money to dangle under her nose. She's been giving it away free to that smug little bastard, from the way it sounded. It would have been a useful education to Clem to see how forgiving money could make a damned woman feel.

But Delia wasn't the core of his rage with himself. It was that charade with Carrie. He should have put a stop to that before it got started. It was bad enough that he'd gulled himself, but he'd let her do it, too. Who the hell did she think she was? She had more brass than a Spanish cannon, trying to act shocked and insulted just because he'd kissed her. Since the moment he had touched her, Willow Bend was as clear in his mind as yesterday, and she hadn't forgotten it, either. If he'd listened to what her mouth and body were telling him, instead of her conventional little conscience, he'd have settled the matter in a way that would have done them both good.

It wouldn't have been the first time. He was supposed to forget about that. That was her big secret. That was why she'd been afraid to accuse the men who'd trapped her in McNaughton's barn. They'd have said the same thing, and her cowardly little mind would have turned against her and confessed. Now she had the gall to act like the grand duchess of all the virgins with him!

But castigating her didn't make him easier. He began to suspect that even his anger was only another self-deceit. His churned and muddled mind, half asleep, wouldn't focus on that matter. Instead, he plowed up ancient fields of trouble in Willow Bend and elsewhere, putting Carrie in the place of other women he had known; finding her at fault each time and leaving her for it, again and again.

He fell asleep at last with a score of uncommitted sins fresh on his head, a prey to anxious dreams until dawn; then he lay in oblivion until late in the morning.

He woke because of some noise he couldn't identify at once and sat on the edge of the bed feeling sour, tired, and old. There was another feeling, nastier than the rest. He mistook it for stale disgust and dismissed it as he started to shave.

He noticed the outside noise again and knew it now for the creaking of heavy wagons in the street. There was a clatter of horses and men's voices raised in excitement. He put down the razor and went to the door to look out.

He could not have been in worse condition to face the coming of the mail-order brides to Arredondo.

He came out of the jail, still unshaven, tucking his shirt into his pants. Two wagons had stopped in front of the cantina, and the women were getting out. The street was filling up with people coming to greet them. Clement Hand was already there, handing them out of the wagons and trying to look happy. He didn't have much cause for rejoicing. It was plain at first sight that there was going to be trouble over them.

They were pitifully few to begin with, compared with what had been expected. They had come in with a military escort of twelve dust-caked, thirsty troopers from Fort Cummings.

"Where are the rest of the ladies?" Clem asked the corporal in charge of the expedition.

"That's the whole shipment, as far as I know," the young man said, slapping the dirt off his coat. "Twelve of them. What'd you expect?"

"Fifty. What happened? Are the rest of them sick?"

"You'll have to ask her—the *señora* there. She's in charge." The corporal was eager to follow his men into the cantina.

A stern-looking young woman with two gun belts strapped around her black bombazine hips climbed out of the first wagon and went straight into Hernando Sánchez's waiting arms. They embraced and kissed as if the street were deserted. Clem waited until they drew back to examine each other with

180

the expressionless passion of matadors before he asked, "Señora Sánchez, where are the rest of the ladies?"

"Flew d' coop," she said briskly. Then, at Clem's blank look, she reported the rest of the tale to Sánchez in rapid Spanish, and let him translate.

"Soledad says when she met the women in Santa Fe there were sixteen of them in the charge of the red-haired one there. Four ladies went for walks from the hotel and did not return. The rest she escorted to Fort Cummings, where they must wait for two weeks to find someone who will bring them here. The soldiers finally do it because the ladies cause so much trouble there the *comandante* put them in the wagons himself." He looked at his wife to see if she had more to tell. She shrugged, and they fell into each other's arms again.

Clem turned to look at the women in despair. Some of them were sniveling with relief or disappointment to have reached their destination.

"Is this it? I mean, is this really it?" one asked.

"Oh, God, don't say it that way! I thought we'd never get here."

"But is this really the place? I thought it was supposed to be a rich town like Denver!"

Clem pushed through the throng, with apologies, to a sturdy-looking redhead who was surveying the street with her hands on her hips.

"Miss—ah, Miss—"

"O'Neal. Mary O'Neal. And who might you be?"

"Clement Hand. Pleased to—ah, are you the lady who was in charge of the rest of the ladies into Santa Fe?"

"That I was, and not by any choice of mine, mister. That man the agency sent with us dropped off the train in Cincinnati, and nobody ever got a glimpse of the creature again!"

"What happened to the rest of the ladies? I understood there were to be fifty of them. We paid—ah, fifty were expected."

"Fifty started out, too. But they started leavin' as soon as they saw nothin' would happen if they did. After Cincinnati, we lost some at every stop. Them as could sew or wash or keep house took a fancy to different towns. There was nothin' I could do about it." She looked at the remainder. "Sweet lot of beggar maids, aren't they? A credit to the female race. But they came. You have to give them that."

"Ah—yes. Well, won't you come in out of the sun and take some refreshment? My sister is supposed to be here to help you get settled." He glanced at a flaxen-haired farm girl who was examining him. "You, too, miss."

She smiled and took his arm. "Süre." They went into the cantina.

Sánchez saw Jake standing on the corner. *"Patrón!* Come over! You must meet my Soledad, the dove of my heart." He took her hand and offered it to Jake. "Is she not beautiful? And so brave! She was a Juarista, this one. She fought the Porfiristas in the mountains for four years, until the bad ones spoiled the revolution. Then she came here, and I caught her in my arms." He explained Jake to Soledad, who looked at him with unblinking jet eyes, and they went into the cantina.

The place was crowded. Prudencia was at the bar pulling draughts of beer for the soldiers. Her face fell at the sight of the well-girded Señora Sánchez.

Two of the subtribe of *lavandería* children burst into the barroom and flung themselves on Soledad. She hugged and kissed them, ruffling their tangled hair fondly. For the first time since her arrival her face relaxed into a warm smile. Then she took off her gun belts, put on an apron, and went to work behind the bar, ignoring Prudencia.

The brides weren't going to be so easily settled. They were already complaining to whoever would listen: about the trip, the heat, the food, and the disappointing size of Arredondo. They had just discovered there was no hotel to stay in. Clement Hand was in the midst of them, listening, nodding, trying to soothe and reassure. He looked as gray faced and nervous as Jake could ever have hoped, if he had cared anything about

182

the matter that morning. Clem saw him at the bar and hurried over.

"Dutch, would you come and say something to these women to convince them they're going to be perfectly all right here when the soldiers leave?"

"Which way are the troopers headed? Back the way they came?"

"No, they're riding on to Fort Bowie on some business of their own. I tried to get them to stay over until tomorrow, but they say they can't do that."

"They're pulling out again today?"

"In an hour or so, yes. When they've eaten and fed the horses. But about the ladies—"

"I guess that gives me enough time."

"Time? Time for what?"

"To pack up and go with them."

"What? My God, you can't do that just when we need you the most! You can reason with the boys here, the way you did the other night. Explain what happened and make them see they're just going to have to be patient until we can decide how to do this thing."

"And how's that going to be?"

"I don't know yet. We'll have to have a meeting in a few minutes and discuss it."

Jake looked at him with disgust. "You'll have another meeting. That's fine! You had months to get ready for this. Why didn't you have your damned meeting before now and make some plans? Why didn't you get some of your people to throw up a barracks to put them in? What did you think they were all going to do, even if they did come? Pair up with a mucker as soon as they got off the wagon, like a reverse Noah's ark?" He drank the rest of his breakfast and put a dime on the bar beside the wet glass.

"You cooked this mess up, Hand. You can serve it out. I wish you luck. My advice is to give each one of the 'ladies' a broken bottle or an ax handle for a wedding present and let natural selection take care of the rest. Delia's girls will take care of the leftovers."

Clem's mouth tightened. "Listen, Jake, you took this job for a month. You promised you'd stay that long. You've been well paid for half that time, and you've had the fines, but you haven't done much to earn the money. If your word means anything to you any more, you won't run out on a job before it's finished. Not if you're the Jake Hollander I used to know."

Jake produced a tight roll of bills from his vest pocket and peeled off five of them.

"What's that for?"

"That's the two weeks' pay you were talking about. I've been here close to three, but I'm willing to chalk the whole thing up to experience. Now, get out of my way. I've got to see the corporal about a ride back to civilization."

But the corporal was unexpectedly difficult. When Jake approached him he was carefully wiping his badly sun-burned young neck with a handkerchief dampened with some of his own beer. He heard Jake out respectfully, then sighed.

"Sorry, mister. We're behind two days already because of the women and all. We'll be traveling light, and we'll need every bit of food and all the remounts we've got for ourselves."

"I'll buy my own horse and bring my own food."

The corporal shook his head. "Sir, if you want to straddle a horse and follow us to Fort Bowie I can't stop you. But unless you have a remount and unless you're used to riding all day, army style—walk, trot, walk—you're going to fall behind, and I'm not going to wait for you. We tried to put up a good show for the ladies, but the fact is, all the stories they heard in Santa Fe were true, and there may be worse they didn't hear.

"There's been three supply trains raided and two ranches burned out this month between Lordsburg and the southern border. That's why they put us back at Cummings. Every kind of Apache you can name has put his paint on. I've got

184

fifty miles of country to cover before I can call my hair my own, and all I want to do, sir, is get the hell through it as fast as I can."

He grinned a little at his own vehemence. "Now, if you had a Gatling gun instead of that old Bill Hickok there I'd make you welcome. As it is, it looks like there's going to be a real down-home shivaree here tonight. If I was you I'd stick around and enjoy it."

Nor would Sánchez sell him a horse, pretending he had none to spare. Jake was seething, but when he remembered the quality of horseflesh he would be staking his life on he began to see he might as well have planned to walk.

He stalked out of the cantina and back toward the jail, his mind almost blank with rage at his latest defeat.

Outside the feed store a wagon was being loaded with sacks of mash and grain. Mrs. Cuddeback directed the work with a stout arm.

"Gut morning, Marshal Hollander," she called to him in her hearty guttural. "I brought you some company you like to see, *ja?*" He walked by her without hearing.

"Tío!" A blur of energy burst out of a door he was passing and flung itself on him, nearly knocking him off the walk. He caught his balance, then reached down for what seemed determined to climb him like a tree and jerked it loose.

"It's me! Paco, Chake! Look, I got a haircut—"

"Get off me, goddamn it!" Paco's rump hit the walk with a solid thud.

"Chake, ain't you glad to see me?" There was hurt and surprise in the voice, but Jake didn't hear it. He saw a woman with a pale face coming toward him. Carrie. He brushed by her and her stunned "Jacob!"

"Keep him out of my way. I've got things to do," he said in a colorless voice. He slammed the door of the jail behind him, and went straight for his valise and the few scattered belongings that were strewn around the room. The front door opened again, but he paid no attention to it.

Carrie stood in the door. "Call him back and tell him you're sorry. It won't be too late, if you hurry. Give him his present and tell him you didn't mean to hurt him."

"Give it to him yourself. And keep him out of my way."

She came into the room and closed the door. "Whatever grievance you have against us, it has nothing to do with Paco. He's just a little boy. He loves you. He's never done you any harm, and you've hurt him terribly, without reason. You frightened Urraca, too. She ran when she saw you, and I don't blame her. You should have seen your face. What's the matter with you?"

He threw his valise on the bed.

"There's nothing the matter with me. I just came into my right mind, that's all. I'm through playing nursemaid and marshal and general all-around sucker. I quit! I'm getting out, and I don't need any company meanwhile."

"You're leaving now, just when we need you? Where? How? With the soldiers?"

"No, they won't have me. And that damned money-grubbing greaser down the street is too civic minded to sell me a horse. But I'm getting out of this patch of quicksand anyway. I'll go up to the Silver Man or even down to the cantina, if he'll rent me a room. If not, I'll pitch a tent until the stage gets here. But until it does I'm going to mind my own business, and you can do the same."

"But why? What is it? You're not afraid of handling the men here, I know that. What is it you're so afraid of?"

"I'm not afraid of a goddamned thing!"

"You are! I can see it. You're sick with it."

He grabbed her away from the door and shook her as if he'd break her neck, then stopped, still gripping her arms.

"I can't remember if I ever hit a woman, but if you say that again, I will. And I don't think I'll lose any sleep over it!"

Her eyes searched his face, widening slightly with understanding. "Did you lose sleep? Did you have a bad night,

186

Jake? Is that what the trouble is? And are you mad at yourself now, or just at me?"

"Yes, you bitch, I had a bad night! Does that make you happy? Make the most of it. I expect to catch up on my sleep and maybe a couple of other things as soon as I'm out of here! How are you going to work it off?"

She blinked rapidly, like her brother, as she registered that, making him want to shake her again. "If you're breaking Paco's heart and deserting Clem because of me—if I'm to blame for your temper and nastiness—why not take it out on me instead of them?"

"Shut up, Miss Hand. I don't want to play any more games with you!"

"Poor Jake! I'm always misjudging your motives. I said you were being gallant last night when you were only being cautious. You were really showing a little weakness, weren't you? You let some old rusty scruple come between you and something you wanted, and went to bed with the colic from it. You must feel you've slipped, terribly. And you're scared. But the remedy is easy, isn't it? Just bury that little weakness in a good healthy rage, then run like you always do! Or take what you want and feel better. Isn't that so? Isn't that what you'd really like to do? Because if it is—if that's all it would take to make you a man again—it's a bargain! Here I am. Hurt me instead of Paco. Help yourself, and then help Clem."

"Lady, you've got yourself a deal!" he whispered furiously, and jerked her forward, crushing her mouth against his; wanting to hurt her enough to make her cry out and fight him. But she didn't.

He staggered, and they fell against the bed and sat down. He ran his hand over her roughly so there wouldn't be any misunderstanding about his intentions this time. She didn't pull away. Things began to go wrong from then on.

He pulled her shirtwaist out of her skirt and reached up under it, then found her fingers there right after him, opening the buttons, loosening her chemise for his invading hand.

187

The valise was in his way. They had fallen against it awkwardly so that it was up under his left arm and she was on top of it. He couldn't get off it or move it because of her weight. Her slight breast detained his other hand, too warm to leave, too tender to bruise.

She put her arms around him; stroked his head and shoulders with gentle hands. Her sharp tongue had learned a soft obedience that was addictive as some Chinese drug.

They sprawled together quietly for a time, touching each other with slow fingers, until he let her mouth go to try for her soft throat and breast. The increased strain the movement put on his supporting arm made him groan and settle for the closer juncture of her throat and ear. The handle of the valise was boring painfully into his side. "Oh, Christ," he sighed, with his mouth against her ear.

"What's wrong?" she asked in a muffled voice.

"I don't know. I've never raped anybody before. I can't seem to get the hang of it."

18

Repeated knocking on the outside door woke them some time later. "Thank God you slammed the door," Jake murmured into her hair. "I think it latched itself."

"Oh, my stars!" Carrie gasped. "We've been asleep! How long? Oh, dear Lord, we have to get up! That must have been Clem, looking for me. What will we do?"

"Go back to sleep."

She started to struggle out of his arms, then groaned and fell against him once more. They made very close company on the narrow bed. "I can't even get up," she said in a small tight voice. "I don't have anything on."

The validity of that made him open his eyes. "So I see. And very pretty that way, too. When did this first begin to bother you?"

"You're laughing at me," she accused him. He was; and stroking her smooth back, which was all he could reach at the moment. "All right. I see it sounds false when I've been so shameless. But I have to dress and I really wish you wouldn't watch me. It's different—and I'm not used to it, and besides, there's nothing very pretty about putting on drawers and stockings and pulling corset strings—oh, shut up!"

"No—no, what you say makes sense. So why don't we just

forget about the drawers and corset strings and what your brother wants with you?"

"Oh-gh!" She sat up and twisted around with her back to him and her arms crossed over her breasts. He touched her near arm lightly with one hand and she drew away from it.

"I feel terrible," she said in a shaky voice.

"You're not terrible."

"They must have already had their meeting. What kind of excuse can I give for not being there? I was supposed to make tea. I was supposed to be in charge of entertaining those women this afternoon."

"Turn your face this way a minute." She did, cautiously, frowning at him. "That's what I thought. You'd entertain them, all right, if you ran out there now."

"How? What do you mean?"

He touched her chin with a careful finger. "You got a bit scoured up by my whiskers, I'm afraid. Sorry. It isn't so bad by itself, but your bottom lip is sort of puffed up."

"Oh, no." Her hands left guard duty to test the damage. "Does it look bad?"

Jake smiled lazily. "A couple of other places, too. Bad? No, just—noticeable. You could say it was due to wind burn, I guess. Or do you fall down much? Maybe you could tell them you tripped over some of that junk out back, and fell and lay there unconscious for—oh, now, don't do that," he said to her tears. He drew her back down carefully and kissed all the afflicted places.

"I'll have to face Clem, and I can't! What's he going to think?"

"If you go tearing out the door right now, he's apt to think you've been doing just what you've been doing. He's a pretty clever man. He's even surprised me." She turned her face away, impatient with his humor, but he turned it back again and kissed her mouth very gently. He was amused, but also somewhat touched by her real distress. So many years had passed since he had dealt with a conscience-stricken woman,

190

he'd almost forgotten how tenderly one must be treated. It was delightful to practice such care with her.

He touched her lips and throat and breasts as if they were made of fine blown glass and might break under the slightest pressure until he felt her hand caress his head, then press it hesitantly down.

"Oh, Lord, how could I have been so thoughtless? What am I going to do?"

"We'll think of something."

Half an hour later, when the first miners arrived from the north with a clatter of mule shoes and whoops of joy, she was dressed and holding a compress of cold water to her mouth and chin while he searched the bed and floor for the rest of her hairpins.

"You haven't laced me tight enough," she complained through the wet cloth. "I feel as if my waistband is going to burst." There had been no second consideration of the esthetics of communal dressing. She had only sniffed when she saw he didn't need to be told how to manage the laces.

"I didn't want to break your ribs. You women are crazy to wear those things anyway. Here are your pins. Let me see your face now." He would have kissed it, but she drew back sternly. "It's just like a little rash. Go home and put some talcum powder on it, and nobody will know the difference. I'll cover for you. Though by the time we get there I imagine things will be too lively for anybody to notice you, and tomorrow chin rashes will be like an epidemic around town."

"Jake, promise me you'll find Paco first, and make it up to him. He must be miserable now, poor little boy. It makes me ashamed to know that I forgot about him, too."

"Sure. I'll give them both their presents and buy them a beer. How's that?"

"No beer! Just tell him you really didn't mean to be so rough with him. If it weren't for the need for that, I'd hope

191

he wasn't even still in town. But I'm afraid Mrs. Cuddeback will have to still be here, doing my job for me. I must go."

He looked out the door for her first; then she left, twisting her hair into a hasty knot, jabbing the pins in haphazardly.

Jake sighed. After splashing a little water on his own face and swiping at it with the damp towel, he picked up the jack-knife and the cedar cat and went out to find the kids.

The cantina was full but not riotous, yet. Nevertheless he had to sidestep a small crowd that had gathered just inside the door, surrounding the flaxen-haired girl. A young giant named Ekman was catechizing her in Swedish. He turned, grinning, as Jake brushed by him.

"Hey, marshal. I found me a perfect woman. Listen to this. Honey, say hello to the marshal."

"Süre," the girl said, beaming at Jake.

"Ain't that something? That's about the only English she knows. If we get married, I'm gonna make it the rule that we don't fight except in English. Honey, do you like me?"

"Süre," said the girl.

"That just tickles me!" Ekman groaned. "Say it again."

"Süre."

Clem was standing at the bar with Sánchez. A half-empty bottle was by his elbow and the gleam of an empire builder in his eye. There were no more than two or three men for every woman, so far. The competition was strong, but the women looked flattered and the suitors good natured and boisterous as boys at a fair. Musicians were already tuning up, and the laundry drudges had brightened and were trying to get an edge on the competition as they hustled beer to the men.

Some of the ladies of the town had prepared large quantities of tea for a reception that never took place because of Carrie's absence, and they were sipping it themselves and pressing it on the newcomers, a noticeable number of whom, however, showed an aversion to tea. Even one or two girls

192

from the Golden Moon had drifted in, attracted to the cheer. It was all very pleasant.

"You see, it's all going to work out fine," Clem said when he saw Jake. "They were just tired and hungry. They began to settle down when Sánchez offered the whole second floor here for their use until they make other arrangements." Jake looked at Sánchez, who shrugged helplessly. "Of course, they felt a bit lost when the troops rode out, but I think we can safely say the crisis is over, if there ever was one. Where have you been, Jake? I knocked at the jail and you didn't answer."

Jake didn't answer again. "Where's Paco and Urraca? Have you seen them?"

"No, are they here? Maybe they're with Carrie. I couldn't find her, either. She was supposed to be here. I can't think of anything else that would keep her away. Why don't you ask Mrs. Cuddeback? She's over there pouring tea for--my God! Well, German women! I guess she ran out of tea."

He chuckled indulgently and poured himself another drink. Jake looked at the bottle, but decided to forgo the risk of liquor on an empty stomach. He saw that Sánchez's mother was making a raid on her son's stock, unnoticed. "Very homey," he said. "When does the rest of the brotherhood arrive? Before the beer runs out, I hope. It'd be too bad if they missed out on everything, wouldn't it?"

Clem gulped his drink and choked a little on it. "Well, I don't think they'll be too rough. These weren't. There's a lot more respect for women in small towns like this than in the big cities, Jake. They get pretty bad among themselves, but you should have seen how these men looked when they first came in here and saw the ladies. It was almost as if they had stepped into a church. All the war whoops stopped at the door. When the rest come in I'll talk to them. I've got a little speech worked out in my mind to get them all in a good humor. They're sportsmen. They'll see the thing in the proper light."

"You sound a lot more certain of that than you did this morning. It must be that Irish courage you've been drinking. Better take it easy. You wouldn't want to grow fur on that silver tongue and mess up your speech." He turned to the listening *cantinero*.

"How's business, Sánchez? Good? Got plenty of everything? Beer, booze, barricades? If you run out, I guess the other saloons will be glad to send you some more. It'd be the fair thing to do, I think, seeing that you've got all the customers, and the best place in town for the celebration. Thick walls, no windows to speak of. I'm sure they'll see it in the proper light when you ask them. Say, have you got any more food? I haven't had a bite to eat all day."

Sánchez, looking suddenly thoughtful, snapped his fingers for one of the girls, but no one heeded him. He called for his wife. "Soledad!" She didn't appear, either. He went to find her, grabbing his mother by her skinny elbow on the way and dragging her with him, protesting incoherently.

Jake decided to have a drink after all. While he was pouring he said to Clem, "I don't suppose any of the women have asked you about the wedding arrangements here—a preacher and all that?"

"Oh, damn it, Jake, you're just looking for trouble so you can stand back and laugh! No, they haven't. That Sánchez woman was supposed to get a minister in Santa Fe while she was waiting for the women—if she could. But she couldn't find one who was willing to come, she said. She's so anticlerical I doubt if she even looked. But it'll work out. They can sign papers testifying to their intention to marry and file them in the county court. It's perfectly legal. People have to do it all the time out here. Then the first circuit rider who comes through, or the first damned judge up for election, can marry the whole lot of them." He looked defiantly at Jake's dry smile. "Are you going to do anything to help if there is trouble, or are you just going to let them tear up the place? I have to know, so I'll know what to do myself."

"Now you're making more sense. I can't handle all of them if they come in with guns. Nobody can. But most of the men at the Hassayampa don't wear guns. We need somebody big, who doesn't get too mad when he's pushed, for a deputy."

"There's Judd."

"He's too slow. Get that kraut Gebhardt and his brother. And Patchy Murdoch. Tell them they're temporary deputies, and you'll pay them for the work. Ten dollars apiece ought to be enough for a day or two."

"Ten dollars for a day's work! My God, the governor doesn't get that much! Where would I get the money anyway? I don't have it."

"Screw it out of Sánchez."

"Listen, Dutch, I can handle a gun and I'm not afraid to use it."

"I know, you're not afraid of anything but Carrie, but guns are for saving your life, not for calming things down. You saw what happened when you helped me make a fool of myself in front of the shooting gallery. The deputies ought to have guns, but tell them to keep them in their belts, for God's sake, and not to go waving them around when they talk. That's why I picked the two Gebhardts and Patchy. They could all stun a mule with their fists, but they've got a healthy respect for the odds."

"But if shooting starts—"

"Just a minute ago you were sure nothing was going to happen. Maybe you're right. Like you say, I come from another kind of town. Maybe I forgot about country boys, but let me tell you what I know about the rest of the race. Rape is ill mannered, but the hurt is temporary and all it breeds is babies, unless the girls have fighting families close by.

"Killing breeds more killing, and that's what you'll get here if you start sticking guns in their faces. If those muckers get the idea that you town people have taken their money and cheated them on their women, they're going to be mad as hell, and they might make it a little sore for the girls. But if they think you're also ready to shoot them down in the street when they come in to get what they paid for as much as anybody did, they're going to turn on this town, and you'll have just the situation you were worrying about when I first got here. They'll tear you apart. Every miner who is killed will have six friends ready to avenge him. The same friends who would've knocked out his teeth in a friendly brawl to see who got to be first with one of these women."

"But if we're not going to do anything what's the use of having deputies at all? If we're just going to leave the women to their mercy?"

Jake sighed. "Because you can't make bets on a hand that hasn't been dealt yet, and neither can the miners." He looked at the celebration in progress. Two of the women had tottered away from their tables and were consulting with one of the waitresses. They made a quiet exit through the doorway she pointed out. Jake's mouth twitched.

"There's your answer, I think. With all the beer and tea they're guzzling, Sánchez's privy is bound to be overworked by both sides. If you can think of some nice way to tell the women that they're welcome to use your privy, I think we could ease them out of here gradually, without making anybody too suspicious."

"But then what?"

Jake rubbed his unshaven face and grinned. "Well, when we get them across the street, we take them down to the jail instead and lock them in. Somebody will have to explain it all to them, of course, so they'll see it in the proper light. We'll put the deputies to the job of guarding the jail, let the miners have the cantina, and see what happens after that."

"But they're bound to find out and come after the women!"

"That's when you make your speech. Tell them the ladies are tired and want to rest up. Tell them they can draw straws tomorrow, or bid for them at an auction, or wrestle for them, or win them at the shooting match—any damn thing you can think up. The main thing is that the women will be out of reach, and the men will have to wait until tomorrow. Hell will pop tonight, but we can hope things will be more settled tomorrow. At least they'll have the satisfaction of all starting even, instead of half of them feeling like they've been thrown out of the game before it started."

"I don't know, Jake," Clem said doubtfully.

"That's the best I can do for you," Jake told him. "If you wanted more you should have talked those troopers into sticking around. I've got to go now. I promised Ca—I promised Paco a present." But new yells and traffic in the street heralded the second wave of men, from the little independent mines, who had been late getting the news. They came in roaring with anticipation and indignation at being the last to know.

There was no need to go looking for the Gebhardts and Patchy Murdoch; they were already there. It began to look as if the whole town were packed into the cantina. The volume of noise grew.

Clem struggled through the press to the Gebhardts and Patchy, and made his offer. They didn't turn it down, provided the salary was paid in advance. Clem looked grave and consulted Sánchez. Jake thought Sánchez looked as if he'd just heard of a death in the family, but he yielded to Clem's insistence.

Jake left them and made his way slowly from the bar to Mrs. Cuddeback, who was laughing and clapping her hands at some japery of one of the miners. Her hat was askew and her florid face made her pale eyes seem almost colorless.

"Where's Paco and Urraca?" Jake yelled when he was close enough.

"Bitte?"

"Where's Paco and Urraca?"

"Ah, they been by Miss Carrie all day."

"No, they haven't."

"Ja?"

"I said, they aren't with Carrie! Where else would they be?"

She shrugged, her eyes flickering from him to the merriment he was interrupting. "Maybe they go see dot Angelina they so crazy for! She's the cook and eferthing for that bad place down the street."

"Why the hell aren't you taking care of them?" he shouted in exasperation.

"*Ja,* I take gut care of them."

He gave up and started out the back way. When he reached the kitchen he remembered he should have told her about taking the women across the street when their bladders forced them to make a retreat. But it was hopeless in that noise. He cut around to Hassayampa again to find the children and get them off the street in case the trouble he expected came early.

Carrie was crossing the street from the *Arrow* to the cantina. He intercepted her and caught her arm.

"Don't go in there."

"But I have to. Everybody will be wondering where I've been."

"Nobody in there would miss the roof if it blew off right now," he told her. "I've got a job for you, but it's on this side of the street."

"Have you found the children?"

"No, I was just going to do that. Don't worry about them. There's a good chance they're down at the Moon with Angelina. If they are, they're safe enough right now."

He hurried her back to the *Arrow* and, after a quick look around to make sure there were no witnesses, he pulled her into the walkway between the two buildings and kissed her hungrily. She responded quickly, then just as quickly pushed him away, looking flustered.

Ordinarily he had no patience with such airs, yet it was strangely true that it was this very thing about Carrie that tempted him. That, and her surprising availability. To see her blush and blow some more, he said, "Are your corset

198

strings still too loose? We could go inside and I could fix them for you again."

"I fixed them myself, thank you. You're behaving like a satyr. And you've been drinking, too. I can smell it."

"Everybody's been drinking. And they're going to go on drinking and dancing and laughing and nuzzling the women. By sundown they're going to pull out all their gold teeth, throw them in a pot, and make themselves a golden calf. A piece of him, anyway. It's hard to watch all that and not join in."

"I'm surprised you left it, then. Are the women that pretty?"

He laughed. "The women are prettier than the miners. That's as much as anybody could give them. Don't worry about them. They'll survive, whatever happens to the rest of us. My guess is that they're all straight out of the Bowery or right off the boat. They didn't learn what they know about men from reading etiquette books. But they may need a breather in a little bit."

He told her his plan for the women and gave her the key to the jail. Looking at her, after all those beer-swilling red faces, he was struck anew by her fine bones and delicate skin. She was a rare find, who would make the rest of his stay in Arredondo a real pleasure. He only regretted that he had wasted so much time avoiding her or baiting her. He could have had her a week ago if he'd paid proper attention. Everybody had told him so, even that bitch Delia.

She was delicious to contemplate now, who a week before had seemed only a thorn in his hand. He made himself a private wager that within two days she'd be thumbing her nose at her brother and the rest of the town and coming to him openly.

He was enticed by her as he hadn't been by any other woman for years. That was the best part of the whole thing. She wasn't his usual taste. She was such a typical, scorn-provoking old maid on the surface; prickly, scruple ridden

199

—and famished for everything she'd been missing. Yet he actually liked her. He was at a loss to explain such a quirk in his feelings, but he knew he'd have to be careful how he handled her, or her conscience would sap the eagerness out of her and spoil things.

He started to touch her again, but to his consternation she looked as if she had been reading his mind. She brushed away his hand when it would have touched her breast, and gave him only her cheek to kiss when he attempted her mouth again.

"Please hurry and find the children. I don't like to think of them being either down at that place or loose on the street."

He surrendered her with a decent grace and started walking toward Delia's house.

As he passed the cantina again he heard someone bellow, "I don't give a damn who got here first. I'm out two hundred dollars, a new bedstead, and a week's digging for a shithouse if I don't get me a woman, and, by God, I aim to have one of 'em!"

He called Paco as he passed the hardware store, the Happy Apache, and the pool hall, and looked between the buildings as he walked, but he saw no one. When he reached the Moon several of the girls were standing out in front in their best bib and tucker, looking longingly down the street. He asked about the kids, but they shrugged their ignorance.

He went to the back door and knocked, and found Paco in the kitchen with Angelina. He had to enter without an invitation and stand in a sudden silence looking down at Paco's still, brown face, with the awful home-style haircut that made his ears seem to be clinging to his head with alarm at their naked exposure. For some reason he couldn't think of anything to say immediately, and the two of them didn't help. Angelina gave him a hostile look with her little obsidian eyes and turned away to her simmering pots. Paco wiped

200

his nose on his sleeve and had trouble swallowing the mouthful he was chewing.

"Hello, kid. Who gave you the haircut, the Apaches?" Jake asked with a forced grin.

Paco's gaze fell to the area of Jake's belt. "Tía Annie," he mumbled.

It wasn't going to be easy. "Annie? Is that her name? How do you like her? Is she a good cook?"

Paco shrugged. "Not as good as Tía Angelina." Angelina smirked at him.

Jake felt foolish standing in the middle of the kitchen floor. He took a seat across the table from the boy, trying to think of something to say that wasn't stupid.

"Where's Urraca?" was the best he could devise.

"She went off to find that cat she likes."

"Maybe you and I ought to go help her look for it. How about it?" Paco shook his head. His mouth was beginning to want to pucker and turn down. He kept straightening it when it did. "You mad at me, kid?" Jake asked him softly.

"Yes."

"Yeah. Well, you got a right to be. I acted like a bastard this morning." Paco nodded his affirmation of that. "I'm sorry about it, boy. The truth is, I didn't even see you, I was so lathered up about something else. It wasn't you, understand?"

"You said you didn't want me around no more." Paco's stiff lip betrayed him and began to quiver as his dammed-up tears started.

"Hey, don't run over! I guess that's what I said. I don't even remember, I was so mad. If you say it is, I guess it's so. But I didn't mean it. Why, I've been waiting for you to come in so I could give you something. Here."

He searched for the jackknife and put it on the table in front of the boy. Paco looked at it, but wouldn't pick it up.

"I've had it for a couple of days. I didn't know when you'd be back. Hell, I thought you might be running the mines by now and be too busy to come in."

"We wanted to come back the first day, but Tía Annie said you was tired of us and she was gonna keep us, unless we got too bad, and then she was gonna give us to the Injuns!"

"Why, that old battle-ax! I hope Urraca wet the bed just for that."

Paco snorted through his tears. "She did. Every night. Tía Annie beat her tail, but she just peed some more."

"Well, the hell with her. She isn't the only rag on the bush. We can do better than that. I'll talk to Carrie about it."

"Will you, Chake?"

"Sure thing. Right now, if you like. After we find Urraca."

"And you ain't really mad at me and don't like me?"

"No! I told you."

Paco slid off the chair and threw himself on Jake, burying his running nose in Jake's vest. "Then I'm not mad at you no more, either. Because I want to stay with you and not nobody else!"

Jake put his arms around the boy, at a loss for any more words. He hadn't meant his offer that way; hadn't even known he was making it. The results of his carelessness left him feeling greasily guilty of betraying both Paco and himself.

A door opened behind them, and the odor of magnolias cut through the onion-and-cumin smell of the kitchen. He got up, still holding Paco, who wrapped his legs around Jake's waist.

"What are you doing down here with that kid? Get him out of here, quick!" Delia's voice was hardly more than a whisper.

He didn't even turn around to look at her. "We were just going," he said, scooping up Paco's knife.

"Well, see that you do. And keep those kids away from here!"

Even Angelina noticed the strange quality of Delia's voice and turned to stare at her. There was a large mark on Delia's

202

cheek, already beginning to purple, that made the old woman take in her breath and start to trundle toward her.

But Jake only tucked the knife into the handiest pocket in his vest and strode to the door.

"Come on, Paco, let's go find your sister." He walked out with Paco's chin boring into his shoulder.

As they went around the side of the house Paco said, "*Tío*, there's a man looking at us out the window." But when Jake turned to see there was no one.

19

They couldn't find Urraca. Calling her was useless, of course. At last Jake took Paco to Carrie and left him, under a strict injunction to stay with her while he continued the search. He would have preferred to stay himself, but with Paco there she wouldn't permit him to so much as touch her while they stood together in the door.

"Where could she be?" she worried.

"Behind any box or barrel, or in any privy or store in town. She's playing with her trash collection or looking for her cat, and she won't know anybody's after her unless they tap her on the head or stand in her sight. Damn! There've been times when I've thought she really could hear and just pretends not to, but— Well, I'll look again, after I've checked across the street. Have you caught any women yet?"

"Only two. One of them became ill, and the other said she'd stay with her for a little while. The rest seem to be enjoying it all." She pinked up when he touched a falling strand of hair and tucked it in behind her ear. He grinned and left her.

He was just coming out of the *Arrow* when two things happened. He saw Urraca appear at the corner of the next building, wagging a cat. She stopped at the sight of him, then ducked back the way she had come. At the same time there was an eruption from the cantina across the street.

The first pairing off had just taken place, and the losers were protesting loudly while friends of the winner cheered and shoved. The young Swede, Arne Ekman, had his arm around the flaxen-haired girl. He was laughing and cursing at the same time, pushing away his rivals as soon as they grabbed at him. His bride clutched her crushed hat and shrieked with terror or delight.

They were about to be mobbed when Ekman picked her up in his arms and swung her around, using her striped cotton legs as a flail. She screamed again as somebody caught one of her plump calves, but Ekman pulled her free and put his big boot in that man's belly, sending him down with two behind him. Then he swung her up onto one of the mill wagons as the miners surged around him again.

"She picked me, now! She's mine! She don't even talk your language, you dumb mick. Get off my wagon, you muck paddler!" he yelled at one of the mill hands. Jake started to join the action, then stopped. Where were Augie and his thick-headed brother? To hell with it; let them handle it. He turned to chase down Urraca while he could.

She had gone behind the feed store. He suddenly remembered the day he'd had to pull her out from under the building. That's where she was, and that's where she'd put the carpetbag, to make a nest for that cat.

She wasn't in sight when he reached the back of the store. He dodged through the barrels, trying to remember where she had gone under before. The noise from in front of the cantina began to sound more like a fight than a contest. He hoped Ekman got away with his pick. It would mean one less damned woman to keep track of tonight. He found two openings in the building foundation, but couldn't see Urraca in either of them. He yelled for her, futilely, and tried to light up one of the holes with a match. But she could be halfway under the building, since cobwebs and bugs didn't seem to

205

bother her. He saw no telltale flash of white britches this time.

He got up, cursing because he'd got himself filthy looking for a kid with a cat. If she was hiding under the store she was perfectly safe, and there was no reason for him to lose any more time and temper looking for her. He'd bring Paco over, with instructions to sit tight and wait for her to come out, then take her to Carrie for a cleaning.

Two pistol shots from the street startled him, and a "Hyaah!" as Ekman whipped up his mules. Jake scrambled to his feet at the noise. Ahead of him, almost to the corner, Urraca suddenly popped up from nowhere. She was turned away from him, headed for the corner behind the Red Front at a trot.

"Urraca!" A white cat scampered across the stage road and she went after it. There was a clatter and rumble that shot him through with sudden fear. He began to run. Ekman's mules, ears laid back, swung the wagon around the corner on two wheels as their driver stood up in the box, yelling his triumph over the mob behind him. Jake, still running, drew his gun and fired, trying to stop the wagon by killing one of the mules, but missed.

"Urraca!"

The galloping team bore down on her as she darted out into the road at an angle from them. Arne Ekman saw her then, too late. He jerked at the reins so hard he fell down in the box, trying to swerve the driving mules. She saw the juggernaut descending on her, wavered, tried to run back, and was struck down just as Jake reached the street.

The cantina crowd came to a momentary halt, frozen with shock as he fell on his knees and hands beside her. Ekman got his team under control and brought the wagon to a stop thirty yards away. He jumped out to run back. His woman was keening thinly, her hands over her eyes. It was the only sound for a second.

Then the miners broke into a roar and surged around

Jake to mob Ekman. He went down, crushed under their fists and boots, while his woman screamed and the deputies shoved and cursed, trying to reach him. Jake heard him crying, "I didn't see her! I didn't see her!" A familiar voice was shouting, "It was an accident! An accident!" But it was drowned in howls of "Kill the bastard! Stomp him into the ground!"

"You Godforsaken animals, listen to me!" a voice above Jake yelled. He looked up from Urraca as if waking from a trance and saw Clement Hand beside him with a double-barreled shotgun. He was raising the gun to blow apart the pack that was killing the Swede, but Jake reached up and caught the barrels.

"Wait!"

Clem's eyes were running tears, and he shook with a rage close to that of the mob. "No! It's starting now, don't you see that? They'll never stop!"

"Wait a minute!" Jake drew his own gun and fired it into the air just over the heads of the crowd. It brought an instant of fear and attention. "Now," he said.

"I'll kill the next man who kicks him," Clem said in a loud, firm voice. "And if he's too far back in the crowd, I'll kill the ones in front of him first, then him. Get away from him now, all to one side, that way. Move, goddamn you!

"This little girl is still alive!"

They began to move, slowly, stumbling over Arne, staring at Urraca.

Jake stood up, his legs shaking with the effort, and beckoned to Augie Gebhardt, who came and took his gun. He saw Sánchez behind Clem with another sawed-off shotgun. No one protested. The miners stood dazed by the sudden cessation of their own fury. The woman jumped out of the wagon and ran to Ekman.

Arne lay in an almost fetal position in the thick dust of the road, his head nearly invisible under his hunched shoulders. There was blood in the dirt and on his hands. Jake couldn't tell whether he was still alive or not, nor did he much care. He stooped to pick up Urraca. As he turned away he asked Clem, "Is there anybody in this hole who's any kind of a doctor?" Clem shook his head, and Jake started away toward the jail. Behind him Clem said, "Somebody look at Ekman and see if he's still alive. Just one of you. All right. One more step out and help pick him up and bring him back to the cantina. Now, the rest of you, get your mules and clear out. These women are tired, and none of you could look very good to them right now. I'm putting them in the jail for tonight for their own protection, in case some of you aren't men enough to remember how to respect a woman. There'll be guards on the jail, in case there are such men, and God help you if you come back tonight or tomorrow carrying any kind of weapon with you. Right now I'd rather kill the whole lot of you than live until Sunday. If that poor Swede dies there could be murder charges put on all of you. Think that over before you call any more attention to yourselves. And get out of here quietly when you go, so this child can have some rest."

He lowered the shotgun while he was speaking the last words, as if there were no doubts about whether they would obey him. Sánchez did the same, and Augie, at a signal from Sánchez, put Jake's gun in his belt. Everyone stood frozen for a moment; then the crowd broke and began to move past the three men, not meekly, but frowning, murmuring, as if digesting the heart of some serious debate that affected them only at one remove. Yet they didn't look at Clem as they passed him, because the women had come out to see and hear, and they were standing in the street now, pale and joyless; alien to the holiday that had ended so suddenly.

Carrie was on the corner by the Red Front; dark eyes in a bloodless face as Jake approached with Urraca.

"Where's Paco?" he asked.

"Down at the jail with the two women. Is she—"

"Then I can't take her there. Where else?"

"My room. I'll get some water and bandages."

"She won't need them. She's dead."

Carrie put her hand over her mouth. "Oh, dear God. Oh, no, Jake. Clem said—"

"He said it to stop them."

She dropped behind him, leaning on the wall to cry soundlessly. One of the new women hurried from the street to catch up with him.

"Mister, listen. I'm not a nurse, but I've taken care of sick people lots of times. Can I do anything for the baby?" Jake stopped, looked at her. She had a plain, strong Irish face and she didn't seem to be drunk. "I know somethin' about broken bones, too. My father and my brothers worked in the mines all their lives." He nodded, blank faced, and let her follow him.

Carrie stumbled after them and opened the doors so he could lay Urraca on her bed. The Irishwoman bent over her, then looked up at him in pity.

"Oh, I'm so sorry, mister. The poor little thing—"

"I know. I didn't say it out there because I didn't want you to go back and tell the other women and start them crying in the street. Everything has stopped now. If it starts up again, it'll be worse." He glanced at Carrie, who was half lying on the bed, crying, and stroking Urraca's hair.

"What's your name?" he asked the woman.

"Mary O'Neal."

"You look like you've got some sense, Miss O'Neal. Can you take charge of the rest of the women tonight? Take them down to the jail. Carrie will show you where it is. No. I will. And we'll get all the blankets and cots we can round up for them. It'll be close quarters, but not as close as the stage was, or that wagon you came in on. When they're settled you can tell them about this, if it makes any difference to them. But make them understand they have to stay in the jail, whether they like it or not. There'll be somebody outside all night if they want anything. Can you do that?"

"I can make them hussies step without raising me eyebrows.

209

I've been like a mother to half the sorry lot of them ever since we started out, including a few that's older than me, too."

"Good girl. Carrie, give me the keys." She offered them, still crying, and he took them stonily. "Have you got any extra blankets here?" He knew she did. She got them from her chest at the foot of the bed, and more from Clem's room. She was looking at him with tearful expectation of some word from him, but he didn't even meet her eyes. He put the bedding under his arm, then took Mary O'Neal out to point the way to the jail. He left her to gather the women while he delivered the blankets.

As he reached the jail door, he remembered Paco would be in there. He could hear one of the women giggling as Paco talked animatedly. He put the blankets down on the chair outside and went to find more. He wasn't ready to face Paco.

He felt cold and queasy inside, as if he had just been kicked in the stomach, but his hands were steady. He could hear his own voice with the ear of a stranger. It gave orders, asked questions calmly. He just wasn't ready for Carrie or Paco. They wouldn't want calm control; they'd want emotion, feelings; and he was not ready yet.

Other voices and acts kept recurring to his mind, monotonously. Urraca running from him; going under the iron hoofs and the ironbound wheels. Ekman sobbing, "I didn't see her!" as the mob beat his face in. Clem, the little man with dreams of valor, with a gun in his hands and authority in his voice: his hour, at last. Carrie sobbing on the bed beside Urraca, her hand stroking the thin hair.

What he couldn't see was himself in it. He had done nothing except pick up a trampled little remnant of Urraca that was so still after that last convulsion; so suddenly changed to nothing that he had to force himself to reach out and touch her.

He kept moving steadily as he looked for his own place in things. Not that he wanted a place there. He wanted out. He got his gun back from a silent Augie Gebhardt, collected more blankets, borrowed cots from the Miners Supply. He still had to bring buckets of water to the close-penned women, look at Carrie again, speak to Clem. And sometime soon he had to tell Paco his sister was dead, then find someplace for the boy to spend the night. He was going to have to force himself to keep moving and do all those things in the same way he had made himself touch Urraca's body.

The miners hadn't gone home. The saloons were full, but the atmosphere in them was subdued. He made his first rounds, mechanically, further delaying the moment when he had to see Paco. In every place he entered he was asked about her. He told them she was in pretty bad shape, nothing more. He said the same thing each time. Their genuine concern seemed to mock his cold control.

Yet they weren't mocking him. He was appalled to see tears in some of their eyes, and retreated from the sight as quickly as he could, before they roused some feeling in him besides distaste and bafflement.

They were the drunken carousers, the woman-hungry howlers, the mob that had mauled Ekman to a bloody crippled heap, and they cried for Urraca.

What was she to them but a homely greaser kid, a deaf-and-dumb curiosity? A little spick pepper bud whom, if she had been above the age of thirteen, not one of them would've minded cornering in some crib or alley to make a whore of and forget. And if some older Paco should object to that, they'd kick him in the ass, or rub his face in the mud, or kill him. But now they cried and patted Jake's back in sympathy because they thought she was only hurt, not dead.

He had to stop thinking like that because that was only going to goad him into some kind of blind, crazy act like grabbing one of them by the throat, and he would be better off if he just quit thinking and kept moving.

When he checked the cantina Clem was in charge, and reported that the women of the town had agreed to take in the new women wherever they could put up a cot tomorrow, and

211

see that the proprieties were observed until they had chosen their men.

"They'd have been glad to do it all along," he said. "I just didn't think so. I imagined they'd resent being asked, somehow."

Jake nodded, scarcely listening. "How's Ekman?" He didn't want to know about that, either, but he had to say something.

"Well, he's alive. His teeth are gone in front, his ribs are broken, and his hands. But he's tough as Spanish beef, so I guess if Sánchez's mother doesn't kill him with some of her concoctions he'll pull through."

"I guess his girl won't think so much of him without his teeth."

"Oh, she's upstairs with him now. She seems to think all the more of him for taking such a beating. I guess she thinks some of it was on account of her, and she's right. A couple of the other women are still here, too, and a couple slipped off with the men, so the number in the jail is reduced to seven. They'll only need two extra cots."

"All right. I'll tell Dugan."

Clem looked at him closely. "Jake, don't you want some food before you go? You look like you could use something."

Jake shook his head.

When he returned to the jail with the folding cots, Mary O'Neal was sitting on the chair outside the door, holding Paco on her lap. Jake put the cots inside first, then came back to her. She was murmuring something to the boy. Jake stood waiting for the worst moment yet. But she looked up and told him in a voice just above a whisper:

"He heard the women talking about what happened, you know. And he wanted to run off and see after her himself. I didn't know what you wanted done, but I couldn't let him go, and I couldn't let him just go on asking about her and wondering why nobody would let him see her. So I brought him out here and told him the truth of it.

"He's a fine one, a brave one, though, aren't you, my boyo?"

212

She stroked his hair as she spoke. Paco's face was hidden from Jake. "You can be proud of your boy," she said. "Oh, we cried some together, it's true. But tears from the heart never did shame to anyone, no fear. Why, even the Lord Jesus cried for his friend Lazarus, and who knew better than He did what a fine place Heaven is to go to? I think he must be asleep. No? Paco, boy, your papa's here to take you now."

Jake didn't correct her. Paco slid off her lap and Jake scooped him up. He clung like a baby opossum.

"I'm sorry we've put you out of your beds," Mary said softly.

"We've got a place, thanks." He was in such need of escape from her warm sympathy he could almost have pushed her through the jail door. But she didn't put him to any further stress. Patting Paco gently on the back, she went in and left them alone.

He'd told her they had a place to go. He didn't know where it was. He would rather have the whole town come and stomp him to a rag, like Ekman, than go back to the cantina or any other place where there were people and submit to more sympathy and talk. He needed to find a place where no one would come. But what could he do with Paco?

Carrie would take him, he knew, but he rejected the idea because, of all the people in town, he wanted least to see Carrie now and have the added burden of her grief put on him. He had never felt so close to panic. Shame for the emotion was the only thing that kept him from flight.

At last he went to the back of the jail, where Paco's box town was, and sat down on something that seemed firm enough to hold them and was backed by the adobe wall. Paco sat astraddle of him, legs hanging down on each side.

When they had been there for a few minutes, the boy sniffed and wiped his nose on his arm, then clung to Jake's shoulders again.

"You all right like this?" Jake asked him.

"Yes." They were silent. "Chake?"

213

"Yeah?"

"Does it hurt when you get dead?"

Jake took a breath. "No."

"Not even a little bit?"

"Maybe, just for a minute. But not after."

"Did she cry?"

"No." He wished Paco were as incapable of speech as she had been. But the questions came, and he answered.

"Mary said you can get dead so quick you don't even know it."

"That's right."

"Did Urraca do that?"

"Yes." He didn't know what he would do about that lie, in the face of so many witnesses, but the truth was unthinkable. There was another pause, for which he was grateful, except that it gave him time to see Urraca's final ten seconds of life again in his mind.

"Chake?"

"What?"

"Did Urraca go to Heaven right away?"

Jake closed his eyes. "I guess so. Sure. That's what they say."

"Did you see her?"

"No. You can't see that. And I can't explain it, either, so there's no use asking me."

"Did Mama go up to Heaven when she was dead?"

"You'll have to ask Carrie about all that, kid. I'm not much of an expert on Heaven." He stirred uncomfortably.

"Me neither." Another pause. "I hope she didn't."

"What?"

"I hope Mama didn't go up there. She didn't like Urraca much."

Jake sighed. "Well, it's supposed to be a big place. Maybe they won't run into each other until Urraca's big enough to take care of herself. Why don't you be quiet and go to sleep now?"

214

"Okay. You won't go away?"

"How can I go anyplace with you right here on top of me?"

"Okay then."

His tailbone began to ache, but he didn't shift his position until Paco's breathing steadied and the looseness of his arms told Jake he was finally asleep. It took a long time. He couldn't reach his cigars or get up. It was turning night cold, and his coat was inside the jail. His lack of faith in the existence of Heaven didn't keep him from feeling he had lit up a new cinder in Hell with his hypocrisy. After a while he stretched out his legs, to take some of the weight off his feet, and closed his eyes.

He didn't know he had been asleep until a touch on his arm startled him. It was Carrie, with a lamp in her hand. Paco only sighed and nuzzled closer.

"What on earth are you doing out here?" she whispered. "Clem's been looking for you. Why didn't you bring him down to me?" He stirred and muttered. "Come on, right now. You can put him in Clem's bed. It doesn't look as if he's going to use it. Come on. Don't be so pigheaded about everything."

He got up with a suppressed groan at his stiffness, and followed her. She went ahead of him and turned down Clem's bed so he could ease Paco into it. He waited a few moments to see if the boy would wake.

When they were out of the room and she had closed the door with care, she said, "Do you want some coffee? I have some hot." He nodded, moving his shoulders to work the cramp out of them.

He drank the coffee while she sat and kept him company without staring at him. He thanked the God he didn't believe in that she didn't talk to him and seemed to be in control of herself. When he was finished she said firmly, "Now, I'm going to put you to bed, too, before you collapse." She made a fleeting effort to smile. "I remember you said you didn't sleep last night, either."

"No. Let Paco have the whole bed to himself. I don't want to wake him up."

"I didn't mean to put you there. I meant my bed." She saw his look and explained quickly, "It's all right. She isn't there now. Mrs. French came down with some new clothes and—and washed and dressed her, and Mr. Farney made a coffin in almost no time. That's the way they have to do things out here, you know. Because of the heat. She'll be buried tomorrow. It's the best way. Oh, Jake." She came and put her arms around him, pressing his face into her body. "Oh, my darling, do come to bed. You look so dreadful." He got up, putting her back with an awkwardness he couldn't help.

"I'll be all right. I'm afraid I wouldn't be much good to you tonight, Carrie." The look on her face told him at once that he'd said something stupid and wrong. He expected her anger for it, but her face showed him a mixture of surprise and something nearer to pity than anger.

"Do you think that's all I could want from you, or all I might want to give you? Oh, you poor— But I can't berate you now, can I? Just take my bed. I meant to sleep with Paco anyway, in case he does wake. If he doesn't, neither of you will even know I'm here."

But shame at his clumsy error made Jake refuse again. He left her and walked the street, making a pretense at his job. The town was quiet and dark. Even the cantina lamp was burned out. Without the light of a half-moon, he would have been blind.

He passed the Happy Apache and the pool hall, and decided to walk on beyond the edge of town. He saw there was at least one light burning, after all—at the Golden Moon. It was in Delia's window, which couldn't be seen from the street until he was past the house. He looked at it without the least desire to know why she was the only one still up.

Beyond the Moon's woodshed and privy, and the chicken yard that Angelina kept, the town ran out.

He stopped and took out a cigar as he stared at the bleak

gray path that Hassayampa Street became as it pushed its way out through the desert to the mines. To consider walking out of Arredondo was unreasonable, but at the moment he could imagine himself doing that as easily as staying and enduring tomorrow. He snapped a match to life and closed his eyes against the sudden painful flare of the light. The cigar took fire, and he drew a healing lungful of smoke.

"Delia told me you was as regular as a banker's watch with your patrollin'."

Jake started and turned quickly, but he was still half blind from the match. He could see little else but a shape that rose from a clump of weeds and moved toward him.

"Keep your hands up where I can see 'em, old man. I don't want to have to kill you when I been waiting out here for so long just to make your acquaintance."

"Who are you?" Jake demanded.

The chuckle that answered him sounded genuine and pleasant.

"Now, that's bad manners, and you know it. But I don't mind. I'm the man you've been playing banker for. Does that help you?"

"Frank Becker."

"Delia said she thought you knew. Well, that's fine, because it saves us both some time. You're not going to believe it, but I'm downright pleased to meet you, and that's a fact."

20

"I think we met once before, didn't we?" Jake asked, taking the cigar out of his mouth with his left hand, leaving his right to look innocent, palm out to Becker, but dropping by slow fractions to his side. It didn't work.

"Don't do that," Becker said plaintively, and Jake froze. "That's right, we did, for a minute or two down the street. I was looking for somebody and you give me directions. You're pretty sharp. I'm glad. It means we can do our business and go our way—except I'm just not going to get comfortable till you let that iron drop off your hip to where it won't tempt you. Tell you what. You take that seegar out in your right hand, and open up your belt with your left and let her drop." Jake obeyed. "Whooee, ain't that a doozy? Kick her over this way. I like old guns."

He shucked it out of the holster and put it in his belt. "Thank you kindly. Now turn around and put your hands behind your back. Pity to waste that seegar. I'll be glad to take it for you in a minute. Just put it back in your teeth, right now."

Jake felt cold metal click around his wrists and took a last draw from the cigar before Becker reached over his shoulder and relieved him of it. "Irons come in right handy," Becker told him, "but I never thought I'd ever be putting them on somebody myself. Now we can talk easy. Just walk a little, too, if you don't mind. I got some horses down the road a piece."

They walked. "I got them irons off old George. You ever meet him?"

"Once. Where is he now? Out there with the horses?"

Becker laughed. "No. He's holed up somewheres south of here."

"He your partner?"

"Nope. Bounty hunter. Sonofabitch."

"You mean he was after you?"

"Started out that way. You're taking all this pretty calm. Delia tells me you used to be a gun, back in Kansas once. That right?"

"More or less."

"I admire a good gun handler. Myself, I'm not too good with 'em, so I always try for the easy places, you know. Hell, if I was to have to shoot you, you probably wouldn't even die for two or three days. I'm not proud of it."

"Becker, if you've got anything to say, why don't you say it now?"

"I want that money of mine that you got. You got it on you?"

"No, and I don't know where it is."

"That's what I thought you'd say. That's why I didn't ask you."

"I'm not stalling you. I don't know where it is. It's supposed to be in that carpetbag, right?"

"Right."

"Well, the bag disappeared. I've been looking for it myself for a week, and I haven't found it."

"Sure thing."

"The farther we get from town, the farther we are from that money."

"But if we turned around now you'd lead me right to it, huh?"

"I told you—"

"I know what you told me. Keep walking."

Becker's animals were picketed out of sight behind a clump of some twisted desert tree a mile off the road north of Arredondo. By the time they reached them, Jake's feet were beginning to feel heavy. Two nights of lost sleep and the emotional strain of the day were taking their toll. Becker swung into the saddle easily and took the reins of the second animal.

"Come up here and put your foot in the stirrup and I'll grab your arm. You got long enough legs, I think you'll make it if you give yourself a good push. Just remember, if you try anything you're going to have to depend on luck more'n you ever did in your life. You believe in luck, Jake?"

Jake didn't. He made it into the saddle with Becker's help, at the expense of a bruised breastbone scraped against the horn. Becker led them away in a wide swing around the western edge of Arredondo until they crossed the stage road again and headed south.

They ran into what must have been Hassayampa Street where it became a wagon-rut trail again, leading to the southern extremities of the Hassayampa Mountains. Becker was cheerful. He whistled the tune to "The Bullwhacker," occasionally breaking into song on the refrain, "Root hog, or die." It seemed to be the only line he was sure of. Jake rode in silence, partly from fatigue, partly because he felt Becker was playing with him, expecting him to talk; bargain for his life; try reason or lies. There was something Becker wanted as much as he wanted his money; maybe the pleasure of evening up his score against the world by making somebody sweat. Jake wished he knew something more about the man, something to gauge him by. He still hadn't even had a good look at him.

When they had ridden for what seemed like an eternity but was really no more than two hours at a walk, holding on to his silence became an almost unbearable strain. If the bastard was going to kill him he'd had plenty of time and room to do it in for the last hour and a half. Even closer to Arredondo, anyone hearing a shot at this time of night would think it was only a miner disputing with a coyote. Either Becker really believed Jake had the money or knew where it was, or he didn't. If he did, why hadn't he searched him for it at once? As he asked himself that, he realized that if he was searched Becker would find his own money in his belt. He hadn't given it a thought until then because the belt was as much a part of him as his arms and legs, which he also didn't think about as long as they worked properly.

He began to worry in earnest, and while he did he made a quick mental inventory of what else he might have on him that could be useful.

Nothing. The .36 was back in his valise in the jail. Not that it would do him any good with his hands manacled, even if it wasn't picked off him the second Becker got him in a good light.

What else? His inside vest pocket held two more cigars and a partial block of matches. His right outside pocket held his watch; the left pocket, his spending money, or what was left of it after he had given Clem back his salary. It couldn't be much. Then why was it so full? He could feel the bulge, now that he was concentrating on that area.

Paco's pocketknife. He remembered picking it up from the table at Delia's and putting it back in his pocket. He'd forgotten to give it to the kid again.

Well, that would be gone as soon as he was searched. He had nothing to use against Becker except his head, and that was empty of useful ideas and being slowly filled with nothing more than the need for sleep.

"You gettin' tired?" Becker asked. Jake's head came up from where it had been bowing toward his chest, but he didn't answer. Let Becker do the talking, since he was so fond of it.

"We're almost to where we're going," Becker said. "T'll help

221

you get off. Just remember what I told you about stretching your luck." Getting off was easier than getting on, except that he lost his balance at the same moment Becker let go of his arm, and staggered back against Becker's horse.

"Hup, hup, ho, there!" The horse was under control and the gun on full cock in an instant. Jake stood perfectly still. There was a little wheezing sound from Becker. Jake thought he might be laughing.

It was very dark. He thought it should be nearly dawn. He hadn't looked at his watch after Carrie woke him behind the jail or since, so he couldn't tell, except that the moon was down now but the sun wasn't up yet. There was only the faintest graying of the night in the east, if that distant, jagged paling of earth was the eastern Animas Mountains.

The ground they walked was rough, uphill, and barren of trees or bushes. Tufts of thin grass brushed their legs and whispered in the dry wind. Becker let out the animals' tethers and anchored them to the ground with a rock, which he found handily without taking his attention away from Jake.

He seemed to know where he was, anyway.

"Up the hill a little way, now." He got behind Jake and guided him with gentle prods of the gun barrel. "Slow, now. We're here." He scrabbled in the rocks to one side of Jake. There was a metallic clink, a rusty creak, and the scrape of a match. He had a hand lantern hidden there. He lifted it, and Jake saw a black hole roughly four feet square yawning at their feet. He felt himself stiffen with apprehension, but he turned his head to get a good look at Becker and asked, "Did we come all this way to see a hole in the ground? What is it, a mine?"

"Well, like my old grandpappy used to say, 'She used to was, but she ain't no more.'" He had the look of a kid who had just given someone a surprise and was waiting to see the reaction. He didn't look like much like the old poster picture. He had grown a mustache and lost the baby fat forever. There was something else wrong with him, but Jake couldn't remember what it was. Becker's face became solemn.

"Now, we got a problem. I can't let you go down by a ladder with your hands shackled, and I can't hardly let you go down with 'em loose, so there's only one thing to do." Jake waited. "You got to jump," Becker finished.

"The hell! How far?"

"Oh, maybe fifteen feet."

"I'll break my damned neck! Then what good will I do you?"

"That's why I say we got a problem."

"Why do we have to go down there anyway?"

"Because that's where George is. Now, when you jump, as soon as you feel your feet touch the ground, bend your knees and roll. Never mind which way. I ain't got time to tell you how to do it good, just how to do it."

As he spoke he gave Jake a shove that sent him into the pit. He hit the stone floor with such suddenness that he had no time to think about bending his knees and rolling. They buckled without his aid, and his left shoulder and his head hit the ground. There was a snap of bone he could hear; a white-hot flash of pain seared him from left to right and ran up his neck to join the stunning pain in his head. He thought he might have yelled.

He passed out for a few seconds or minutes, though the echoes of agony were still running riot in his skull and body. They were joined by the hollow sound of Becker's voice coming down the rock shaft from above.

"That's the way George did it. Now, myself, I've got to take a ladder."

There was silence for a while. Jake lay still, wondering whether he had broken his neck, his back, or just his arm. He couldn't move; he couldn't localize the agony. Then he realized his feet and ankles hurt as much as the rest of him. He could feel them. You weren't supposed to be able to do that if your spine was snapped. He tried to move them and

223

succeeded at last, at the expense of fresh hurt to his shoulder and chest. His arm or collarbone was broken, then. Not so bad.

Jesus, he thought. Not so bad as what? He was fifteen feet down in a hole, out in the wilderness, with a crazy man coming after him, and he couldn't use his arms.

There was a scraping noise over the top edge of the hole, followed by a heavy thump. Light appeared with Becker, coming down a long, crude wooden ladder that looked silver with age and dryness, like driftwood.

"Hurt yourself in the fall? Afraid you might, but I çouldn't see no way around it." He reached the bottom and held up the lantern. "Leg?"

"Collarbone, I think," Jake breathed. He had heard a grating sound there when he tried to roll over onto his right side.

"Well, that being the case, you might as well stay where you are for a while. Just turn your head a little bit and look over there and you can see old George again, though." Jake looked where the lamp directed. George Ramey was slumped against the wall. The old bloodstains dried on his shirt indicated he had been shot. He was unconscious. Becker walked over to him and kicked him lightly in the side. Ramey gave a sharp cry and opened his eyes weakly.

"George, I brought you some company. This here's Dutch Hollander. You heard of him? Sure you have. You two have got a lot in common. Yes, sir. You both had my girl, and you both want my money. I thought it was about time you two bastards got to know each other better."

He sat down on the upper edge of a boxlike thing that was the remains of an ore wagon and put the lantern on the floor beside him.

"Now, where's Rosie and where's my money?"

Jake frowned into the light. "Delia told you everything else. Didn't she tell you that?"

"Never mind what Delia told me! You tell me. Where is she?"

224

"She's dead. In Tucson."

Becker looked at him without expression. "You kill her?"

"No! I didn't even know her. I just happened—"

"Mister, when you've been down here as long as old George has, you might get tired of tellin' lies, if you can still talk at all, that is. Might save a lot of grief if you just quit now."

"I'm not lying to you! Ramey must know she's dead." He saw that Ramey's eyes were closed again. He also began to see that Ramey might *not* know Rosie was dead, if he had had to depend on hearing it from Delia. He still didn't know who Ramey was, or how he had been involved with the others. "You can check me on it. Ask Delia. Ask the sheriff in Tucson if the county didn't bury a woman named Robles last month and send her kids on to Arredondo with me."

"How am I going to ask a sheriff?"

"Send him a wire from the express office back in town." Becker blinked at him for a second. "All right, make Delia send the wire for you. That wouldn't make anybody suspicious. Rosie was on her way to see her." He waited for Becker's reaction. Even to him it sounded like a lame-brained suggestion. Looking at Becker, he remembered now what else it was about him that was different from the poster picture.

It was the scar. It pulled down the corner of his right eye, so that side of his face looked perpetually sad and bewildered. Looking at him was like trying to watch two different people at once.

"All right, then," Becker said quietly. "You tell me about her."

Jake told him about her, from the moment she got on the train at Yuma. He was brief, but he left out nothing of importance that he could remember, including his reluctance to be saddled with her kids, his efforts to get rid of them at Delia's, his suspicion that there must be something hidden in the carpetbag other than what appeared, and his discovery that Delia thought so, too.

Becker heard him out and asked a few questions to test

225

details of the story. After that he sat with his head bowed, thinking about it. Jake couldn't tell whether he believed any of it or not.

There was no sound in the pit but that of their own breathing. He began to feel cold and sick; as if he might pass out again. His right arm was tortured by the weight of his body on it, and he didn't dare move for fear of creating more havoc with the broken bone. His left ankle was throbbing, too, more than the other one. If he hadn't broken it, he had sprained it severely. He rested his forehead on the cold stone floor trying to stay conscious. Whatever Becker was going to do to him, he wanted to see it coming.

"George," Becker said at last, starting echoes down the tunnel behind him. "If you're such a good bloodhound, how come you didn't know about this?" George didn't answer. Becker woke him with a louder call and repeated the question.

"I didn't know nothing, Frank. I swear I didn't. I told you Rosie got away from me while I was making arrangements for you to get free. She was scared of you. I couldn't help that. And I told you, I didn't let on to Delia that I even knew Rosie. I thought she'd come in from wherever she was hidin' in a week or two, and I'd just wait for her. That goddamned Delia wouldn't hardly let me stick my head out the door while I was there. She knew there was paper on me, and she said he"—moving his eyes in Jake's direction—"might start asking a lot of questions. He was jealous of her, she said."

"Oh, hell," Jake breathed.

"But you knew what Rosie's kids looked like. You lived around 'em for months. How come you didn't say nothing to me about them bein' in town?"

"I never saw them! I heard that old woman cluck about some kids, but I never knew which ones she meant. I didn't know! I was just waiting for you or Rosie to show up and—"

"And lead you to my money. That's all you had the brains

226

to think about, wasn't it, George? You smelled out my girl and took her. You tried to root out my money. And when you got it you were going to turn me back in to the law for the reward!"

"No, I wasn't! I helped you get out, Frank. Don't forget that. I made all the plans. Rosie never thought of it. She wouldn't have done it, even if she'd had the sense to think of it. I was the one who bribed the guard, and got you set up with money and clothes when you got loose; not her! Without me, you would still be in Yuma right now, dragging leg irons and breaking your back on those rocks. And she'd be dead anyway. You owe me something for that!"

"I guess I do. My girl run off, afraid of me, because of a damn baby you give her, and died of a fever from it. My money's lost or spread out across the territory instead of sitting safe and easy the way it has been the past six years, without nobody knowin' it was even there except Delia, and she couldn't have touched it without your help. While I was laying out in the desert this past month, frying my brains out every day and spending the nights with the ague from a cold ass and an empty gut, you was snug in some hotel or whorehouse. I owe you just a hell of a lot, George, and I'm obliged to you for reminding me." He pulled Jake's gun from his belt and fired point blank at Ramey before the other man could cry out a last protest.

There was a rumbling in the tunnel beyond him as something gave in to the shock of the explosion. Ancient dust billowed out of the tunnel mouth as the rumble faded into a gravelly trickle.

Jake struggled to sit up and did so, even though the effort made the pit grow black for him for a moment. He expected he would be next. But Becker was admiring the old Colt; rubbing the warm barrel on the sleeve of his shirt to burnish it. He ignored Ramey, who didn't move again.

"Hope you didn't mind me borryin' your piece," he told Jake calmly. "It sure does the job, don't it? My pappy had one of these, or almost like it. A Confederate piece, but it was all right. Called a Griswold and Grier. Brass frame. Pretty fair copy. Them damn Yankees had all the patents, but they didn't have all the gunmakers by a long sight." He put it in his belt again with a sigh and looked down at Jake. "I don't know about you, but I'm about tuckered out. For the past week I haven't slept no more'n a she-cat in season." He saw Jake's tenseness and smiled at it. "What's the matter? Did I get you worried?"

"Well, you're kind of sudden, and I wasn't ready for this mine to come down on top of me. What are you going to do with me?"

"Nothing but straight business, if you'll have it that way. I told you that before, just like I told him I was gonna kill him. Say, are you hungry? I got some jerky and tack here."

"Have you got any water?" Jake asked, fearing that food would turn on him now, even though he had fasted since breakfast. Becker brought him a canteen and held it to his mouth. Holding his head back for a drink put a strain on his injured chest, making him wince and spill the water. Becker looked concerned.

"Say, I bet you hurt like hell. Tell you what, I'll fasten them irons in the front for you, so you can rest on your back. You'll be a sight more comfortable. I can't do anything about the collarbone, though." Surprise, and the certain knowledge that he didn't have a chance to take Becker in a struggle, kept Jake quiet as the change was made. It did make some difference.

When he was shackled again, Becker took him under the arms and helped him scoot back until his shoulders were against the wall. For a while after that he couldn't do anything but lean there and try to keep from making any sound until the pain ebbed.

When it did, he breathed a shaky sigh of relief and opened his eyes again. Becker put the canteen beside him, and brought him a filthy blanket and a piece of hardtack.

228

"You just try to gnaw on that when you can. I know how getting busted up can make you thirsty and tetchy in the gut at the same time. I've been hurt a few times myself. The jerky would make it worse, but that tack will stay down if you take it slow."

He wrapped another blanket around his own shoulders and stretched out on the floor, close to the foot of the ladder, with a small saddle pack for a pillow.

"Oh, God, I'm done in," he sighed. He looked at the pale square of sky visible through the mine shaft. "It's sunup." He yawned. "I reckon by this time all your friends are awake. They'll be missin' you sore."

His breathing quickly deepened, while Jake sat watching him with a puzzled frown. In a moment he began to snore.

21

Jake sat brooding over those words. "Your friends will be missing you sore."

He had always been proud of the fact that he never counted on friends to do anything for him, much less miss him. But now he wondered. Somebody *would* miss him, certainly. Paco, for one. He'd promised the kid he wouldn't go away while he slept; he'd be awake soon, and asking for him. So would Carrie, and Clem. Even Sánchez would expect him to come in for breakfast.

What would they think—and do—when he didn't show up? They'd have to know something was wrong when they saw he was gone, because a man didn't just run off in the middle of the night without his coat, or his valise, or even a horse to carry him away, damn it!

They'd look for him. Then what? Somebody would find his gun belt, since it had been dropped at the most traveled end of the town street; that would be a dead giveaway.

Then he remembered it would also be a time-wasting false lead, because he and Becker hadn't gone north from that point; they had swung all the way around the town and come south.

But Sánchez knew about Becker, if he gave it some thought. So did his cousin Ramón. He'd shown them both the poster. Of course, he hadn't given either of them any indication that he was more than casually interested in the man. Hell, no, he'd been too clever for that, hadn't he? So they might not think of the poster, after all.

What else?

Delia knew about Becker, and the money, and possibly even where he and Becker were tucked away right now.

Lots of luck there, he told himself bitterly. She knew because she had been the one to sic Frank Becker on him in the first place, in an effort to get a piece of what was in that carpetbag. Becker must have left her thinking she would get it, too. Or else he hadn't left her alive at all.

That possibility didn't give him any pleasure, even when he was hurting like hell in the dark. She deserved something for her greed, but he didn't bear her enough of a grudge to condone the spoiling of that cream satin throat.

He leaned his head back against the rough wall and closed his eyes. His shoulder had stopped hurting so much, but his ankle was beginning to swell inside the thin leather boot. He wished he dared to move, to remove the boot while he still could.

So nobody would know where he had gone or why, and there wasn't a decent clue left to tell them. And the people most likely to care about the matter had other things to think about this morning: settling the new women, cooling off the disappointed miners. Burying Urraca.

They'd be doing that early this morning with or without him. When he didn't show up they'd think he was holed up somewhere, drunk or sulking because the cavalry wouldn't give him an escort yesterday. Or too fainthearted for funerals. No, too guilty. Because he had as much to do with Urraca's death as Ekman did, or more.

The lantern guttered out while he was considering that, leaving him in the dark with more pain and remorse than he had been able to feel for a long time.

She had been running from him as much as she had been

chasing that cat. He'd scared her white, handling Paco the way he did. Carrie had told him that. So that later, when he was trying to get her out of harm's way, she'd— God! He must have been put in the world to kill cripples. First the Yaeger boy, now Urraca.

It wasn't a thought he could afford to dwell on, injured and in the dark. He tried to turn his mind to something less destructive.

Carrie.

Carrie loved him; she had said so yesterday. He hadn't been much interested in her finer feelings at the time, he recalled. Still, she loved him. Would she believe he would disappear in the middle of the night just to escape the unpleasant duty of burying Urraca and giving comfort to Paco?

Why not? He hadn't left her much reason to believe otherwise. Hadn't he been stopped from running out on them yesterday only by her throwing herself into his arms and his bed? And he certainly hadn't allowed her to think for a minute that that interlude meant anything more to him than simple physical relief.

No, he had made it pretty clear to her last night about what he thought she was good for, when she tried to put him to bed. He was too much of a realist to deny the thought, even now, when he could use a beneficial doubt about himself. Still, the memory of her face when he made his blunder shamed him.

When he didn't appear this morning she was just going to think he had recuperated his spirits enough to be down at the Golden Moon in bed with that conniving Delia.

He had made a fine mess of everything. Nobody would waste time looking for him, and Becker was never going to believe he didn't know where the money or that damned carpetbag was.

Becker was crazy. He'd killed Ramey like a fly on the wall. But he wasn't crazy enough to believe Jake's unlikely story, or to let him up out of this mine alive, with or without the money.

He was going to die down here with Ramey, and be picked clean by the desert ants. He had wondered a few times lately, when he couldn't sleep, where he would be and what he would be doing in ten years' time. Now he knew.

On that thought, inexplicably, he went to sleep. Dreams came to indict him that were much like his waking thoughts. Carrie told him what a poor excuse for a man he was and always had been. Urraca fled like a rabbit through endless mazes of back-yard trash while he followed her, mired in mud, held back by every obstacle that had let her pass, and the wagon wheels thundered closer with a sound like an approaching train.

He felt Paco's light body in his arms again; heard him ask, "You won't go away?" And he answered, "I won't go away," while all the time he was wondering how soon he could put the kid down and slip off, as he always had before. How many other voices had he heard asking, "You won't go away?" It had always been like the shot that started the race to freedom, because what had he ever dreaded more than he dreaded need?

A slight noise woke him with a start that sent the hot pain running again. He gasped, and heard Becker say, "Hurtin' pretty bad, ain't you?"

The man's air of friendly concern maddened him. Becker behaved as if they were old friends, and the trouble was in some way Jake responded to him. He ought to be a lot madder at Becker than he was. If he was going to die here, he ought to have the privilege of being angry with his executioner, yet he couldn't seem to make himself feel that way. Instead of the comfort of anger, he had nothing but a profitless curiosity about the whole Becker–Rosie–Delia intrigue. And if he wanted anything besides life and freedom and a stiff drink to numb his pain, he wanted to know what it was about them that was going to be the death of him in a little while.

Becker climbed up the ladder and went to take care of the horses. Although it must have been broad day above-ground, nothing but the palest twilight came down the shaft. Jake was left alone in the pit so long he began to be gnawed by a dry-mouthed certainty that Becker wasn't coming back. Panic swelled in him. He'd rather Becker came back now and shot him like he had Ramey than leave him like that.

But at the same moment he realized the ladder was still in place and he might be able to crawl up it and die in the sun instead, he heard a foot strain the top rung again. The old wood creaked threateningly as Becker descended into the mine.

"Bet you was gettin' worried about me comin' back, huh?" he asked cheerfully. "One of the horses strayed off. Both, in fact, but I caught one. I had to find him some kind of graze, too, and that ain't easy out here." He rummaged in his pack. "You hungry now? I sure am. How about a bit of jerky?"

Jake took it willingly because he was famished. When he had washed it down with some of the water from the canteen, he asked, "What are you going to do now, Becker?"

"I was hopin' you'd tell me." He shuffled around in the dark for something. "You know, I'm not much of a planner myself—let the damn lantern burn out. Never was. I find a lot of people like to plot and plan, and I let them do it if they want to. I just wait and follow along. You might think that's dumb"—he struck a match and grinned at Jake—"but you'd be surprised how good it works out most of the time."

He used the match to find Jake's last two cigars; put one of them in Jake's mouth and the last one in his own, and fired another match to light them. "Much obliged," he murmured, and settled back on his blanket.

"I'd hate to play poker with you," Jake told him.

"Would you?" He sounded pleased. "Poker was never my game, but you might be right. You ain't so easy to figure

234

yourself, you know. Does that come from playing poker all the time? Bluffin', they call it, don't they? Sit tight and say nothing. By damn, you're a real boss when it comes to that. I figured you'd start dickerin' and complainin' a little when I come back. Most people don't like the dark much. And bein' alone in it too long makes you kind of crazy. I know. They put me in solitary half a dozen times back in Yuma."

"Do you mind if I ask you a couple of questions about that?"

Becker laughed. "Why, shoot, no. You just fire away. I'll answer—if I take a notion."

"What makes you think that carpetbag still has your money in it after all this time?"

"Hasn't it?"

"I don't know. I told you that. It was heavy enough to feel funny, but what if Rosie double-crossed you and put newspaper in it instead? How do you know you could trust her to keep it?"

Becker's cigar glowed and faded. "Why would she put paper in it? Why would she still be in Yuma if she found the money? Why would old George have worked so hard to help me break out of jail if the money wasn't still missing?"

"So Rosie never knew the money was in the bag at all?"

"That's right. She was a good old girl in her own way, and I thought a lot of her. We even talked some about gettin' married. But a man can trust a woman just so much. Hell, you know that. Look at what your girl Delia did for you."

Jake spared his splintered bones the snort that deserved. "I thought she was your girl."

Becker cackled. "Oh, Lordy, I hope to tell you! She was never anybody's girl but that old rattlesnake's."

"You mean her father?"

That made Becker laugh again. "Father? You talkin' about old man Mooney, that had the Marvel Show? I seen his old tent back in town. If he was her pappy, they had a funny kind of family life. Like Mister Lot and his girls back in Bible times—if you recollect. No, sir. I thought a lot of hard things

235

about that old sonofabitch while I was shillin' for him, but I never called him her pappy. What made you think he was?"

Jake thought about it. "She called him Pop."

"Oh!" Becker laughed. "He had some kind of a old-timey name: Popul-eenus, Pop-pilly-something. Crazy. Hey, I bet she told you how I named him in on the job and he died of a busted heart right there in the jailhouse, huh?"

"Something like that."

"Yeah. Well, let me tell you, mister. He *was* in on the job. We was supposed to be fifty-fifty partners. Only he wasn't fast enough that time. I got to thinkin' about some of the little tricks he'd worked on me before, and I decided to work one on him. Instead of throwin' the bag back in his wagon and runnin' like hell till he caught up with me outside of town, I just took it over to Rosie. I stuffed all my extra clothes in it, put a few dollars on top for her to find, and told her to keep it until she heard from me again."

"Was Rosie part of Mooney's show?"

"No, she was just my girl, like I told you. Except that she'd caught the *mamacita* fever and was swelled up too big to come along with me then. She was working as a cook in a parlor house there in Yuma." He pulled on the cigar and laughed again.

"Now let me tell you about old Delia. Did you ever wonder how a girl like her could afford a big fancy house like she's got here? Well, when old man Mooney was in the jail with me she came in bellerin' like a sick cow for them to turn him loose. Then, when she saw how good they had us both tucked in, she hopped back to the wagon, packed up, and hightailed it out of town with everything the old buzzard owned. That's what killed him!" He enjoyed the memory of that for a moment, then noticed Jake's silence. "What're you so quiet about over there?"

"I was thinking about how smart we all were. Rosie, Delia, Ramey, and me. We all had a chance to open your bag, and none of us knew it at the right time because we were busy being smart. Now some cat's probably making a bed on your cash, or the town rats are chewing it up. Urraca took it off to play with, and she's where your string runs out, Becker."

"Who's Urraca?"

"Rosie's daughter. Didn't you know?"

"Oh, yeah, María something-or-other. Simple minded."

"No, deaf, thanks to Rosie."

"Well, if she really took it and you're not trying something on me, she can show me where it is."

"I told you the string runs out there. She's dead."

"Dead? Hell, since when?"

"Since yesterday. She ran out in front of a wagon she couldn't hear coming, chasing some cat; the one I figure is sleeping on your money now." He could hear Becker getting up, coming toward him. A match flared so he could study Jake's face. "Hollander, you got more bull in you than—"

"No bull. The kid's dead. Check me out if you want to."

"Check you out with who this time?"

"Delia. She'd know what happened yesterday."

"Delia can say anything she damn well pleases. That don't make it so. No, this all seems to fit too neat. Everybody who knows anything about that bag just happens to be dead, except you and Delia."

"Becker, what good is it going to do me to lie to you, in the spot I'm in? I'm not going anywhere, am I? That bag is put away in some hiding place of Urraca's, and she's dead. I'm as good as dead. If you want to drag Delia out here and kill her, too, you'll do it. But you'll be stuck."

Becker was silent for so long that Jake had trouble keeping still himself. He began to hope his snare was going to work.

"What's that other kid's name?" Becker asked then.

"Paco. But he doesn't know any more about it than I do."

"It's interesting you should put it that way. Paco," he mused. "Paco. I'll be damned. I never gave him any study before. He's my kid, ain't he? Sure he is. Why, he's even

237

named after me! Paco, why, that's like a nickname for Francisco, and that's the same thing as Francis, ain't it?"

He laughed in delight at the discovery. Jake felt like a Judas for mentioning the boy. There was no hope of keeping Becker from following through on the thought he had obviously begun. Anything he said would make things worse.

"By damn, Jake, you just did us both a big favor, bringin' him to mind. Hey now! Why wouldn't old Paco know somethin' about his sister's little hidey-holes? Don't they play together?"

"He doesn't know. Don't you think I asked him when it first disappeared? He helped to look, but we couldn't find anything. That's the truth, Becker."

"Well, maybe he'd look again for his daddy. How about that? He ought to be glad to see me, wouldn't you think? I'm the only folks he's got left now."

"He thinks you're dead."

"Does he? Then he ought to be double tickled when I show up. A boy needs a daddy to show him the way to go, ain't that right? To buy him some new boots and stick candy? That little booger—you know, I never have laid eyes on him? Does he look anything like me?"

"No. I guess he looks like his mother," Jake muttered tonelessly. Christ! Why couldn't he have kept his mouth shut? The last thing he wanted was to make Paco the goat for him, no matter what Becker did.

"Well, I guess that figures. What comes off the tarbrush don't wash away easy."

"Let the kid alone," Jake said. "He's had a bad enough time in his life without adding you to it. If he is your kid you ought to think about that. Even if you could make him find that bag, the chances are somebody else like Ramey is already looking for you. If he finds you he's apt to shoot you on the spot to make things easier for himself. Or hang you to the nearest tree and let Paco watch. That's a hell of a treat to give your own flesh and blood!"

238

"You kind of like old Paco, don't you?" Jake didn't answer. "He like you, too? I bet he does, or you wouldn't like him, right?" He seemed to wait for Jake to say something else damning.

"You know, old man, you could be right about me and that boy," he said softly. "A boy might not cotton to havin' a jailbird for a daddy. He might not want to help out kinfolks he's never seen. Little boys can be right stubborn. I was myself." He paused again. "It might be that he wouldn't do half as much for his daddy as he would for you. He was just bein' muley with you the other time; not wanting to give away the little girl's secrets. But if I was to bring him out here to see you now—and you asked him again—he'd think on it more serious. What do you think?"

"Get me out of this goddamned hole and take me back to town! I'll find that lousy bag of money for you! Make up any story you like about finding me beat up and robbed and I won't deny it. I give you my word. You can stick to me night and day until it's found, then lock me up in the jail or bring me back here when you've got it."

"That's a pretty big offer," Becker said solemnly.

"Well, what do you say?"

"I say you sure as hell must like that kid a lot better than I thought." He chuckled at Jake's silence. "Yes, sir. A kid couldn't help but want to do what he could to please a man that thinks so much of him."

22

After Becker had drawn up the ladder and left him again, Jake lost all sense of time. The pain of his ankle had grown steadily worse as it swelled in his boot, until it blotted out everything else. He broke into an icy sweat trying to pry the boot off with his other foot. It wouldn't budge, and he was on the point of nausea when he remembered the knife in his vest pocket.

He took it out gingerly, trying not to move his upper arms doing so. It was new and therefore difficult to open. Twice he fumbled and dropped it in the dark, and spent an agonizing time searching for it, to the detriment of his temper and his collarbone.

When he finally got it open, and his foot propped up on his other knee to slash at, he was shaking with exhaustion. As he sawed and jabbed at the tight boot with his manacled hands he repeatedly struck himself with the knife tip. The additional hurt scarcely impinged on the agony of his swollen, throbbing foot by then. He was half ready to amputate if he couldn't get the boot loose.

He cut it down to the top of his foot, grabbed the front of it, and ripped it toward the toe. It came away enough that he could push it the rest of the way off with his other foot.

After that he did nothing for a long time but sit with his

legs stretched out, panting and sweating. When he tried later he found he could move the foot a little, so there was a chance it wasn't broken, after all, but only badly sprained. He wondered what difference that made now.

It was like the water. There wasn't much more of it, and he was dry mouthed from the struggle. He might just as well have drained the canteen at once and had one short spell of comparative ease before the end. But he didn't. He held himself down to one mouthful and kept the little that still tinkled in the can for later.

There was a lot of later. He slept and waked, slept and waked again, without knowing how long the periods were. They could have been minutes or hours. The darkness became like a living thing that had swallowed him alive and kept him in its maw to digest at leisure.

His sense of direction grew confused and twisted. At one time, half asleep, he thought he was up high somewhere instead of in a pit, and all he had to do was crawl to the shaft hole, roll himself over the edge, and drop through it. The fall would kill him, he knew, but he would be out of the dark.

He tried to do it, wriggling along on his good side, shuddering with the effort, until he came to the place where the ladder had been; where the hole ought to be. When he rolled over on his back to rest and saw the little square of light above him instead, he could only lie there and stare at it stupidly, fighting down the feeling that he must be stuck up on the ceiling like a fly.

He slept there for a time and woke to find the quality of the light from the hole unchanged. It was still daylight, but whether of the same day he couldn't guess.

He knew he was delirious when he began to think Ramey wasn't dead. He knew it was his own breathing he heard in the dark, made a little more hollow and resonant by the empty stillness. Yet the idea persisted and grew that there was someone besides himself there, breathing at almost the same rhythm. He changed his speed and even held his breath to

241

convince himself this was nonsense, but nothing shook the illusion until he heard himself whisper, "Ramey?" with such a timid quaver that the very terror in the sound broke the idea's hold on him.

He lay laughing helplessly at his fear, and at the damned mess he had got himself into, and even at the ludicrous way he was going to die—not of drink, or a sore loser's bullet, or the ills of the aged and useless, but simply of neglect; the very thing he had courted all his life. He felt better for the laughter and went back to sleep under the unreachable but comforting escape hole.

He dreamed about Carrie again. She didn't come to accuse him this time, but pressed herself to him as she had done before, worrying about being naked in broad daylight. It was a serene and sunny daylight, and they were in a comfortable bed somewhere. Once more he made her give up thoughts of dressing for a time and let him love her again. He wanted her so much, and she was full of that awkward, shy hunger that had made him want her before. But he couldn't have her. The dream wavered, blurred, and began to repeat itself impotently as he tried to force it on. She faded like some sweet reluctant succubus, and left him awake and hurting from the memory.

He saw that the light from the world above him was much dimmer. Darkness was an abomination, but still he was glad to see the difference. Something had changed. Time was working again. He rolled over and began to work his way back to where Becker had left him, because he felt that if the man was going to return at all he'd come soon.

As he crawled across the floor he tried to measure the distance from where the ladder would come down to where he would be propped against the wall. It wasn't far; no more than four or five ordinary steps, if he could take them. His ankle felt much better out of the boot, and even his shoulder was numb now unless he moved it. His left arm and hand

242

were numb, too, and felt swollen. But the rest of him ached like a rotten tooth from the cold.

He sat against the wall and waited, half awake, until he heard scuffling noises overhead; then he let his head fall like Ramey's, eyes closed. Under his right hand, open and hidden, was Paco's jackknife.

The ladder slid over the edge and hit the floor with a crack. He heard Becker talking to someone in a wheedling voice. Someone answered: Paco. He didn't seem to want to come to the edge of the hole. Smart kid. Becker argued some more, his voice taking on the whine of reproach.

"All right, stay up here, then, if that's the kind of baby you are. I'm goin' down to where Jake is. If you don't want to come down and help him it's all fine with me. But it's gonna be dark soon, and them wolves and coyotes'll be out for their supper. Bawlin' and cryin' won't keep them off you, no, sir."

He started down the ladder, and when he had come five or six rungs he called out in a loud voice, "Jake? You still here? I brought your little pal out here to see you, but he don't think enough of you to put his head in the door and say, 'How are you?'"

Jake didn't speak, but Paco, taking the bait, leaned down and sobbed fearfully, "Chake? Chake!" and Becker caught him and pulled him in, choking off the boy's alarmed cry with the strength of his grip on him. The ladder groaned as Becker wrestled him around so that, coming a few steps farther down, he could swing him out by the arm and let him drop. He didn't fall far enough to hurt himself, but the shriek that burst out of him shook Jake.

"Paco!"

Paco sobbed in relief. *"Tío!* I can't see you!"

"Over here." Paco scrambled to him in an excess of joy, considering the occasion. Jake made an attempt to fend him off his own injuries and only made things worse for himself. He cried out uncontrollably as Paco fell on him and flung his arms around him.

243

"That damn *bandido* said you was hurt and he was help-ing you! I bet he did it himself, huh, *tío?* Where you hurt, Chake?"

Jake, when he could get his breath, tried to move Paco's weight off him. He pushed the jackknife down between his legs to hide it. "Ease up, kid. Oh, God."

Paco began to cry vocally. "What's the matter with you, Chake?"

"I broke my shoulder, sort of— Don't pull on me."

The boy began to pat Jake's arm as he would have com-forted a beleaguered dog.

Becker scratched a match on the wall and held it up to look at them. "Ain't that a picture! Glad to see us, Jake? I just bet you are. I brought us some food and more water, and" —he produced it from a pocket—"a candle stub. A present from Angelina. That's where I found your little pal."

He lit it and set it in a spot of its own wax on the edge of the unwheeled ore wagon he used again as a seat. It was heavy enough not to rock when he sat on it.

"Now, here we all are, comfy and snug. Little Pack-o and his Uncle Jake and me. Uncle's got a little favor he wants you to do for him, Paco, so he can get out of here. You ready to tell him what it is, Jake?" But Paco had seen Ramey in the wavering light and yelled, grabbing at Jake.

"That's nothin' to be scared of. It's just George," said Becker. "You ain't scared of old George, with me and Uncle Jake here to protect you, are you?"

"That's the *bandido* that stayed with Mama once and made her cry. Hey, did you kill him, *tío?*" He took courage from the sight of a dead enemy to lean forward and yell at the corpse, "You damn bastard! I'm glad my *tío* killed you!"

Becker burst into a spasm of laughter at that. "Hey, he's a chip off the old block after all, you know it?"

Jake questioned him silently, and Becker shook his head, still grinning. He hadn't told Paco who he was. When he fin-ished chuckling, and Paco was glaring at him like a bear cub

244

from the safer side of Jake, Becker said again, "You want to tell your boy what he has to do to get you out of here?"

Jake didn't answer at once, and Becker said with growing temper, "Listen here, cardsharp. I been mighty easy with you up to now. You might think you're hurtin', but if you give it some study you'll see you could be a lot worse off. Right? And now you ain't the only one, if you know what I mean. So if you've got anything to say to that kid, get it said, or him and me will take a little trip off together and I might bring you back a souvenir you wouldn't like to see."

"It'll be the same thing when you're through with him, won't it?"

"No sirree! You both act right and do your part, and I won't lay a hand on either of you. Word of honor!"

"How do I know what that's worth?"

"Why, the same way I know what yours is worth when you tell me how that bag disappeared before you got it open. We'll just have to see. Like in showdown poker. Now, I've got the high hand here, but you get one more card and it better be a good one."

"Paco," Jake said softly, "you know your mama's traveling bag that Urraca was playing with? This man wants it. Do you think you can find where she hid it?"

"That's my mama's bag. It ain't his!"

"It is his, and he wants it back. Now think."

Paco thought. "Maybe under Gebhardt's, maybe under Tía Carrie's. Hey, Chake, maybe she put it down in the silver mine we dug!"

"If he takes you back to town, can you get a candle from Angelina and look there?"

"If you want me to."

"And don't make any noise, you understand? Don't let anybody know you're out there." He looked at Becker. "That's impossible. He's missing, and they'll be looking for him."

"You just leave all the worry to me. By the time we start lookin' everybody'll be in the bed asleep. And if they ain't

245

they'll wish they had been." He got up. "Okay, Paco, we got a two-hour ride back to town. Then we can rest up until it's late enough that nobody'll see us. We'll sneak in there like a pair of Apache Injuns and find that old bag that my pappy give me when I left my happy home. It's the last thing he ever did for me, when he give me that old bag of his. You wouldn't want to keep me from having a keepsake like that, would you?"

"How did my mama get it if it's yours, *bandido?*"

"Get up off your tail, kid, and don't talk smart to me!"

"What about you, *tío?*"

"I'll be all right until you get back."

"Sure he will, Paco. When we find that old bag we'll put a note on the jail door telling anybody who wants to know where he is." He grabbed Paco by the waist and boosted him up the ladder.

"I'll tell Tío Clem when we find it," Paco promised Jake. Becker patted him on the rump.

"Sure you will. Get on up there."

"Wait a minute," said Jake. Becker paused, three feet up the ladder. "You gave me your word you wouldn't hurt the kid. What are you going to do with him if he finds what you want?"

"Why, I told you. Nothing. I might even give him a little joy ride down to Mexico with me. You can't tell, we might learn to hit it off yet."

Jake took a slow breath, listening for Paco. He heard the light feet slide on the stone lip of the shaft.

"What if he can't find it?" The sound was fading. Paco was going down the slope to where the horses must be tethered.

"If he don't find it I'm going to bring him back here and peel him in front of your eyes. Or maybe I'll peel you in front of him, depending on who I think is lying to me the most. Now you just sit back and pray he knows where to look."

"All right, you win," Jake sighed. "You bluffed me out.

Come back down here and forget about him. You'd be wasting your time."

Becker descended one rung of the ladder, staring at him. "What are you tryin' to pull with that 'bluffed me out' stuff? You're tryin' a bluff right now, ain't you? It's wrote all over you."

"No bluff. I've got the money on me. I was bluffing you before, but you're such a dumb bastard you fell for it. You're such a dumb sonofabitch you didn't even think to search me for it. Come on over here and see! It's in a belt around my waist. You could have had it last night without all this trouble if you had any brains. But you were too busy trying to throw a scare into me and shooting off your big mouth to think of it."

Becker's foot touched ground again, cautiously. He took Jake's gun out of his belt and leveled it at him.

"I don't know what you're trying to pull off, but if you so much as blink your eyes while I'm searchin' you I'll blow your damn head off."

He advanced on Jake and pulled his vest and shirt open roughly. "Well, I'll be goddamned," he breathed. "You sure had me fooled. Why did you wait till now to give in?" He unstrapped the belt and pulled it free, then laid it over his knee while he opened first one flap, then another. "Sonofagun, there it is." He looked at Jake, pleased but puzzled. "What do you want for this? To have me shoot you now, instead of leaving you here?"

"Let the kid go, that's all."

Becker stood up, throwing the length of the belt over one shoulder. "Sure thing. I'll drop him off somewhere across the border."

"No! I mean outside of town. He has someone there who will take care of him." He was beginning to gather himself for a one-chance lunge, the knife hidden in his hand, his good leg tensed to push him up the wall. Becker saw the motion and came back to jerk his arms up by the handcuffs and shake

247

the knife out of his fist, while Jake sucked in his breath against the sharp pain and fell down again. Becker folded the knife and pocketed it, letting go of the handcuffs. While Jake was still limp and the light was swimming in his vision, Becker blew out the candle.

"For that, I'm going to let you live in the dark a while instead." Jake heard his boot bear down on the first ladder rung. "Don't fret yourself about that boy while you're waitin' to die—*tío*. If he takes after either his ma or pa, he'll get by all right. After all, he'll be down there with his own kind of people, won't he?" He went up the ladder carefully in the dark.

Jake rolled over on his left knee and got his good foot under him, then launched himself blindly at the invisible ladder. He hit it with his whole weight behind the lunge, striking it with his right arm first. He felt the ladder crack apart, the way his whole chest seemed to crack apart as the force of the blow sent him past it, stumbling to the ground. He screamed or Becker screamed, or both. He heard the heavy descent of Becker's body and the hard crack of it as it hit the ore-wagon bed.

He was sobbing with the effort to keep moving. With his head against the far wall, he put his feet up to feel for what was left of the ladder and kicked at it. The old wood split again and the ladder fell apart. He lay on his back, tangled in the debris, and gasped with relief and with the overwhelming pain. He could move no farther, but he tried to reach Paco with his voice.

"Paco! Get to the horse! Grab the reins if you can't get on him. Do you hear me? Grab the reins and don't let go! He'll take you home. Paco!" There was no answer.

He heard a faint moan from Becker. It surprised him. With the best of luck, he didn't think he could possibly have done more than stun him. He'd clear his head in a second, and Jake would be a dead man. But at least Becker wasn't going anyplace for a while either.

Becker moaned again. It was almost like a sob; very child-

248

like. It sounded like Paco. There was no movement from the direction of his voice.

"Becker?" he whispered. He felt nothing now himself except pain and cold and exhaustion. What was holding up his execution? "Becker?"

"I—think my back's broke," Becker said faintly. "You play a—rough game—old Jake—but you still lost the pot—this time. That kid won't be able to find this place again. We're both of us goin' to die down here—now."

Jake heard him, but couldn't answer. Becker didn't speak again. Jake had closed his eyes to dream one last dream. He saw Paco running after the horse, falling down and losing the end of the reins, but getting up again to follow the animal in the darkness.

What Becker said was true. They were both going to die now because Paco wouldn't be able to find his way back with someone to get them out. But Jake wanted him to find home again. He willed it, clinging to the fading image of the boy running as long as he could; summoned up welcoming lights to guide him, searchers to find him and take him home to Carrie.

Then he was too cold and tired even to dream.

23

He never knew when they came for him. They found him and pulled him out of the pit by a rope tied under his arms. They hauled him back to Arredondo tied across a mule's saddle, because it looked like he was going to die soon anyway, and there was no other way to do it without losing four more hours on another round trip into town for a wagon. It was a rough haul, but he was too deep in shock to feel it by then.

When he did feel it and began to moan, somebody poured whiskey down his throat and nearly choked him. Somebody else complained angrily about that; somebody jabbered, someone was crying quietly.

He was lifted, stripped, tortured in some incomprehensible manner so that his arms would no longer move at all, then put down at full length on a bed that smelled of sun-sweetened fresh sheets.

A soft voice was speaking to him. It was Carrie's. He knew that much, but both the will and the ability to answer her were lost to him. He slept for a very long time. Even when he was awake for a few minutes together, he clung to the pretense of sleep, keeping his eyes closed and listening to know if there was anybody in the room with him ready to pounce on him and made him wake and talk.

An infection set into his chest from the mauling his splintered bones had given him. He ran a fever for several days and felt such pain when he breathed that he lay like a dead man, trying not to breathe at all. Whenever he opened his eyes in the silence, either Mary O'Neal or Carrie seemed to be there, bending over him with a cold compress and a somber look.

When he believed he was going to die, he had a lot he wanted to say to Carrie, and couldn't form the words. But when he knew he was going to recover, it all seemed foolish, like a fever dream. By that time she was very cool with him, never staying longer than it took to feed him or straighten the bed. Yet he knew she had been there before, night and day.

She had certainly been there once with a hammer while he was too far out of his head to hear. The first time he woke and tried to turn his head he found his money belt skewered to the wall a foot from his nose with a nail that reminded him of something Biblical. It was Jael and Sisera, he found out later, though at the time everything about their story evaded him except the nail.

He found he was strapped into a remarkable set of splints. The break in his collarbone put his left arm out almost at a right angle to his body, making it impossible for him to move in bed at all. He also seemed to have broken his right arm in the rush on the ladder. It was bound and strapped to his side with a sling. His ankle had been only badly wrenched and was soon mended, but the rest left him embarrassingly helpless in every possible way. He could not feed himself or shave or attend to the simplest necessities. He was humiliatingly dependent on the others for everything. As he recovered, his humiliation deepened and soured. He became a foul-tempered and ungracious patient. Paco was kept away from him, and Carrie was once reduced to tears, trying to feed him the approved invalid's diet.

"Very well, don't eat it, then, if you think it's swill! Don't

251

eat at all! Because if you can't eat this, you can go hungry. Call me when you find an appetite and some decent manners." She snatched the tray off his lap so suddenly that the soup bowl and cup flew from it and smashed on the floor.

With all the concentration and care of a furious woman, she cleaned up the mess from the boards in a deadly silence. He wasn't going to give her the satisfaction of a retreat into reason, so he kept silent, too, while she collected the shattered china on the tray again and stalked out with it.

Mary O'Neal appeared a few minutes later and looked down on him as if more in sorrow than in anger. He did feel he had behaved badly, but he was ready to defend himself whenever she chose to open the attack. Instead, she closed the door and tipped her head down as if peering at him over spectacles.

"You're not fit to live among Christian people."

"I wish to hell I didn't! Unchristian people might either let me alone or give me what I ask for."

She continued to study him. "Let me guess at it," she offered. "Is it a drink you want, or somebody's fist in your mouth?"

"A drink! Oh, my God, all I want is a drink and some food that's solid. A steak, or beans, or even some of Sánchez's rotten stew."

"Meat is inflammatory to the system—like bad temper. But if you tuck in your evil tongue and give that poor woman who's been slaving for you a pleasant look the next time she comes near you, I might see my way to bringing in a small glass of beer and a bit of chicken."

"All right, even beer would be something. But, Christ, Mary—"

"Don't blaspheme to me! There's a little child out there who keeps asking to see you, but Miss Carrie says he's not to come in until you can stop cursing with every breath. And don't take me up on it! Remember, you must get on the good side of me to have your beer." She started to leave, but paused in the door to break into a sudden giggle.

"Get out of here, O'Neal."

"Ah, I'm sorry. But it came to me all at once that when you scowl like that you remind me of my father, bless his black heart." She left him stunned. It was the final indecency.

He was much subdued and silent when she came around again. She carried a cloth-covered tray, which, being unveiled, supported a terra-cotta bowl of fragrant chicken stew and a respectable mug of beer. "Now," she said firmly, "you can't have more than a sip to start with. Then you will either eat Carrie's stew or watch me drain the rest of the mug right before your eyes."

He ate, feeling like a pet monkey as she fed him each mouthful, half opening her own mouth with each bite in her total concentration on the job. The beer went down slowly, too, with little administrative wipes at his mustache in between.

"I'm that pleased with you, now," she said, putting down the empty mug. "Why, you can sip it as fine as a lass at her first wake."

"I feel like livestock," he muttered, "being fattened for the market." She saw he was in low spirits and not just sulking, and put the tray on the floor for a moment in order to study him.

"It's hard for a strong, healthy man to abide a sickness, I know. But you've been more than a little lucky if this is the first time you've ever been down on your back with the womenfolk pecking at you. Most people have had more than one taste of it, though few of them go to such lengths to splinter their bones just to be waited on by the ladies."

That wasn't what troubled him now, she saw. "Where's the pinch? Are your wrappings too tight?"

"No. How old are you, O'Neal?"

"Twenty-two," she answered, surprised.

He closed his eyes wearily. "God. I guess I am old enough to be your father."

"What's that?"

"Nothing. I've just been wondering how long it takes for bones to mend—in older people."

"Are you a Catholic? Would you like for me to ask Señor Sánchez to send out for a priest to give you the last rites before you die of old age?"

"Oh, shi—I beg your pardon. I just wondered how long I'm going to have to be tied up like this, that's all. I guess a kid's bones heal faster than somebody's my age. What does it take? A month? Two months? Six?"

"Six to eight weeks, young or old. Now, you take my father. He was caught in a cave-in down in the mines when I was a tiny bit of a girl back in the old country. Broke his collarbone and his arm, just like you. He was back picking coal and swinging his belt strap after my skirts in a bit over two months."

He nodded bleakly. "I see."

"Did I tell you before that you remind me of him? You do. Of course, I could only guess how he'd have looked at your age. How old are you?"

"Forty-five," he said grudgingly.

"Ah, well, I wouldn't know about him then, for sure. You see, he was coming on to sixty when he fathered me, and I have a sister two years younger back home." She got up with the tray, the napkin over her arm. He had thought her very plain at first, and much older than twenty-two. She had carroty hair like Delia's, and the same milky skin, but heavily spotted with healthy freckles. Her face was soap-and-water shiny like Carrie's, however, and for all her efficient ways she blushed like Carrie when he asked her, impulsively:

"Have you picked out a man yet, O'Neal? Or does the medical profession keep you too tied down?"

"I've been studied over and inspected, like that livestock you mentioned, and I've done some inspecting myself. But

I'm in no hurry. A woman can be a long time married, so there's no need to rush. There's somebody else out here to see you, so I won't take up any more of your time."

The somebody was Paco. His chopped-off hair was beginning to recover from Mrs. Cuddeback's shears, and his clothes were clean and well mended. He had his pocketknife in hand and a sample of work for Jake to see: a short piece of board with a portrait gouged out of it.

The face was long and pointed, the eyes deep slits, the mouth a tight line, the mustache flourishing. It bore a striking resemblance to Simon Legree. Jake studied it for some further clue.

"It's you, Chake. See? I was gonna put some teeth in it, but Tío Sánchez said teeth was too hard to do. Some man came down here last week with a camera, and made a picture of me and Tío Clem and Tío Sánchez and those dead *bandidos*. They wanted to make a picture of you, too, but you was sick and Carrie wouldn't let 'em. So I made one. You like it?"

"Yeah. Thanks. Put it over there on the table for me, will you? I'll use it when I start shaving again."

Paco examined him curiously. "Why you got all them things on you still? You don't look sick any more."

"Did anybody ever find that bag of your mama's?"

Paco shrugged. "They all looked. Some *hombres* came here in round hats from the place that *bandido* robbed and just about tore up the feed-store floor looking for it. And all the boxes and my good stuff, too, that I made in the back. They took it off and tore it up, but they didn't find nothing."

"What about your silver mine?"

Paco broke out in a crow of joy. "Oh, man, that was a funny part. Las' week, before they got here, the Gebhardts put a privy on it. They said it looked like that's what it needed to keep somebody from fallin' in. So those round-hat men tore up the privy, too, and got down in it with shovels and buckets! Man, Gebhardts was mad, and the men was

255

mad, too, 'cause there wasn't nothing at the bottom but a lot of rocks and crap!" He fell over on Jake's knee, nearly strangled with the humor of it. Jake chuckled at him. They both grew solemn faced for a moment, looking at each other. Then they broke out laughing again.

The door opened enough to show Carrie's face. "You can't stay very long, Paco, if you're going to be so boisterous."

"He was just telling me about the Wells Fargo detectives digging up Gebhardts' new privy."

She started to smile, then tucked her bottom lip under. "Just the sort of topic I might have expected the two of you to fall on."

"Come on in, then, and raise the moral tone of the place. But let the kid stay for a while."

Paco glowed at the reprieve and climbed up on the bed with Jake, while Carrie took the chair and smoothed her skirts thoughtfully.

"I understand they couldn't find the money. Tell me what else happened while I was out of my head."

"Well, it's been very busy here. The sheriff came for the two—bodies. He said there was a reward out for one of them, the one named Frank Becker. He wasn't sure about the other one. And the express company is going to pay a reward for the return of the stolen money, if it's ever found.

"We had a judge in from the capital, day before yesterday, to hold a hearing, and while he was here he performed marriage services for eight of the twelve women who just came, and two of the women from the Golden Moon. He also promised Clem that as soon as the legislature meets again we can be certain to get our papers of incorporation, and a circuit judge, too, since the railroad is drawing so close."

"What's Delia doing?"

Her mouth tightened. "Miss Moon isn't here any more. The day you were rescued from the mine she sold her house to Mr. Sánchez, took back her tent, and left, just behind the stage for Mesilla. I'm afraid you've missed another one."

256

"Sold out to Sánchez? My God, what's he fixing to become here, the merchant prince of—" He floundered, unable to think of any way to edit the comment at the last moment.

She appeared not to notice. "No, Mr. Sánchez is going to turn the place into a hotel. It's going to be the Arredondo Carriage House from now on." She had more trouble with the corners of her mouth and turned pink. "It's because he wants to cater to the carriage trade—respectable travelers— not for the reason that must have instantly occurred to *you.*"

Jake began to shake with laughter, joined by a mystified but eager Paco. She smiled at the two of them reluctantly at first, but their amusement was contagious. The dimple woke again that he had seen only once before, since she had smiled so infrequently in his company. She looked away from his examination of her. There was a pause. Paco lay on his back beside Jake, making an investigation of his splinted left arm.

"I guess Clem's in his element with all the comings and goings, then," he said, to fill her silence.

She drew a deep breath and looked thoughtful again.

"Yes, he's very busy these days. When Miss Moon left us so suddenly he was—disturbed more than I thought he should be, until— Some of the people in the League have suggested that when we have our first election he ought to be mayor. He says no, of course, but he's flattered that they'd think of him. I believe he wants it."

"Why not? He'd make a good mayor. He's got the kind of guts that people look for in a politician." She looked at him in surprise. "I mean it. It took a lot of nerve to put a shotgun on that mob of miners and make them back off. Enough of them had guns that they could have made Swiss cheese out of us both if he'd flinched a little. But he made believers out of them right there. He's not very big, but he's man enough."

Carrie glanced at Paco. "Yes. He—we had a talk about something last week that we should have talked about years ago." She looked at Jake helplessly.

"I know," he told her.

257

She shook her head, her fingers beginning to pick at the lap of her skirt. "I don't understand why he didn't tell me before. How could he think it would hurt me to know he was all right? Why did he do it? It makes me feel as if I've spoiled his life. I never wanted anything like that from him. Why couldn't he have been honest and set us both free?"

"Maybe because you weren't entirely honest with him."

She studied her fingers. "I suppose not. But I was afraid and ashamed."

"There was nothing for you to be ashamed of. It wasn't your fault."

She gave him a long look. "Some of it was. You were my fault, weren't you? And that's why you left Willow Bend. That's why there was only Clem to meet them when they came looking for you." She looked away again. "But if you mean—the rest of it; if you think the matter of whose fault it is has anything to do with who gets the blame—" She shook her head. "Haven't you ever read stories of Indians capturing white women? The women who survive or who are rescued will tell of being beaten and insulted and starved, but never anything else. Never. Haven't you noticed that? I have, and I know why.

"It's because they know they'll be treated as objects of curiosity and pity. And blame. People say they're 'ruined,' because if they don't have the delicacy to die as a result of their experience it must be because they're really depraved at heart anyway.

"I tried to die. I wanted to at first. But then I thought I had to live, for Clem. And if I had to live I never wanted to see him or anyone else look at me with the pity and curiosity I'd seen on their faces when they talked about someone like me."

"Now that you've told him, you see it didn't matter that much, though."

"Told him? I haven't told him. I never will!" She stopped

258

in disbelief at herself, staring at him. "But I told you. Why is that? I'd still just want to die if Clem knew."

Jake smiled faintly. "I guess it's easier to talk to another depraved soul than to a strong-minded, virtuous type like your brother." He sighed a little. "It's a pity neither of us had his resources."

She examined his face carefully, but could find nothing to substantiate a charge of mockery. He seemed to be concerned only with checking a drowsy Paco beside him.

"Well," she said after a moment, "I won't have to be Clem's keeper much longer, I'm sure. He looks so absent minded now every time Mary O'Neal speaks to him, I'm certain to be supplanted in a very short while. She's had an offer of marriage from every remaining bachelor around here and she's turned them all away. I hope he doesn't wait too long to speak to her. She's a wonderful girl, and he isn't getting any younger. None of us are. I'll be taking new quarters soon, perhaps in the hotel."

"I don't think they'd throw you out, Carrie, even if they did get together."

"Well, I certainly wouldn't want to stay and be a fifth wheel and an intruder in my own kitchen! I like Mary fine. I believe I could love her. But one woman in a kitchen is the rule that every woman knows the first day she takes a skillet in her hand." She stood up preparing to go. "I won't be a beggar, though. I'll take your advice. There are plenty of things I can do. Maybe I'll start a school here. Heaven knows we need one. Perhaps if Clem becomes the mayor he'll have one built for me. After all, a rise in the literacy rate would be beneficial to the newspaper. Paco, you're half asleep. It's time you were in your own bed. Don't break your uncle's bones again, climbing over him."

She leaned across Jake and took Paco under the arms to lift him. While she was close he breathed in the clove and soap smell she always had about her. In spite of her present self-possession, he wished for a moment that Paco was locked

259

in the back cell, and he had his arms free. He could think of no words to convey this wish to her that wouldn't go beyond what he wanted to say.

Paco yawned and looked sleepily at Jake. "Good night, Chake." He scrubbed at his head and lingered.

"What's the matter with you?"

"Mary said I ought to kiss you good night, but I don't think you'd like it." He and Jake frowned at each other in mutual suspense, then Paco leaned forward quickly and made a peck at Jake's jaw, wrinkled his nose at the sensation, and escaped from the room. Carrie stood a moment longer, without expression; then she said good night and closed the door, leaving him alone, planked to his boards like a banquet fish, to congeal slowly in his own gloom.

He also mended slowly. When he was allowed on his feet he made a venture in the direction of the cantina and was stopped a dozen times before he got there by people who wanted to congratulate him for killing two dangerous criminals without help, and to modestly indicate their part in saving his own life afterward. It seemed that the whole town had turned out to look for Paco and him. The inaccuracies in the rest of the tale going around made him groan, but Paco's version of what had happened in the mine was firmly planted in the town's mind. To Jake's disgust he was the walking wonder of Arredondo, who had overwhelmed two outlaws unhampered by a pair of broken arms. His disclaimers were approved as decent, manly modesty, because everyone knew how closemouthed he had been about earlier exploits in Kansas.

He discovered from occasional winks and painful nudges that there were a few cynics who thought he had the stolen money stashed away himself.

Paco was his shadow and personal attendant, getting out his cigars and lighting them, and handling the drinks until his one arm was freed from the sling. Paco, learning to count

260

better all the time, played poker with him during the uneventful days of his convalescence, shuffling the cards, dealing, and putting them in Jake's right hand, then pulling a long, shrewd face over his own.

Augie's brother, Rance, stayed on as a deputy, though Jake still patrolled the streets at night, with Paco trying the door handles for him.

Another stage went through town on the way to El Paso. He watched it load and go, morosely. Arredondo was beginning to smother him like an overprotective parent, but El Paso seemed remote and flat; an idea whose time had passed.

He had to go someplace and soon. The urge to migrate had never been so strong.

Everyone else had business and interests to keep them going from dawn to dark. Only he seemed to be an idler. Yet the townsmen were always ready to pause from their labor and speak to him as he roamed aimlessly. He would have been welcome at any supper table in exchange for a retelling of the killing of Frank Becker.

He refused to oblige them, even returned to the habit of taking his meals in the jail rather than in the cheerful company of Sánchez's cantina.

Sánchez had become one of the busy ones. He started wearing a full suit every day and spent his time running from the bar to the New Arredondo Carriage House Hotel.

His sternly handsome wife, Soledad, had become the hotel manager and made an impressive sight behind the new desk in the hall, even without her gun belts. But Sánchez pretended to think she was unable to make a decision without him, and traveled back and forth all day.

Clem and Mary O'Neal were undoubtedly coming to a rapid understanding, and Mary continued to look younger and prettier every time she came to inspect Jake's splints, which was less often every week. The week before the June stage to El Paso was due, she took them off and let him free, to flex his weakened arms and dress himself properly at last. He felt strangely light and unbalanced without them, like a swimmer coming to land again after hours in the water.

Clem declared a celebration in honor of his recovery. The five of them crowded into the closet-sized kitchen for dinner while Clem talked about the future of the town, and between times exchanged such private looks with Mary as made them both smile and the others feel like intruders.

"Well, what about you, Dutch?" Clem asked. "You didn't think much of the place at first, but do you like us any better now, or do you still want to get back to the city lights and the fancy hotels?" It was not a question phrased to invite Jake's reply. Carrie got up from the table suddenly and left them with a murmur of excuse.

"We're going to El Paso and buy a big saloon," said Paco with his mouth full.

Clem looked from him to Jake. "Oh? Well, that's fine, I guess. Though you look a little small to tend bar, young fellow. Is that what you plan, then, Dutch? Because if you want to stay you know your job's good here as long as you want it."

"Maybe nobody's really asked him to stay," said Mary, who had been watching him since Carrie left the table.

"Of course they have. Everybody wants him to! Why, he's the reason Arredondo's going to be put on the map now. This town is proud of him!"

That was enough for Jake. He got up, pushing back his chair.

"I'll keep it in mind. But the stage comes in Wednesday, and I guess I better be on it. The man I was going down there to see expected me in March. He'll give me up for dead if I don't."

He'd give himself up for dead if he didn't. He'd have to use Paco's carving for a mirror if he didn't, because he'd never be able to look himself in the face again.

He left, muttering his good night. Carrie wasn't in evidence outside. He and Paco walked their rounds and returned to the jail. Everyone who saw them together smiled on them.

Jake felt like an honored thief. Wednesday he would take that stage, and the whole town would turn out to see his perfidy, and chew on it for the rest of the year. Because he had no intention of taking Paco with him.

24

He didn't sleep as well that night as he thought he would. His bed, which he felt would be a couch of luxury once the confining splints were off, was the same old nest of coiled vipers. He got up sometime after midnight and went outside to wander listlessly until he found himself behind the jail where he had once sat holding Paco.

He wasn't rehearsing his explanation to Paco or his good-bye speech to Carrie. That was the sort of thing he never let himself in for. He'd just pack and go as he always did. Paco would find himself another hero, and Carrie would be better off than anyone.

He once thought he would ask her to come with him at the end, but he saw the terms wouldn't suit her and he could make no others. He also thought that getting away without good-bye speeches and explanations was going to be damned difficult in Arredondo.

Standing there he suddenly felt he wasn't the only night watcher. Somebody down the way was sitting outside. He knew who it was, but he didn't acknowledge her.

It made him uncomfortable just to stand there pretending not to see her, and know she was watching him. What was more uncomfortable was the slow realization that he was actually *lingering* there waiting for her to come over to him.

He was ashamed enough of that discovery to go back inside again.

She didn't move.

The last four days were hell. Everyone heard the news, and everyone did his part to try to make Jake change his mind and stay, except Paco, who was charged with excitement at the prospect of becoming a saloonkeeper, and Carrie, who didn't come near the jail all that week.

On Wednesday he lay back down on his cot after a late breakfast while Paco went out to say good-bye to everybody. He had reached a point in guilt that was almost catatonic. He despised himself for not telling Paco he wasn't going to get on that stage with him, but he couldn't say a word.

When noon approached he got up and took his valise out from under the bed. The front door opened and closed too softly to admit Paco, and he heard the brush of skirts in the outer room.

Carrie came quietly in and sat down on the chair to watch him pack. He moved deliberately, because there wasn't much to put into the valise and he didn't want to finish and have nothing to do while she was there. Her absence had annoyed him for several days, but now that she was here he wished she'd go away.

He thought prolonged speech with her would be the worst thing that could happen, but it wasn't. In his silence she began to cry. She made no sound, but a side glance at her discovered tears in her eyes. Jake began to marshal all his old resentments against other people's intrusive emotions. He remembered how he had fled the possibility of another woman's tears in San Francisco only three months ago, and now he could scarcely recall her face. But to keep himself clear of those tears and reproaches he had run from her without a word, straight into this place and this woman, who never did anything by halves. There would be such a flood here in a moment they'd both be washed out into the street.

He groped for something to say that would stop her; make her mad, make her leave him. That had always been easy enough in the past, but now he couldn't think of a thing except the bare truth about his plans, which didn't include Paco. He felt too numb and gray mouthed to start with that. Damn the woman.

"You're not taking Paco with you," she said quietly.

He stopped in the act of wadding up his recently unwashed laundry to cram into the bag. At least she let him have the option of answering briefly.

"No."

"I thought not. But I felt I'd better come around to make sure. Shouldn't you have told him by now?" She seemed calm and unaccusing.

"It depends on which you think is better: to whittle off somebody's leg a couple of inches a day, or make a clean job of it all at once."

"Who's suffering this amputation, Jacob, you or Paco?"

"You know he's got no business going with me, Carrie. You've said it yourself, so why try to make it seem like I'm double-crossing him instead of doing him a favor?"

"That wasn't my intention. I only thought you might have prepared him for the favor somehow, before the stage comes. But I'll do it if you can't. I think he likes me a little, and I love him, so I'll be glad to have him stay. Every woman needs a child, I suppose; even we determined spinsters. Clem will have Mary to look after him soon, and a houseful of babies, I hope. So I'll need Paco as much as he needs—someone, too. Perhaps, when he's past the shock of being left behind, he'll come to understand why it was best, and even feel a little sorry for you, as I do."

He stared at her. Sorry for him? Malarkey. This was the way she had decided to slip the knife in, or else it was the build-up to a plea for him to stay. She saw his rigid look.

"You don't think I feel sorry for you? I do. God knows I've tried to work up a lasting anger against you, this last

266

month. I've made myself take a hard look at your sublime selfishness, your self-deceits, your callous way of treating other people as if they were just figures in your landscape —all your endearing traits that have made me so mad at you at one time or another. But I can't seem to get mad enough. I want to. But I've seen too much now and it only makes me sad for you.

"The way you feel you must live is so—unrewarding to you. I mean, several people here have benefited in some small way from your stay in Arredondo, but not you. Clem and I have come out of our separate cells and can live a bit more honestly. Mary had the leisure to find a man who loves her, while she was nursing you. The town got its little reward from the world. Paco will have a home here, at least, and someone who really cares about him.

"Only you get nothing. Today you'll board a stage alone, and make a solitary journey to a lonely town, with a bad meal and an empty bed at the end of the trip. No one here wants you to go and no one there cares if you come. The worst thing about it is that you aren't doing it easily. It's hurting you. It's hurting you to do this to Paco and to yourself, but you won't help yourself. I even understand, from things you've said, that you call this peculiar form of purgatory 'freedom.' "

"That's right," he said shortly, then cleared his throat and jammed his clean shirt down on top of the dirty ones. He saw there was nothing left to pack.

She got up, wiping her tears away with her fingertips, quickly. Now, he thought, she'd be the clinging vine; hang around his neck and sob on his shoulder. He tensed himself for that, and there was even a sort of satisfaction in his certainty.

But she only smiled at him with the sort of fleeting pity she'd have turned on a beggar at a street corner, and put her hand out to be taken. The great emancipatrix.

He took the hand involuntarily; heard her say, "Good-bye, Jacob. I don't believe I want to see you off. I'd better find Paco instead and tell him he can't go with you this time. I don't mean to imply that I think there'll be a next time, but it's the only lie I can think of at the moment that will let him down without breaking his heart.

"Take care of yourself wherever you go. I hope you find something you want in El Paso." She slipped free of his hand and turned away.

Amazement sat on Jake like a startled owl, until pure outrage rushed to rout it. His hand shot out without his volition and grabbed her arm, pulling her back. He heard himself whisper, "You're not going to get away with *that!*" and saw her startled face—truly startled and not smug—as he took her roughly by the jaw and kissed her.

They stood blindly locked together until they began to sway, then sat on the edge of the cot without noticing what they did. Her mouth had the taste of every sweet thing he had ever known. The sudden release of his pent-up resentment left him weak.

Presently he pushed her down gently on the cot, burying his face against her soft body, fumbling with her buttoned shirtwaist until she put her hand up and took his away.

"I want you," he said indistinctly from the haven of her breast. She touched his head lightly, then slid her fingers between his lips and her breast. He took them away and kissed her there again. "I want you," he said again, feeling her stir under him.

"Tough luck," she said in a clear calm voice.

He raised his head, disbelieving, and saw her eyes held a trace of amusement as well as tears.

"Those aren't the magic words, dear Jake. Try again."

He kissed her mouth again, harshly, to squelch that impudence. It seemed to him that for somebody who was saying no, she was making a very warm response. When he let her go, he said as much. She smiled, and the tears spilled over the planes of her cheeks.

"I didn't say I didn't want you, too. And I'm not so unselfish that I can't enjoy the last of what I'm going to get."

"Well, then—"

"I said, 'Tough luck.'"

"And you think I'm just going to let you get up and walk out of here on 'tough luck,' after this? The hell you do!"

"If you don't let me go," she whispered, "I'll cry rape so loud you'll be deaf right up to the day they take you out to hang you."

He snorted. "It's a little late for that, isn't it?"

"As they say, 'Better late than—'"

"You won't do it. You want—"

"Try me."

They lay looking at each other.

"You're tougher than Delia the worst day she ever lived."

"I think you're right."

"And you came in here just to make me crawl so you could have the last word and walk out like a victorious bitch!"

"No." Her eyes were solemn. "I never wanted to hurt you. I love you. I always have. And I certainly never want you to crawl to me or to anyone. I want you to be a man. Dear Jake, how I want you to stand up and be a man, but you won't, so it's just as well you're going. If you're afraid you're crawling to me when you say what you did, it's because you're like a proud, stubborn little boy who won't use his company manners even if it means missing out on the Christmas feast. That's you; going hungry and thirsty and naked in your heart all your life because you won't admit you need anyone."

"I said I wanted you."

"And I said those weren't the magic words. Say 'I love you, Carrie.'"

Nothing.

"Say 'I love you, Carrie.'" She touched his clouded baffled face. "Poor Jake. You better get up now or you'll miss your stage again."

A dozen impulses flashed through his mind, all of them

269

destructive and inconclusive. He wanted to do something to humiliate her now. But she lay under him, looking at him with those thick-lashed wet blue eyes, as if he were Paco who had hurt himself. Her damned arrogance! He wanted to hurt her. He just wanted her, in spite of his rage. His whole body ached for her.

He ran his hand slowly and possessively down her body until he could pull up her skirts and caress her firm thighs up to where they joined in cotton-swathed chastity. She let him, watching his face unblinkingly; even relaxed a little for him.

He thought of all the damned clothes he'd have to snatch off her while he tried to keep her from making good on her promise to scream. The same thought must have occurred to her, too, because she choked on a tearful little laugh.

He let her go and sat up in disgust to put his head in his hands, feeling closer to both murder and tears than he had ever felt in his life. The cot springs creaked as she pulled her skirts free and got up. She paused with her hand on the door-knob, looking at him.

"Don't do that. Don't pretend to, either. Leave it for later; you'll have time. In twenty years, or even in ten, when Paco has forgotten you and I'm an old woman. Then you can do that, alone. I'll have shed all my tears by then."

The door closed.

She was gone several minutes before the door burst open again and Paco rushed into the room. "Hey, *tío,* look at what Angelina gave me! A roseberry of holy beads, and a basket of good stuff to eat on the way!"

Jake hadn't moved since Carrie left him. Paco bounced on the cot beside him and swung the rosary around, enjoying the glint of the dark amber beads. He noticed something left out of the packing. "Chake, you didn't take your picture I made for you." He got it, admiring it anew, and put it in the valise, then strung the beads around his neck and dropped them down inside his shirt. "That's the way to do it," he whispered to himself. Jake scrubbed his hands over his dry face roughly and looked at Paco.

"Let's go now, Chake, so we can watch the stage come in."

"Sure," Jake sighed. "Hell, yes. Why not?"

No one told Carrie when they left. She had let Paco stray from her mind while she grieved on her own bed. When she remembered him she jumped up in alarm and ran out through the office. Clem and Mary O'Neal looked at her in astonishment.

"Carrie, dear, what's the matter?" Her face was badly damaged by her tears and she looked wild.

"Where's Paco? Have you seen him?"

"What do you mean? You know he's gone."

"No, he isn't! He's here someplace. I've got to find him!"

"You've been sleeping and had a bad dream."

"No! He wasn't going to take him! He's still here! Oh, God!"

Clem frowned. "But of course he was going to take him, if you mean Jake. And he did. I saw them both off myself. We all wondered at you for not being there." He looked around for Mary's help. "You went to sleep and missed them." Carrie flew out the door with another strangled denial. "Mary, sweetheart, go after her. I don't know what's wrong. I've never seen her like this before."

Mary followed her down to the empty jail and found her in Jake's room, face down on the cot, sobbing.

"Oh, Carrie darlin', don't. There now, lamb. Don't cry for the likes of him. I'm sure he wasn't worth a drop of your tears if he could leave you so, the blackguard! For all that he could be a fetching man if he tried, he had a cold, lonesome heart in him, I could tell. It's the kind you never warm up if you burn your own heart out trying. I've seen the like. He's like one of those little fox cubs we used to find in the fields back home that looked so much like puppy dogs. Oh, we'd smuggle them home and feed them and favor them and give them names. But when they grew up they were foxes, just wild foxes, and nothing else."

"He took Paco with him," Carrie sobbed, with her face in the pillow.

"I know, the poor little beggar. I only hope he treats him fair and tries to find a decent home that'll take him in."

Carrie lifted her head and rolled over. Mary saw with surprise that, although her face was crumpled and stained with tears, she wasn't in either sorrow or despair at Jake's leave-taking. She looked almost radiant.

"No, no, you see, he took Paco with him—he wasn't going to. I know you all thought he was, but he wasn't going to do it. I knew! He just didn't have the courage to tell Paco. He was going to sneak away and leave him at the last minute."

"A better thing if he had, too. But what a mean, low trick, to ditch the poor child without a word!"

"But he couldn't do it! Don't you see? He couldn't do it! Maybe there's hope for him after all."

She lay back on Jake's pillow with a groan of relief and anguish. "Oh, Mary, I don't know how anyone can be as relieved and mad and miserable and happy as I am right now. Would you mind if I asked you to leave me alone, until I get myself in hand, so I won't go making a fool of myself on the street again?"

"To be sure, dear. I'll just tell your brother you're all right." But Mary was less reassured than puzzled by Carrie's outburst and explanation.

When Carrie returned to the office she was calm and full of purpose. Clem and Mary watched her, waiting for some sign that would permit them to question her further on the matter of Jake and her tears, but she gave them no opportunity.

In a few days they began to believe it must have been some sort of dream that had made her fly out the door after a phantom Paco. They avoided mentioning either the boy or the man to her, as if they were dead.

Carrie seemed not to notice either the concern or the new reticence. She wrote, edited, swept, scrubbed, and dusted with total concentration. In the evenings she shut herself away in her room early after supper, pleading fatigue, which was reasonable. She didn't look now as if she were either grieving or brooding. If anything, Mary thought, she looked better than she had in recent weeks. Her hair took on the shine that long sessions of brushing must have given it as she sat alone.

Once, when Mary glanced into her open doorway, she found the room so clean and bare it could have been unoccupied.

"Dear God," she thought, "has the woman gone and taken private vows? It looks like the cell of a nun." But Carrie wasn't a Catholic.

Others in the town seemed quickly to forget Jake and his protégé. Rance Gebhardt took over as full-time marshal and occupied the jail, glad to be out from under his brother's heavy humor. Patchy Murdoch regained his reputation as the man most to be watched at the card tables. But without a suitable rival to oppose him his audience waned and bar profits rose accordingly.

In the weed-tangled field behind the cantina where the glorious tent had once stood the Sánchez children found a dirt-caked cloth bag full of dead kittens. Or, rather, their skeletons, for the invading ants and other insects had found their way inside and picked the little bones clean.

There was a thick paper stuffing in the bottom corner of the bag, visible through a hole chewed in it by the field mice. They tried to pull it out, but it was wedged in too tightly. It wasn't very interesting, compared to the delicate little bones, but they hauled the whole thing in to their grandmother to see if she wanted to make use of the remains for her spell medicines.

Sánchez found her and the children polishing up the tiny skulls on their sleeves. He stood as if bemused, until they saw him, too, and scattered away prudently. When they were gone he picked up the filthy remnant of the bag and carried it into his private office. No one remembered seeing it, afterward.

When the westbound stage to San Diego made its stop in late June the streets were so broiling hot not even the Anglos were out on them. The stage driver advised the passengers to try the new hotel down the street if they were planning to stay, and gave notice of a thirty-minute lunch stop to the rest. A hardware drummer took the longer walk; two mining types went into the cantina. The last two passengers crossed the wide street instead.

"Remember, you only get thirty minutes here, mister," called the driver. The man nodded. His companion made running circles around him in the street to stretch his legs, then straightened out into a beeline for the kitchen of the Arredondo Carriage House. The man let him go and continued across the street at an angle to the newspaper office.

Carrie was alone in the office, proofreading copy and fanning herself listlessly with a palm-leaf fan, while her brother and his intended bride dawdled over their lunch together in the kitchen and made plans for enlarging the living quarters of the building. Carrie heard the door open behind her and turned around, then got up slowly.

"Is Paco with you?" she asked when she didn't see him.

"He went down to see Angelina."

"Oh. How was El Paso?"

"I don't know. We didn't stay long enough to find out."

"I see. You must enjoy traveling, to do it in this heat. Are you going back to California now? Or did you forget something here?"

He shut the door behind him firmly.

"No. That was the whole damned trouble. I didn't forget

274

anything here," he said gracelessly. He sat down in Clem's chair and took off his hat. He looked hot and ill tempered.

"This is never going to work out," he muttered. She sat down again facing him, knee to knee. "You wouldn't like keeping a saloon," he told her.

"No, I don't believe I would."

"Or living in a hotel with a gambling room downstairs, either."

She looked pensive.

"And I couldn't spend the rest of my life shut up in a flea park like this." He indicated Arredondo with a slight motion of his head.

They stared at each other.

"Isn't there anything else?" she asked.

"I don't know what—"

"I mean, isn't there anything else you want to tell me?"

He looked as if he had come to confess to a murder.

"I love you," he said at last.

She blinked back her first tears.

"I know you do. But I'm so glad you came back to say it."

"It doesn't make me any different. Or you, either. It doesn't do anything for either of us, except mess up our lives."

She nodded wordlessly, her tears spilling over.

Then he pulled her out of her seat and into his lap, holding her hard, with his face against her shoulder as she clung to him; until she had her cry and began to laugh.

"How long will it take you to pack?" he asked after a while. "We haven't got much time."

"I've been packed ever since the day you left. That's what I was laughing about."

He dumped her off his lap onto her feet again as he stood up.

"God, I can see this is going to be a massacre. The only possible good that can come out of it is that I won't have to sleep with Paco any more. Whatever we do, that kid has got to have his own room. I don't know what the hell you're laughing about. You're going to be sorry. I'm going to be sorry!"

But when Paco burst through the door a short time later Jake was still kissing Carrie.